ELIXIR

ELIXIR

Charles Atkins

This first world edition published 2020
in Great Britain and the USA by
SEVERN HOUSE PUBLISHERS LTD of
Eardley House, 4 Uxbridge Street, London W8 7SY.
Trade paperback edition first published
in Great Britain and the USA 2021 by
SEVERN HOUSE PUBLISHERS LTD.

British Library Cataloguing in Publication Data
A CIP catalogue record for this title is available from the British Library.

ISBN-13: 978-0-7278-9050-4 (cased)
ISBN-13: 978-1-78029-705-7 (trade paper)
ISBN-13: 978-1-4483-0426-4 (e-book)

All Severn House titles are printed on acid-free paper.

Severn House Publishers support the Forest Stewardship Council™ [FSC™],
the leading international forest certification organisation.
All our titles that are printed on FSC certified paper carry the FSC logo.

Typeset by Palimpsest Book Production Ltd.,
Falkirk, Stirlingshire, Scotland.
Printed and bound in Great Britain by
TJ International, Padstow, Cornwall.

To Harvey and Cynthia Atkins

ONE

At six and a half, Jen Owens knew she would not have a seventh birthday. It didn't bother her, not that part, at least. What hurt, and she fantasized about it for hours every day, was the kitten she would never have. It would come as a present in an open-topped box with pink or blue satin bows and shiny rainbow paper.

From her child-sized chair that overlooked the parking garage for Boston's St Mary's Children's Hospital, she spun her beloved fantasy. She'd have hair, not the half inch of blonde fuzz that fell victim to every new bout of chemo or radiation, and wear overalls with bright red suspenders. Like a smooth river rock, the details fit. Parts she left open. Like when she finally got to look in the box, would it be a fur-ball white Persian or a green-eyed tabby? Sometimes with short hair, but more often with the luxurious coat of a Maine Coon. She pictured white-tufted ears, symmetrical markings, and little noises it would make as it looked up at her and tried to climb the walls of the box. Tears streamed as she saw herself reach in and touch it for the first time. She whispered to no one, the names she'd picked out, Stewie if it were a boy kitten and Gracie if it were a girl.

She closed her eyes and imagined kitten fur against arms and her cheek. She heard the soft purr in her ear.

'Jen.'

A familiar man's voice intruded.

She sighed, and it all evaporated. She opened her eyes. 'Dr Frank.' Not as good as the kitten, but her favorite adult, though she did love Mommy and Daddy. She liked the way he looked straight at her, when so many others, including Mommy and Daddy couldn't look her in the eye. But not Doctor Frank.

She'd sometimes glimpse him in the hall, surrounded by white-coated doctors and nurses, always in movement, always in a hurry. Like the ducklings in one of her favorite books set in the Boston Gardens, which she'd never seen, though she knew it was close. But not now, now he was quiet. His warm brown eyes were focused on her.

'Are your parents here?'

'No.' It was the middle of a Monday, they both worked. 'Is it a holiday today? It's not Saturday or Sunday.'

'They asked me to meet them.' He pulled out his cell. 'I guess I'm early.'

'You're always early.'

'You're observant.'

She watched as he settled cross-legged on the small Thomas the Train carpet in front of the window. Even so, his head was higher than hers as she sat in her chair. 'You're tall. I like that. I can see you from far away. You need a comb. You got happy hair.'

He smiled and pulled his fingers through a mop of dark curls. 'It starts combed, but as the day goes on, it gets happy, does its own thing.'

'Better than mine,' she said, staring out the window at the bustle below. Ambulances, medical personnel, and just people passing by the hospital on their way to wherever. She felt his gaze.

'Thinking about kittens?' he asked.

'Yup. You should have one up here.'

'You know we can't.'

'They have therapy pets on other floors.'

'I know.'

She wanted to keep going, but she knew the reasons, and she didn't want to waste her time with Dr Frank on something neither one of them could change. Like her never having a seventh birthday. 'Why do Mommy and Daddy want to see you?'

'They didn't say, but said it was important.'

'OK. So what did you bring me?'

From a lab coat pocket he pulled out an iPad. 'I found this.'

She waited as he opened an app that filled the entire screen with a kitten.

Her breath caught. 'Let me see.' Enthralled, she took it. Then she started to cough. Dr Frank's calming hand landed on her back, as one cough blossomed into another and then another, like they'd never end.

'Ssh.' He smoothed circles between her shoulder blades as

she struggled for breath. Her fingers clenched the tablet as the kitten stared back at her. 'Ssh. Tighten your tummy muscles,' he instructed. 'That's right.'

He sounded calm, and that helped. His voice stayed deep and like a rock she held onto it. She squeezed her tummy and hated the pain that ran from the back of her mouth all the way to her belly. It burned. She stared at the kitten, and then up at Dr Frank and into his eyes. Those were real. And then behind him, in the doorway she saw Mommy and Daddy and a man she didn't know. She tightened her tummy hard as she could. She didn't want Mommy and Daddy to see, but Mommy's eyes looked scared.

'I'm OK.' She wheezed and forced a smile. The burn at the back of her throat was bad, and a tickle threatened to reignite her cough. 'I'm OK.' She felt Dr Frank's hand leave her back as he stood and, before greeting her parents, he walked over to the bed, turned a dial, and came back to her with the greenish breathing thing that went in her nose. He handed it to her. She looped the pieces around her ears, stuck the little bits up her nostrils and then tightened the slidey thing around her neck so it wouldn't fall off.

'You good?' he whispered.

She nodded, clenched, and smiled.

He pulled a grape Tootsie Pop from his pocket, and gave it to her.

She nodded thanks. Too scared that if she spoke the coughs would start and she wouldn't be able to stop.

She watched as he turned to her parents and the strange man. He was different with them, just as with the white-coats who followed him around. She wondered what the difference was, like a switch on a machine.

'Jim, Marnie.' He shook her parents' hands, and made eye contact. His gaze darted to the strange man in the dark-blue suit. Like the game where you name the different emojis, she tried to imagine what was going through Dr Frank's mind.

He doesn't like that man. Does he know him? She moved from her chair by the window, letting the sweet grape candy coat her throat, but taking careful ninja steps, both to not get the cough restarted and to not make her parents take what was shaping up to be an interesting morning out of her room. She hated that. The 'We don't want her to hear.' Or, 'It'll upset her.'

'You had something you wanted to discuss,' Dr Frank said.

Her mommy cleared her throat, and wouldn't meet his gaze. 'Jim and I wanted you to meet Mr Crisp. He's with Doughton Pharmaceuticals and he—'

'Where's your badge?' Dr Frank asked the man in the suit.

Jen braced up against the bed, fascinated by the tone in Dr Frank's voice. *He's mad.*

'Dr Garfield, I was hoping to talk to you today about stage three trials we're doing with Robenazide. And little Jennifer here is exactly who—'

She saw Dr Frank's fists clench and his jaw twitch.

He's real mad. I've never seen him mad. Mommy is scared and Daddy wants to run away. And what kind of name is Mr Crisp? Is Dr Frank going to hit him? He wants to.

'Dr Garfield,' her mommy spoke, 'I hope you're not upset, but I was online looking at different experimental drugs and it seemed like this might be a fit for Jen. I contacted their hot-line and then Mr Crisp got in touch with us and said Jen was exactly the right fit, with her type of . . .' she lowered her voice, 'cancer, and . . .'

Jen felt Mommy's fear, she talked too fast, and didn't know where to look. *Daddy doesn't want to be here. And we all know I have cancer, so why whisper like I don't know.*

'Marnie, Jim.' Dr Frank's voice now sounded calm, but his face was pink, almost red, from the tips of his ears to an inch below his hair. He reminded Jennifer of a cartoon character about to explode. He looked back at her and shook his head.

Mr Crisp spoke, 'Dr Garfield this is really a unique opportunity and there would of course be no cost to the Owens and you'd be credited as an associate investigator.'

'Shut up,' Dr Frank said. He stared at Mr Crisp. 'You need to leave. You don't have clearance to be here. And if I find that you've crossed any lines with the Owens, I will report it to the FDA.'

'But we invited him,' Mommy said.

'We should have called first,' Daddy said. He looked at Dr Frank, 'I had a feeling this was a bad idea.'

'Dr Garfield,' Mr Crisp persisted. 'I understand your concern here, but frankly Robenazide could offer Jen additional time. I think you owe it to her and the Owens to at least—'

Jen repositioned herself as Dr Frank's broad back blocked her view of Mr Crisp. Then when she caught his expression, she gasped, *he's going to hit him.*

Dr Frank's voice became different than she'd ever heard. 'I am familiar with your drug and its failed studies. I am amazed that it's been approved for stage three studies. But I imagine there's been clever maneuvering to try and create an indication for extending life by two to three months.' He turned to her parents. 'Which I don't want to discount, but what Mr Crisp neglected to mention is that those two to three months would be a nightmare, and that's why Robenazide's prior trials failed. I will not go into the details with Jen here but you do not want to put your daughter through that agony.'

Mr Crisp interrupted, 'Dr Garfield I think you're overstating—'

'Shut up,' he said. 'What you have done here . . . you need to leave. And if you don't I'm calling security to have you removed, and I will contact the FDA.'

Jen saw the moment Dr Frank lost his cool.

'How can you do this to people?' He closed in on Mr Crisp, who initially stood his ground and then backed out the door and into the hall. 'To children? Are you even aware of the poison you're peddling?' He started to yell. 'And you make them promises while hiding the horror-show that awaits. And then when you get enough kids to live another three months of agony, with one organ system shutting down after the next you take your results and get your poison onto the market. I can see the ads already, smiling children with puppy dogs. And in pages of tiny print that no one reads, you bury the truth of how they were tortured, and how their families had to watch, and how three months of unbearable pain and suffering was worse than the disease itself.'

Jen wheeled her portable oxygen tank, and chomped down on the fudgy center of the Tootsie Roll Pop as she followed the action into the hall. But too many adults obscured her view. She listened and pictured Dr Frank with a sword and happy hair as he shouted at Mr Crisp and ordered him to leave. Though she wondered if two or three more months wouldn't be a good thing. But she knew her months and counted on her fingers; it still wouldn't get her a seventh birthday or a kitten.

TWO

F rank stared at his mentor, white-haired Jackson Atlas, and wondered why he even tried. 'You don't understand.' *He doesn't get it. What can I say to get a yes? There has got to be a way.*

'I do,' Jackson replied from a leather chair, stained with sweat on the armrests. 'But just because you *can* do a thing, doesn't mean you should.'

'They're children.' Frank argued. A wave of young faces raced through his mind, most of them dead . . . but not Jen Owens, not yet. *She doesn't have long. You need to make him say yes.* While he knew from painful experience not to get attached to his patients, it was not a trick he'd managed to achieve. Jen's imminent death felt real and awful. *And I could save her.*

'That's how it would start.' Jackson said. 'I'm telling you, the minute the drug companies get their hands into a thing it goes sideways. It always does, and you will have no control. Zero.'

Frank's gut tightened. He let out a breath and looked around at Jackson's familiar study, a conservatory in a Tudor in one of Brookline's oldest neighborhoods. The smell was dank, traces of tortoise dung and guano from Jackson's pets, Killer the Galapagos tortoise and Harvey his potty-mouthed Macaw. 'You're wrong,' he said. 'You know how I work. I write down nothing. It's all in my head. I can control that.'

Jackson snorted. 'Not likely.' He sat up and fixed Frank in his gaze. 'You're young. You don't understand, with pharma it's all about the dollar. But wrapped in a Madison Avenue moral shellac. Smiling faces, puppies, direct advertising to consumers desperate for a pill to fix what's wrong. And doctors . . . we're the worst. We don't read the small print and believe what comes out of the mouths of sweet young marketing reps who don't even have a degree in science. They are, without exception, pimps and whores, Frank.'

'Pimps and whores. Pimps and whores,' the macaw echoed, and then attacked a seed-embedded toy.

'I'm not arguing about that,' Frank said. 'But if I don't pursue the natural course of my research, someone else will. It's just a matter of when.'

'Maybe.' Jackson said. 'Eventually. It's a can of worms you should not open. Or should I say, open further. And I'm sorry to do this. It hurts. You are, with the possible exception of one other, the most-brilliant researcher I've had the privilege to work with.'

'Who was the other?' Frank asked.

'Not important. Though she is an object lesson . . . at least she was to me.'

'If you're shooting down years of my research it seems I'm entitled to something. Tell me who she is . . . or was.' *Tell me how I'm going to get you to agree, old man.*

'I'm sorry, Frank. It's just . . .' Jackson gripped his chair arms and stood on knees that had both been replaced. He grimaced and headed towards a carved Victorian sideboard covered with stacks of journals and a liter-and-a-half bottle of Kentucky bourbon. He poured two tumblers half full, took a swig, and with his back turned, spoke. 'Her name was . . . is Leona. And it was a long time ago.'

Frank waited as Jackson returned and handed him his glass. 'And?'

'I don't want to talk about this.'

'No. In a world where everything is caused, there's a reason we wandered to the topic of your most-brilliant student. So out with it. What's the object lesson worth shooting down the cure for cancer?'

Jackson snorted. 'I didn't say that to make you jealous.'

'I'm not. I'm curious. Leona who?'

'Let's leave her with a first name. She was even younger than you, whizzed through her doctoral work with a thesis that was complex, logical, and could have set her on the path for a brilliant academic career. She was one of the first to look at the so-called garbage DNA sequences and lay out serious questions as to their true purposes.'

'There's still pushback on that,' Frank said.

'There always is with anything new. What was it that Planck said? Science advances one funeral at a time.'

Frank looked up from the amber depths of his drink to Harvey's birdcage, and the brilliant green and blue bird as he savaged a swinging feed toy. He spotted a mangled head of fresh lettuce on the floor and watched it disappear under a worktable that was Killer's favorite lair. He walked over and knelt. The tortoise's wrinkled head and beak-like mouth were mostly hidden inside the bulk of his shell. But it wasn't the tortoise that ran through his mind, it was thousands of related articles around his thesis. And then it hit, 'Leona Krawsinska, 1988, *Genetics International.* Volume 52.' He paused and mentally flipped pages in his mind. 'Hypotheses Regarding the Nature of Leader Sequences in Human DNA.'

'Fuck you, Frank. I should have kept my mouth shut,' Jackson said.

'Glad you didn't. What happened to the brilliant Dr Krawsinska?' Frank paused, and let his mind drift as he meditated on the name *Krawsinska.* 'Why aren't I seeing other articles? With that big a topic someone should have published her thesis . . . strange. And as we both know, she was onto something big.'

'She was, and now you are, thirty years later.' Jackson mumbled into his drink.

'Spit it out.'

'I didn't say anything.'

'Jackson, you're trying my last nerve. What happened to Leona Krawsinska?'

'What do you think happened? She met a man, got married . . . and was never heard from again.'

'Not exactly the dark side. People get married. Where's this object lesson?'

'I merely brought it up as a cautionary tale.'

'Which makes no sense without the details.' Frank stood and left Killer to his salad. 'What was so bad? She was your student and you mentored her. Your name was second on that article. It's not like you slept with her.'

And Frank, who sucked at social clues, read Jackson's silence as a confession.

'Seriously?'

'I'm not talking about this,' Jackson restated.

'Yeah, you are. This was your conversation. You tell me that I need to suppress what we both know is ground-breaking work. I'm sick to my core of watching children die when I know I can do something about that.'

'I get it, Frank. And why you chose pediatric oncology, I never understood and still don't.'

'Don't change the subject.' Frank felt a pressure in his temples and started to pace. Horrific images of his childhood, never far from the surface, intruded. Chief among them, a crazy mother locked away in a forensic hospital since he was nine. 'Tell me about your affair with Leona Krawsinska and I'll tell you why working with those kids is the one thing that keeps me going. Because children shouldn't have to suffer, and they do. And you're saying that when I can completely change the game and give them a whole life without people stabbing them with needles or poisoning them with chemo that destroys the very cells they need to survive, I shouldn't. I don't get it Jackson. Make me understand, because none of it makes sense.'

Jackson winced.

'What?' Frank asked. 'Just spit it out . . .'

'You don't know how things work.' He drained his glass and headed for a refill. 'Leona was my lesson. Not my only one, but the one time I was unfaithful to Ruth. It nearly destroyed my marriage, it kept me from getting department chair, though there were other reasons, and . . . it just about broke me.'

'You were in love with her.'

Jackson grimaced. 'I was.'

'And she married someone else.'

Tears popped at the corners of Jackson's eyes. 'Like you, she was at a decision point. Thesis in hand. Ridiculously young to have a PhD . . . and while these things shouldn't matter, they do. She was the most-beautiful young woman I've ever met. What happened between us was shameful. A fifty-year-old married man and a twenty-two-year-old. Like an accident in slow motion. You think somebody should stop it, but no one does.'

Frank struggled to make sense of Jackson's strange revelation. *What does this have to do with him refusing to sponsor my next trial?*

'I remember the moment we crossed that line. It was in this room. Just like you, she'd come over. At first, maybe once a week to talk about her work, or new papers. I thought I was the hip supervisor who had students coming and going. Ruth liked that I did most of my office hours from home. She'd sometimes bake trays of cookies or brownies. That I hurt her is the worst part of this. She found out. She asked me if I wanted a divorce, if I was in love.' He choked on his words. 'I lied and told her I didn't know. That was a lie.' He gazed out through a darkened conservatory window. 'I asked Leona to marry me. Told her I would leave Ruth.'

He became quiet. The room was silent save for the crunch of lettuce, and the squeak of Harvey's swing's toy.

'She said no, that she'd met someone else and intended to marry him. I realized what an absolute fool I'd been. It was the last time I saw her before she graduated. Ruth and I stayed together, though she never again trusted me. No more trays of cookies and not till she got sick did we really talk. I hurt her more than I could ever atone for.'

'Jackson, that's . . . I'm sorry. But I don't see the parallel.' Frank's cell rang. He glanced at the screen and hit decline.

'Recruiter?' Jackson asked.

'Yeah.'

'Pimps and whores. That's the parallel, or rather the fork in the road, or the devil that speaks with forked tongue. Leona left, got married . . . and went into industry. That last paper of yours should never have been published.'

'Not again.'

'You chummed the waters, Frank. How many recruiters from how many drug companies have called today?'

'Enough. I get it.'

'No, you don't. The minute your work leaves your head, you have no control on how it gets used. When you published that article on telomere manipulation and how that influences lifespan, you basically said, "I can make you live longer."'

'Your name is on that piece, too.'

'My name is on thousands of articles. I should never have agreed to it. Did you at least get rid of the rats? And that's a whole other can of worms. You had no permission for an animal study. If I'd known, I would have shut it down myself. Are they gone?'

'Yes.'

'All of them?' Jackson asked.

Frank hesitated and did something he rarely did. He lied. 'Yes.'

'Good.'

The whiskey had both muddled and cleared Frank's thoughts. He felt manipulated and realized that Jackson had confessed to something big, but had never made his point. 'You left something out.'

'Damn,' Jackson said. 'I hoped you'd drop this.'

'Where's the object lesson, old man? I didn't sleep with those rats . . . or anyone else for that matter.'

'I didn't just betray Ruth.'

Frank let the silence stretch.

'I did something worse. I've never told anyone.' He looked down. 'I let her read my other students' theses.'

'What?'

'You heard me.' He met Frank's gaze and looked away.

'Why?'

'She asked. I was in love. I knew it was wrong. What I didn't know was how she'd use it.'

'Blackmail?'

'If only. No, it was during a wave of bone-marrow research. The underpinning of all the toxic chemos. I had three doctoral students who'd found a way to destroy nests of stem cells. She stole it. Within six months of her leaving the university . . . and me, the first of those poisons was on the market. She took something that was never intended for human use, at least not in that form, and it's resulted in untold human suffering.'

Frank wanted to feel bad for Jackson. He looked old and defeated. But what roiled in his chest was disgust.

'I need to get out of here. As you said, she was your object lesson. Not mine. You're trying to control something that will come out, whether it's from me or someone else. What makes this worse is that I feel like . . . no, I know for certain, that I could take what I did with those rats and apply it right now to those kids on the eighth floor.' He gritted his teeth. 'They don't have to die, but without your help, and university backing I've got no options. Maybe I can get approval for an animal study, but not without your sign-off. I have zero intention of going with a drug company. I need you to say yes.'

'Pull it back, Frank. You can't let this out. Not now, not yet. You need to think through how others will use it. There's at least two sides to every great scientific advance. You just see those kids. I get it. But that's not how others will use you and your work. You're going into the very structure of the DNA and what can work to lengthen life and kill a cancer . . . there are other ways it could go. For God's sake it could be weaponized. Instead of stabilizing DNA, it could unravel it.'

'That's absurd.' Frank glanced at the clock, it was ten-twelve. *And he's drunk and this is going nowhere!* He grabbed his knapsack and looked at Jackson. He stopped himself from saying anything further. It was no use. Without a full professor, and a Nobel Prize winner at that, signing off on grant applications or requests for an animal, or God forbid, human study, his work was dead. 'I've got to go.'

He left through the front and nearly slammed the door. *Chill.* He stopped and checked to make sure it was locked. *He's old. There's got to be a way. He slept with a student. She stole.* He swallowed hard and thought of his own work and his inspired twist that made the impossible possible.

Cool air brushed his face. He looked towards the lit bus stop at the end of the block, but too much raced inside his head to sit and wait. He mapped the distance from here to his one-bedroom on the Cambridge/Somerville line. About six miles.

He started to jog. The muscles in his legs loosened up. He focused on the sound of his feet as they pounded the sidewalk and pushed faster and faster. He thought of Jen Owens, who had maybe a month to six weeks, and all the other children he'd treated. An army of them at his back, mostly dead. *There's got to be a way. Jackson is wrong. There has got to be a way.*

THREE

D alton Lang adjusted his ear bud and repositioned the directional feed on the *Big Brother* wireless eavesdropper. From his black BMW X hidden in the shadow of an ancient beach at the edge of Jackson Atlas's Brookline property, he listened with rapt attention. The conversation between the two, not his first he'd listened to, tripped a nerve – Leona Krawsinska. *What were you up to, Mother? You and the professor . . . shocking. Interesting. And stealing others' research.* But something stung, *why didn't she tell me?*

It now made this assignment – recruit Dr Francis Xavier Garfield, for UNICO Pharmaceuticals – more personal. It also fueled his discontent as the only child of Leona Lang, née Krawsinska. He often wondered what she'd do if he just said no to her. *I'm not your lackey.* But then there was the other piece, the thing that caused his chest to ache. *What would it take for you to say I did something right?* No, for her nothing was ever good enough. 'You had an affair with the old man. Why?' He calculated back to when his mother got her PhD. It was the same year she married Lionel Lang. 'Of course, she wasn't going to marry you,' he said aloud, as if part of the conversation between Frank and Jackson. 'You don't know my mother.' *Do I?*

As he listened to the conflict inside, he pictured his father. With each year he felt it grow harder, but the one memory that did come, was bad. Lionel Lang's head covered with blood in the shower. Water and blood down the drain. His mother, naked and too calm as she dialed 911. *'There's been an accident. My husband slipped in the shower.'*

He tried to block that, but there were smells, metal and feces and soap. 'Shit!'

Then the front door to Atlas's house opened. Garfield, tall and with a mop of dark curls, stood lit in the overhang.

'Frankie boy, what's it going to take?' Dalton said to himself. Thus far all attempts to lure the young doctor to UNICO had failed. Even getting him to pick up the phone was a challenge. The last two recruiters he'd sent, who'd snuck into his class, had been shut down and escorted out.

Though he now had gathered good information, about Garfield's past, *which, if I thought my mother was bad at least she's not an ax murderer. Although* . . . He shook his head, as graphic memories of blood and water threatened to overwhelm him. With them came the unanswerable question. *Was it an accident?* Then, as he jogged closer, he focused on Frank Garfield.

He sank down and ticked through intel he'd accumulated. Frank's best friend since childhood was another pediatric oncologist and researcher, Grace Lewis. Gay, no boyfriend, and he'd been seeing shrinks most of his life. But why Dalton was here had to do with Frank's work, and his mother's uncanny ability to ferret through scientific journals, like a douser for water, for the next big thing. Even Dalton, with his lack of scientific interest, sensed it. *He's got the Holy Grail. And Mother wants it. All I need to do is get it for her. Simple . . . not.*

He contemplated his next move, the two men's talk had crystalized Garfield's dilemma. *He wants to use his research to save his patients.* He snorted. *Which I'm certain is not Mother's intent. And that's why the old man wants to keep this in the bottle. He knows her . . . why didn't I know that? Did she think I wouldn't find out?* His thoughts spiraled down. *And that's how much she thinks of me. And if I fail . . . just another example of how I don't measure up. But* . . . and inspiration hit. The thing that could dislodge Garfield from the ivy towers of Cambridge. *He wants to save those kids . . . that's it. But . . . but . . . but.*

But the old man isn't going to let that happen. So . . . And inspiration hit. *Sorry, old man.*

He pulled out the ear bud and studied the quiet lamplit street. He mapped a path of shadow from his car along a dense hedge that hemmed the property. Then he inventoried what he'd need and how best to do it. *No time like the present.* He wondered what Leona would say. She hated it when he went off script and didn't run things by her. *But she never has to know it was me. After all, she keeps secrets.* It rankled. *What else haven't you told me, Mother?*

He got out, felt the heft of the Glock in its holster, and moved with grace up the lawn towards the brightly lit conservatory out back. He spotted Jackson, back turned, at work on a computer. He surveyed the options: ground floor and second story windows, French doors at the back and another entrance off the kitchen. *There we go*, an open window on the second floor. *Too easy.*

He tested his weight on an ivy-covered trellis. It held, and he climbed. Years of gymnastics and martial arts made it easy.

Like a boa he eased his head and shoulders through the window, then lowered his body to a bathroom floor.

Did she love him? he mused as he padded down a broad curved staircase. *What will she think about this?* Excitement bubbled as he saw the light from the conservatory. *She hates surprises. Hates not being in control. This is fucking perfect.*

He unsnapped the holster and screwed on the silencer. He heard the lettuce-crunch from the giant tortoise and the click of the old man's fingers on the keyboard as he came up behind and squeezed off a single surgical shot through the occipital cortex of Nobel Prize laureate, Jackson Atlas. There was minimal recoil, and a gasp of breath, like an uncapped soda bottle through the old man's lips. Then maybe a second, and he crumpled forward.

But Dalton's focus was pulled by the screen as it went black – it had been an unsent email to Frank Garfield. Without thought he pressed the enter button to bring it back, *shit! Should not have done that.* Aware of the error, that every keystroke created traceable meta data, he focused on Atlas's final words to Garfield.

Dear Frank:

It pains me to be your stumbling block. Yet, through the lens of my decades I see what you cannot or will not. Your research has ramifications far beyond your admirable and altruistic aims. Yes, I believe you could save those children. But at what cost? That's the rub and until you can address it in a manner that assuages my concerns, I see us and you at a crucial point. For me to continue to offer my support I would like you to terminate your current research. Perhaps develop a new project that focuses on one of the many rich and related topics. I believe for someone as brilliant as you, this should not be difficult. However, should you decide not to terminate your current efforts

Dalton read the ultimatum and imagined its end. Do what I say or else. *Sounds familiar.* He lingered and stared at the stark white hair on the back of Atlas's scalp. He resisted the urge to pull up other files, to search for traces of his mother. The revelations from earlier, burned. How stupid of her not to tell him she'd had an affair with Frank Garfield's supervisor. *She didn't think I'd find out.*

He wondered if the unfinished and unsent email would put Garfield on the radar as a murder suspect. *There's a motive, but that's not how I want this to play. What to do?* And taking more time than he'd intended, Dalton spread Hansel and Gretel breadcrumbs to serve as a mundane reason why an esteemed researcher and professor would be shot dead in his home – a simple break-in and burglary gone wrong. But, the assassin-style single shot set the wrong tone. *It won't do.* He paused and eyed the near-empty tumbler of bourbon, too drunk, too old, and too preoccupied to hear the burglar enter. A scuffle would have been better, but to move the body now would be a mistake, each drop of blood on the keyboard would leave a trail of post-mortem manipulation. It's what came next that had to set the stage. And like a director's suggestion in one of the many acting classes he'd attended at NYU's school of the arts, he thought, *if I were a heroin addict what would I do?*

He set to work, opening drawers, pocketing whatever small bits could be easily pawned or bartered for drugs. But as he passed through a study with a wall covered with framed class photos, a discordant note hit. He zeroed in on the doctoral class of 1988. Twenty-four mostly smiling, and mostly bespectacled faces in front of the physics building. Jackson Atlas, a proud parent on one end, and his mother on the other. She had stared straight into the lens, younger than all, blonde, and even with her hair tied up and back and her prim white buttoned blouse, lovely, like a fairy princess with sapphire eyes, a pointed chin and perfect symmetry to her East European features. He wondered why she stood as far from Jackson in the photo as possible. 'Something's not right here.' *Why didn't I know this? Well, she would have been dating my father when this was taken . . . was she already pregnant?*

He stared at the picture. The trees had leaves, but new ones . . . April, maybe May. Which even then . . . June, July, August, September, October, November, December.

Nausea flooded his mouth. He felt the weight of the jewelry he'd taken from an upstairs dresser, and the heat from his gun through the leather holster. The story went that he'd been born a month premature, even so. *She was pregnant in that picture and when she married Father.* Sick to his stomach, he returned to the conservatory and stared at the fallen man.

No. Did I just kill my father? Why didn't she tell me she knew him? What else is she keeping from me? I am so fucking tired of her pulling my strings. He stopped. *Don't let her get to you. You have a busy night ahead and information she didn't want you to have. Good things. And this anger . . .* Song lyrics formed, and with them came a melody in a minor key.

I am not my lady's lackey.

I am purpose and intent.

I will feed my baby's hunger, with the burn of discontent.

He checked the French doors to make certain they weren't alarmed, and humming, he left.

FOUR

F rank felt sick to his core. He'd lost all sense of time, from the moment he'd found Jackson's cold body to dialing 911, 'Someone's dead. I think he's been shot. His name is Jackson Atlas. He's a professor.' To now, seated in Jackson's kitchen at the paper-strewn and coffee-ringed table with a dark-suited, Brookline detective named Sean Brody.

'Dr Garfield, can you think of any enemies Dr Atlas had?'

Frank looked at Brody, not much older than he, early thirties, sandy blond hair, hazel eyes, well-pressed suit, white shirt and burgundy tie. Not like yesterday's Mr Crisp with his five-thousand-dollar suit, but like he knew his way around an iron or used a dry cleaner . . . *Do detectives make that much?* His cell buzzed. He glanced at the number, didn't recognize it, figured it was a drug company, and rejected it.

'Dr Garfield? Please focus.'

'Enemies, yeah, lots.' *And was I becoming another? Am I a suspect? Shit.*

'Tell me about that. Who in particular?'

Frank swallowed. *Jackson is dead. Someone shot him.* But the pieces wouldn't fit. He'd come over early, before classes, for breakfast. He was determined to move past last night's impasse. His run home had cleared his head and brought him to a decision point. Jackson either would support him and his work, or he'd find a different faculty sponsor. A grim prospect. But with children's lives, Jen's life, in the balance, he could not roll over and bury research that might save her. *He didn't get it . . . and now he's dead.*

'Dr Garfield, I know this is upsetting, but please concentrate.'

His gaze now connected to the detective's. *This is his job. This matters to him . . .* 'Of course. Jackson made a lot of enemies and torpedoed a lot of projects.' *Including mine.*

'I need specifics.'

'OK, here's one. Someone here had a cancer drug heading toward a stage three human investigation study. That's the final hurdle before a drug company gets the FDA approval to bring it to market. And by the time you hit stage three, millions have been invested and careers are on the line. So this drug, Robenazide, was being pushed hard for small cell lung cancer. Jackson got asked to review a study for one of the journals. He shredded it, said the toxic effects outweighed any possible benefit. The study was terminated, though the drug company is now trying again with a different indication.'

'They can do that?'

'Yeah, it's called finding a hammer for the nail. Happens all the time. It made Jackson furious. He was usually right about these things.' *Was he right about my work?* Like an amputee who still feels his arm, Frank desperately wanted to talk with his mentor. *He's gone.*

'How many of these Robenazide scenarios were there?'

'Lots. Jackson was a one-man crusade. Especially cancer chemotherapies. He believed the entire cancer industry had gone in a wrong direction. That most of their treatments made things worse, and ensured that the bulk of patients would die in the most expensive manner possible.'

'That's a bit cynical,' the detective said.

'No. Factual.' Frank's words felt disconnected, as scenes from last night's fight played over and over. *Answer his questions . . . why is he smiling? Nice smile.* 'Most chemotherapy attacks the immune system. How can an organism heal when its defense weapons are taken off the field?' Frank glanced up at the kitchen clock. 'I was supposed to teach a class at eleven. Can I make a call?'

'Go ahead.'

Frank pulled out his cell, and under Brody's scrutiny he dialed his best friend. 'Grace.'

'Frank, what's wrong?'

'Lots.' He spoke fast. 'Jackson was murdered . . . shot, sometime after I left him last night. I'm being questioned. I'm not going to make my eleven o'clock. Can you cover or call out for me? And you should let them know that Jackson won't . . .' He couldn't say it.

'Oh my God. Where are you?'

'Jackson's.'

'I'm on my way.'

'OK.'

She lowered her voice. 'Are you a suspect?'

'Maybe . . . Yes, I think so.'

'Do you have a lawyer?'

'No.'

'Frank be careful. We know you didn't do this. Right?'

'Of course.' He knew it was a joke, but he couldn't feel the humor.

'Just checking. And Frank, you've been through worse, you'll get through this.' And she hung up.

'What do you teach?' Brody asked.

'Genetics.'

'Where?'

'MIT.'

Brody nodded and held eye contact. 'Smart guy. So, you were here last night and again this morning. That usual for you?'

And here it comes. Should I get a lawyer? Should I stop answering? I didn't do this. I should tell the truth, the whole truth, and . . . he's got nice eyes. Green . . . hazel, little gold flecks. 'Yes. Jackson doesn't keep office hours, so we'd meet here. He was my doctoral thesis advisor and has sponsored my research ever since.'

'Explain that.'

'Which part?'

'The sponsor thing. You're a doctor, right. Is that MD or PhD?'

'Both.'

Brody smiled. 'Like I said, smart guy. So why do you need a sponsor?'

'I'm junior faculty, on a tenure track, but whether or not I ever become a full professor is a crap shoot and depends on my ability to get grants, do successful studies, and publish what will be considered important work.'

'In genetics?'

'Epigenetics. But trust me, you don't want me to explain that.'

'We'll see. So keep going with the nuts and bolts of your relationship with Jackson.'

'He was my mentor, and it was his name and reputation that got my last two NIH grants funded. It's his sponsorship that gets me the office and lab space I need.'

'And without him?'

'I either get another sponsor or . . . I don't know what. Go somewhere else, I guess. Although—'

'What?'

Tell the truth. 'Jackson and I had reached an impasse about my work. He felt it was dangerous and I should go in another direction.' He waited, knowing he'd just lobbed a motive onto the table.

'You fought?'

'Yeah.' *He'll find out anyway.* 'Seems all we did lately was disagree. I'd come to where I knew he wasn't going to give in, and I'd have to find someone else, or go somewhere else.'

'I'm glad you told me,' Brody said. 'Did your arguments ever get physical?'

'No, of course not.'

'Good. So why did Dr Atlas view your work as dangerous?'

Frank thought of something Grace would say, and bit back a grin.

'What made you smile?'

'In scientific circles you have to be careful what you ask. We live in super-specialized niches so that no one knows what we're talking about. It's why you never ask a doctoral student about his thesis . . . because he'll tell you, and tell you, and tell you some more.'

'Give me *The Reader's Digest* condensed.'

'Sure, there's little bits of protein on the ends of our DNA. They're called telomeres. They keep everything folded the way it's supposed to be. But every time a cell divides the telomeres shorten and their ability to keep the DNA in its most-stable configuration is compromised. And it's why cells can't reproduce forever, something called the Hayflick limit. My work focuses on reinforcing the telomere.'

'Pure theory or have you actually done it?'

Frank looked at the detective who had just asked the big question. Jackson's voice rang in his head, *'Once people know what you've done. Then it's not theory.'*

'Just theory.' He lied, not about to tell this detective about his small clandestine study with tumor-riddled Norwegian rats. Or that they all lived . . . until he sacrificed them, dissected them and found not a single malignant cell. 'Jackson didn't want me to publish my theory, said it was like chumming the waters for the drug companies.'

'Those recruiters you keep blocking?'

'Yeah. He wasn't wrong.' *And now he's dead. Did that article have something to do with this? Did I?*

'Come with me, please' Brody said, and he walked back through the house to the conservatory.

Sunlight streamed through the windows and skylights. Even so, bright tripod lamps had been set up around Jackson's body, as he was photographed from every angle.

'Where's Killer?' Frank asked.

'Excuse me?'

'Killer,' Frank crouched and looked in the direction of the tortoise's hangout spot under a stainless-steel potting table.

'Who or what is Killer?'

'A Galapagos tortoise. And no one woke up Harvey.'

'Who is?'

'A Macaw in the cage over there. He swears.' Frank turned around. 'Shit! Who left the door open?'

He headed towards the gaping French doors.

'Dr Garfield,' Brody followed him. 'Don't touch anything. This is how the room was found, correct?'

Frank stopped and turned. 'Yes.'

'Think hard, did you move anything, anything at all?'

'The chair. And then I knelt down, and felt for a carotid pulse. There wasn't one.'

'And?'

He paused, and could feel Jackson's flesh, cool and rubbery, against his fingertips. 'He was cold, he must have been dead for hours. It must have happened not long after I left.'

'Which you said was at ten.'

Frank heard the unmistakable thump and drag of Killer from under the back deck. 'Yes, ten. What will happen to his animals?'

'Professor Atlas has family?'

'Not close.'

'And what's with the weird animals?'

'Not weird, long lived. Killer has documentation going back a hundred years. Jackson's had him for over thirty-five. What will happen to them?'

'If there's no family they go to Animal Control.'

'Could I take them, even for now?' *Unless I'm getting locked up.*

'Let me get back to you on that. What I'd like you to do

now, is take a careful look at everything here and tell me if anything is missing or different from how you remember it.'

Frank looked. 'It's all here. Except for Killer. We shouldn't leave him outside. He's not fast, but he wanders. Maybe I could grab him and we could shut him up in the kitchen.'

'Sure,' Brody said, but sounding less than certain.

Frank headed out into the spring morning; it smelled of cut grass. *This is how the killer must have left.* He looked back and spotted the open second-floor bathroom window. 'That's how they got in.'

Brody nodded. 'Seems like, access up there and egress through the conservatory.'

'He's under there. I can hear him.' Frank got down on all fours and searched in the sun-dappled shadows under the deck for Killer. He spotted the tortoise semi-burrowed next to the stone foundation where he munched on a patch of weeds.

Mindful of his suit, Brody knelt next to Frank. 'Sweet Jesus, how big is he?'

'Four-hundred plus.'

'You want to take care of that?'

'I suppose. I just hope what he's eating doesn't give him diarrhea. There's nothing worse than sick tortoise shit.'

'How are you going to get him out of there?'

'Food, and there's a hydraulic cart in the garage. We fill it with lettuce, make a path, and leave the door open. He'll go in.' He then blurted his question. 'Am I a suspect?'

'Did you kill him?'

'No.'

'Then for now, you're not a suspect. Though you are in the middle of things.'

'I know. Will you help me get Killer out?'

Brody turned and faced Frank. Mere inches separated the two men as their gazes connected.

Frank's breath caught. Relief surged, *not a suspect.* But there was something else, as a silence stretched under Brody's scrutiny.

'Sure.' He smiled. 'Let's get some lettuce.'

FIVE

From her power position in UNICO's Manhattan Auditorium, capacity five-hundred, CEO Leona Lang sat perched at the top of the pharma heap. *And where do we go from up? But down. That will not happen.* She pressed her Botox-kissed lips into a serene half smile, fixed her jaw at an upward angle to decrease lines in her neck, and scanned the capacity crowd assembled for the annual meeting. On the periphery, reporters hung, including ones from *The Times* and *The Journal* and jumbo flat-screen monitors provided lesser shareholders with poor seats a better view. On her right, son Dalton, who she'd recently promoted to COO and on her left her board chairman, J. Robert Henry, IV. Bob to his friends, of whom she was not.

She half-listened to her current head of R&D, Dr Bradley Gordon, drone on about *his team's* accomplishments over the past year. To Dalton she whispered, 'I want him gone by the end of the week.' Even the man's voice annoyed her . . . *Useless.*

'Yes.'

'Where are we with Garfield?' she asked.

'I've found an angle.'

'Yes?'

'Terminally ill children. Six of them. He wants to save them.'

'Interesting.' On a screen, she now caught her and Dalton's images. She flinched. At forty-nine, she'd reached the outer limits of Botox, Collagen and Dr Ramon's temporizing miracles. But Dalton; she inventoried his looks, her cheekbones and piercing blue eyes, thick hair, and not a wrinkle on his face. She ached for the beauty she'd once had.

'A very good year,' J. Robert offered from her other side. 'Lionel would be pleased.'

'He would,' she said, knowing the Lionel he referenced was not her dead husband but his father, a scion of industry who had put UNICO on the map with great government contracts after WWII and the development of powerful antibiotics, still on the market, albeit with new derivatives that extended the patents. She then followed J. Robert's gaze fixed on her breasts. *Great, he still finds me attractive.* Her earlier years at UNICO had been punctuated with J. Robert's unwanted advances, even when her husband – the other, and arguably lesser, Lionel – still lived.

The applause swelled as the soon-to-be terminated Dr Gordon turned towards her, 'And now a few words from our esteemed leader. The CEO of UNICO Pharmaceuticals, Dr Leona Lang.' She stood and smoothed down the front of her navy Chanel suit. She weighed the applause – *fair, not great.*

'The numbers speak,' she began, as the monitors displayed her smoothed-out features, luminous blue eyes, and trademark spiked blonde coif. As a young woman, she'd been compared to a blonde Audrey Hepburn; her looks a tribute to her Polish mother and the Swede she'd bedded in a drunken encounter.

Leona needed no notes or teleprompter. 'We are a single entity you and me. Without you, our shareholders and supporters, UNICO does not exist. Without us, well, this is our twenty-third consecutive year with double-digit profits. How rare that is.' *And the reason why Bob and all his desiccated cronies can't fire me.*

A cell phone with a marimba riff distracted her. She noted Gordon silence his ringer and scroll through messages. *Moron.* 'But here's the thing,' she didn't miss a beat. 'Everything we do, every penny invested in cutting edge research is based on the UNICO mission and vision. It's simple and it's true. *Here to help; here to heal.* When other pharmaceuticals sit on past laurels we finish the year with innovative products, which have either already made it to market, or will be released in the next twelve months. We do not make me-too drugs, but rather, the new, the now, the next . . . the needed.' She felt the energy in the room. It fed her and she it. And she would give them what they wanted. *And what do they want more than anything? What we all do. Money, power, beauty.* But that wasn't it and she knew it. There was something more. 'Yes, we will finish this year strong. But that's not the point . . . is it? We till the soil for next year, the year after, and the years beyond. It's not a question of what we've accomplished, but of what is to come.

We, you and me, will move ahead boldly. We will bring miraculous new drugs to market. We will transform lives. Because we are UNICO.' She stared out into the crowd, her voice like thunder. 'Here to help; here to heal.'

The room erupted, as she bowed her head slightly and returned to her seat.

Dalton whispered, 'Flawless.'

But she heard undertones, and felt the moment slip away. *Sharks are circling. Is he one of them?* She glanced at J. Robert, who'd made it clear he felt a woman in the role of CEO was unseemly. She knew that all it would take was a single negative quarter, two tops, and she'd be on the chopping block. *But look at how old he is.* His hands like crepe paper, his jowls loose like he'd swallowed bags of marbles.

'Do whatever it takes to get Frank Garfield,' she whispered to Dalton; she heard desperation in her voice. 'Do it soon. Before someone else gets to him.'

'Yes, Mother.'

As the Chief Financial Officer took his turn at the podium, Leona scrolled through her messages, which included news feeds and synopses from major scientific and medical journals. But it was Frank Garfield's work that obsessed her. It connected to her own, nearly three decades ago. A progression of how science carves away at the material world, laying bare the essence of creation. *What the hell?* She stopped. Her attention drawn to an email from her alma mater, MIT. The subject line – *Professor Jackson Atlas, unhappy news.*

> *Dear colleagues:*
> *It is with a heavy heart that I must inform you of the passing away of Nobel Prize laureate and professor, Dr Jackson Atlas. While the details have not yet been released, Brookline police stated that Dr Atlas died from a single gunshot wound and that a homicide investigation is underway.*

She reread it. Wavy electric lines spasmed in her right visual field. *Just what I need.* She sought for the term that described the onset of what could turn into a crushing migraine, scintillating scotomata. Her vision blurred. *Jackson dead.* She swallowed and looked at Dalton. She passed him her cell, so he could read. *Murdered.* She tried to study her son's response, though his image was now distorted like a Picasso by rainbow-edged jagged lines.

He seemed surprised. 'That's Garfield's mentor.'

Dalton is a good actor. Like mother like son. Why is he looking at me so intently? Like I care . . . I do care. Jackson is dead. What did you do, Dalton?

He leaned into her. 'But, as you've taught me, Mother, never let a crisis go to waste. This could help dislodge Garfield.'

'Do it.' She bit her lip as her vision danced. *Do not cry. I will not cry. You made your choice. Look at how far you've come. You could never have been happy with him. But you were.* And Leona willed away her grief, a technique she'd learned as a young girl. *Head in the game. Eye on the prize.* And despite the certainty of the headache soon to come, because she'd be damned to show weakness and take a pill while on the stage, she smiled. *Here to help; here to heal.*

SIX

Usually more than half empty, Frank faced a packed auditorium of one-hundred and fifty undergraduates, mostly pre-med and nursing students. They rarely came to Friday class, as most studied from notes they'd take turns writing and then distribute via email. And, if he let his paranoia get the better of him, he suspected there were one or two pharma recruiters who'd become more aggressive after his last article. *Was Jackson right?*

Since Tuesday, and finding his mentor dead . . . *shot*, he'd struggled to put one foot in front of the next. But routines, like rounds on his young patients and his teaching responsibilities helped. He tapped the smart board and started a film clip. 'The luminescent bits at the ends of the genes are the telomeres. Observe the differences in stressed rats and . . . happy rats. And this has been observed in humans,' he flipped to images from a recent article, 'protracted stress shortens telomere length, which in turn has implications for morbidity and diminished life expectancy. Longer telomeres equal longer life.'

He pictured Jackson. It was in this class that Frank first had his mind blown by epigenetics, the field of science that asked basic questions about what causes a cell's DNA to do one thing or another. And Jackson lit that fuse.

A hand shot up.

'Yes.'

'I don't get the telomerase thing.'

'It's the enzyme that maintains the telomeres. The less telomerase, shorter telomeres, more disease, and a shorter life. Even before birth, if you stress the mother, her offspring have shorter telomeres.' He flicked a tab at the bottom of the screen and pulled up a study to illustrate.

The student persisted. 'But not in cancer. That's the part I don't understand.'

'Yes. In cancer it's the other way around. The cell's nucleus decides it wants lots of telomerase. Division goes rampant with tumors comprised of mostly undifferentiated cells.'

'But if telomerase is supposed to be a good thing, why would having a lot of it lead to tumors?' she asked.

Frank heard Jackson's Boston twang in his head. 'Good and bad are manmade constructs that have nothing to do with nature.' He dragged electroscopic images onto the screen. 'Here we have healthy cells with robust telomeres and a normal amount of telomerase. But over here is a tumor with short, almost absent telomeres and a whole lot of telomerase. This is what happens. As the telomeres shorten, the DNA – and get all those tidy pictures of the double helix out of your head – unravels. Think in three dimensions, four if you can. Parts of the DNA that were never meant to be exposed to the cellular environment are now bare and ripe to be copied. That's how the cancer starts.'

He glanced at the clock and started. Beneath it stood Detective Brody.

Frank's mouth went dry – *how long has he been there? Am I about to be arrested?* Adrenalin surged. 'As I'm sure you're aware, Dr Atlas has passed away. I'll cover both his and my seminars for the rest of the semester.' *If I'm not in jail.*

Hands popped.

Here it comes.

True to form, worried questions about grades and what would – and would not – be on the final exam all came. Jackson snickered in his head, '*Follow the bouncing dollars.*'

He dismissed the class. Students swarmed the podium. He fielded questions and requests to have grades re-evaluated. Then an attractive young couple in crisp suits, presented business cards.

'Doctor Garfield, hi, I'm Andy Anderson and this is Victoria Claybourn, we're with—'

'Not interested. Leave, or I'll call security.'

'But Doctor Garfield, we were hoping . . .'

He stared at preppy Andy and blonde and perky Victoria. 'Leave.'

'But—'

Frank pulled out his cell.

Andy held up his hands. 'Got it' – he threw cards and a glossy brochure onto the podium – 'but Galaxon Pharmaceuticals is very interested in your work. Any time you want to call and—'

Frank, pressed the number for security. 'Hi, I've got a couple unauthorized people in the Briarcliff Auditorium.' He looked up. 'Never mind, they took the hint. Thanks.'

As the two left, Detective Brody approached. 'That was interesting.'

Frank picked up the heavy stock cards and prospectus, showed them to Brody, and tossed them. 'Recruiters.'

'I meant your lecture. Telomeres are the secret to aging? Seriously?'

'Part of it.' His cell rang. He glanced at the readout and rejected the call.

'Your name was on a bunch of those slides you tossed up. This is your work. And this is what Jackson wanted you to step away from. It seems too important to do that.'

Frank was at a loss. *Why is he here? Those eyes, not quite green. Am I going to jail? And why does he pretend to be interested in my work?*

Brody continued. 'The stuff you tossed out on Tuesday, about how Professor Atlas made a lot of enemies, and that maybe robbery wasn't the motive. You said he shot down some cancer drugs. That's billions of dollars. But it's also related to this stuff. These telomeres.'

'I don't know . . . maybe.' Frank looked at the detective, and pushed past vivid memories of being handcuffed to a gurney in psychiatric emergency rooms when he was ten, eleven, and twelve. It suddenly was hard to breathe. 'Why are you here?'

'That's blunt. I need someone to decipher what's on Professor Atlas's computer. I figured that could be you.'

'Right.' *Not what I expected . . . is it a trap?* 'When?'

'Now, if possible.'

He swallowed. *Is this how he does it? Get you to come without a fuss.* Phantom bands of padded leather clamped around his wrists and ankles. 'Not a problem.' *You didn't kill Jackson. Yeah, and you didn't kill your father either, but they locked you up anyway.*

SEVEN

'Why Garfield?' Dalton asked, as he stared out at the passing scenery of the Taconic Parkway. He cracked the window to vent the reek of her perfume.

'You really don't see it,' Leona replied.

Her disdain, like a slap, felt familiar. 'I'm not an idiot. But you've pursued others. Garfield seems somehow different.' He pulled out his cell and flipped between his Twitter, Instagram, and Facebook accounts. He scrolled through the most-recent comments on his latest YouTube music video. Over ten-thousand hits, the majority of the responses were good. A few, like, '*dude sounds like someone's torturing a cat,*' hurt. But one, from a true fan, was what he needed. '*Voice of an angel. Soul of a poet. And those eyes . . . I love you, Dalton. Shine on.*'

'He is different,' Leona said.

He paused in mid ego-surf and looked at her in profile.

Well, no longer beautiful. That's what this is about. 'Then, tell me.'

'I see you handled Dr Gordon,' she said, referring to the recently termed head of R&D.

'Yes, papered and out the door. And he didn't fight.' *And you didn't answer me. Typical.*

'That would be stupid . . . and—'

'Yes Mother, the office is being remodeled and will be ready for its next occupant, the reluctant Dr Garfield. And now that his roadblock of a mentor is no longer among the living . . .' *Let's see if she bites.*

Leona took her eyes from the traffic to look at him. 'You had nothing to do with that?'

'Of course not.' He waggled his fingers in the air. 'A strange twist of fate.' He liked the way those words rolled in his mouth. A possible lyric, though he wondered if it were too close to some oldie. 'What I'd not realized, was that you and the good Dr Atlas had history.'

'I told you before I knew him when I was at MIT.'

'You never mentioned he was your thesis supervisor.' *Or that you had an affair with him. And this is how much she thinks of me and my abilities. You didn't think I'd find out. And now you don't think I know what you're after.*

'He was.' She flicked her signal for the Hyde Park exit. 'Thank you for coming today. I know you don't like to. I appreciate it.'

Nice, a change of topic, and a few breadcrumbs of . . . what to call this . . . right, what makes Mother squirm. And a compliment to boot. 'You're wrong. I haven't seen Grandma Karen in a while, and we needed to talk through a few things. It's a twofer.'

'You're not going to bring up that silly singing thing again.'

I was, but when you put it that way. He wondered how it was she did this to him. Forty minutes in the car with her and he was reduced to a petulant twelve-year-old. In clearer moments, he saw the truth of their relationship. If he did what she wanted all was well. But the one thing he wanted, which he'd tasted earlier in life, she was dead set against. 'No need, you couldn't have been clearer, though I appreciate that you've stopped trying to take down my videos.'

'It's not that they're terrible,' she said.

And here it comes. He braced.

'It's just they're not who you are. Who we are, and what we can be. We are not Kardashians or some pop tarts hungering for fifteen minutes and a hundred-million hits on YouTube.'

'Speak for yourself. Father would have understood.' *If he even was my father.* He pictured Jackson Atlas, the back of his head as he aimed and fired. *Did I kill my real father?*

'True, and that was as much a problem with him. More. I never told you this but he wanted to sell our control of UNICO. He had a different vision of where he wanted to take our family. A risky one.'

'He wanted to make movies,' Dalton stated. 'I read two of his screenplays. They're good. Though I think he modeled his leading ladies after you. Tough, beautiful . . . cruel.'

'Yes, they were . . . are I suppose. But to sink hundreds of millions of our dollars. He would have run us into bankruptcy in no time.'

'Technically, *his* family money.'

'There was no pre-nup. Though his mother, may she rot in hell, wanted one. Half of everything he had was mine, the minute I said: "I do."'

'Which is why you married him,' Dalton stated.

'It didn't hurt.'

'Come on Mother, rich, handsome, heir to the controlling interest in one of the world's largest pharmaceuticals.'

'Lionel had a lot to offer,' she admitted.

'I remember he was handsome, but the thing I most remember,' *blood and water . . .* 'you fought all the time. I'd hide in my closet and wait until it was over. You'd scream at him and there'd be broken glass. Then someone would slam a door, and a car would peel away. And this is what it was about. He wanted to be an artist and make movies and you wanted to control UNICO. Seems like you got your way. And he . . . wound up dead.' He studied her profile, her once tight jawline now sagged. *She used me to blackmail him. 'You even think of divorce, and you will never see your son.'*

'Ancient history. What progress have you made with Dr Garfield? Time is ticking.'

'He's as ready as he'll ever be. We lead with our best pitch. It's not going to be money, or the promise of accolades, or even power.' *Essentially Mother, nothing there for you to relate to.*

'You said something about a Christ complex. God help us.'

'Yes, he wants to push his research into human trials. As you're aware, he works with children with advanced malignancies . . . they all die. He thinks he can change that.'

'And Jackson . . . Dr Atlas, didn't.' She added, 'Quite a problem for an up-and-coming academician. Motive for murder?'

'There's a detective who's pursued that. Sean Brody, young, clean record. But it was a sad burglary for drugs. Jewelry was taken.' He kept his answer short, minimal embellishment. Nothing more than what could be found on an internet search.

'What a waste. Jackson was brilliant.'

'When's the last time you spoke to Dr Atlas?' he asked.

'It's been some time.' She turned down a manicured lane that led into the sprawl of the Roosevelt Acres Retirement Community.

'Months, weeks, years?'

'Months, certainly,' she said.

'I see. So, it wasn't just that you happened upon Garfield's work in some journals.'

'No, though I never trusted what Jackson said, not a hundred percent. He was a crafty old dog.'

Who slept with his beautiful young student. Something doesn't add up. 'What did he tell you about Garfield?'

'It doesn't matter. But enough to pique my curiosity. He was hiding something and when those last couple of articles came out, I knew where Frank Garfield's work could head, and I knew why Jackson wanted to keep me and pharma away. While it was a waste,' she glanced at Dalton, 'Jackson's death is useful.' She pulled into a visitor's lot on a road dotted with gray wood-shingle condominiums with green shutters and trim, like a New England seaside community. She flicked down the visor mirror and dabbed on lipstick. 'Let's get this over with.'

Dalton trailed behind as she headed up the path towards Unit 8C. The two-bedroom, two-bath residence of his Grandma, Karen Krawsinska.

Leona rang, as Dalton took in the grounds with their bright arrays of German Iris, spidery purple and white bachelor buttons, fresh-planted violets and vivid annuals. A door creaked. He smiled at the first whiskey-cured tones of Grandma Karen.

'Why if it isn't warden Leona.' And then she spotted him. 'Dalton, get over here. Give grannie a hug.'

He turned. From yards away, he smelled the booze and the cigarettes, but those were not what caused his cheeks to ache with happiness. 'Grandma, how the fuck are you?'

He took stock of his rail-thin grandmother, her bleached blonde hair tied in a bun. It was middle of the day and she was still in her pink-fleece slippers and a house robe. He pulled her into a hug. 'How the fuck are you?'

'Fucking great living in this hell-hole.'

'Mother,' Leona interjected. 'Do you have any idea what this hell-hole costs?'

'Of course, and it's always about the money. Isn't it? Why thank you warden, my jail is lovely. Acres and acres of fucking walking paths, two golf courses. Which, in case you forgot, I don't play, nor do I plan to. And let's not forget the bridge clubs and Mah Jong. Woo hoo.'

As she ranted, Dalton and Leona entered her vaulted living room. Light streamed from second-story windows onto mahogany furniture and tasteful couches and armchairs. It reminded him of a furniture showroom, or one of the glossy brochures for Roosevelt Arms. He looked closer. She hadn't burned holes in the upholstery and the ashtrays had been changed recently. A beautiful room, and he and Grandma had spent a fun weekend picking out the furnishings and bric-a-brac. And how tickled she'd been when they'd purchased the antique liquor bottles with silver labels that let you know which was whiskey, rye, or bourbon. He suspected these were the most-used items in the home.

'The place looks good,' he said.

'It should,' Karen replied. 'You designed it for me. It's good to know someone in the family has taste. Want a drink?'

He watched Mother wince.

'Why not, it's five o'clock somewhere,' he said.

'Good boy. I hate to drink alone.' She snorted and started to cough. 'Who am I kidding, I love to drink, alone or with someone. Doesn't matter.'

'It's a little early, Mother,' Leona said.

Karen headed towards the sideboard and parroted Leona. 'It's a little early, Mother. It's a little early, Mother.' She looked to Dalton, 'Bourbon, right?'

'Sure.' He ignored Leona's glare. *She wanted me here. This could be fun, and maybe I will learn something new . . . something useful.* And Grandma Karen could do what he couldn't, push Leona's buttons.

'Mother,' Leona said through a clenched jaw, 'how have you been?'

Karen's hands shook as she poured generous tumblers for her and Dalton. 'Leona, do you need to ask? You stick me in this hell-hole and expect me to be what . . . grateful? We both know why you did it. You don't want anyone to know where the great Leona Lang came from.'

'That's not true, I just want to make sure that you're safe and—'

'Cut the crap, dear. No reporters here. We're family. And as far as I know, I'm the only real family you have. And Dalton, you be careful of those Langs. They'll rip you and Leona to shreds in a heartbeat.'

'I am aware,' he said as he took the bourbon, and tried to remember if last month her shakes had been this bad. 'Beware the cousins,' he grinned.

'True,' Leona said. 'But as long as the balance sheet is in the black and the shareholders get their twice-annual dividends, they can't touch me.'

Dalton peeked down the hall to Grandma's bedroom. The door was open and he saw the unmade bed and mounds of clothes on the floor. *Not good.* From there he meandered to the galley kitchen. The sink held a few dirty dishes and the fridge was well stocked with the easy-to-prepare foods Grandma liked. Though he knew she drank most of her calories.

'I'm sure you're being careful,' Karen said to her daughter. 'That is your special power. Especially now that your looks are in the crapper.'

Direct hit, Dalton thought. Wondering how many times in

the space of their visit Leona and Karen would jab each other. *This is why she wants me here. Fine. I'll be her shield . . . for now.* 'Grandma, I don't get it. This place is pretty lux. Is there something else you want?'

'Ah sweetie,' Karen sank onto the sofa. 'Give me liberty or give me death. This place sucks. There's nothing to do. No one worth doing it with.'

'There's no bar. That's what you're saying, Mother.'

'Well, now that you mention it, the only thing that halfway passes as a club, is the lounge in the member's hall. I won't bore you with the details. The music sucks, and no available men under eighty. Should I continue?'

'Call an Uber?' Dalton suggested.

'Been there, done that. It's this town. It's—'

'Give it a rest, Mother. You're over seventy. It's a miracle you're still alive, and we both know why you're upset.'

'I don't know what you're talking about.'

Dalton could almost read his mother's thoughts. Would she pursue the topic or not? He sipped bourbon and waited.

'Men, Mother. There are no random men here. That's what this is about. And frankly, whether here or back in Boston, who's going to want to take a hag like you to bed? If my looks are in the crapper, and thank you so much for saying that, have you checked a mirror lately? Have you ever considered that there might be other things you could do to occupy your time? This place is filled with activities and theatre trips to Manhattan.'

'And that,' Karen said with a rise to her voice, 'would be a better place for me. Why can't you get me some swanky apartment in the city? Tons of suitable activities for an old hag like me.' She winked at Dalton.

'Not an option, Mother.'

'Yes, and what Leona says, goes. That's how it's always been.' Karen swigged back her drink, braced against the sofa arm, and propelled herself up towards the sideboard.

'No, Mother.' Leona's face grew red. 'That is not how it's always been. And everything I've achieved has been through my efforts. Nothing, absolutely nothing came from you. At least nothing good.'

'Hah!' Karen turned. 'Your looks. You got those from me. But beauty fades.'

'True and the drunken Swede you took to bed . . . and can't even remember his name. And growing up, all the questions. Who's your father, Leona? What does he do? No idea. No fucking idea.'

'Oh boo hoo. Poor Leona. Here comes the pity parade. It's not like things have gone so wrong for you. Did you ever wonder how maybe I had something to do with that?'

Dalton finished his drink and wondered about a second. But his current buzz was pleasant, and the drama was too rich to derail. He knew his mother. While she appeared in control, the twitch in her jaw foreshadowed an eruption.

'In certain lights,' Leona said, 'I do owe you. For not having clean school clothes. For coming home and finding you passed out on the couch, and the time you burned down our apartment with a cigarette smoldering in your bed. You made me lie to the fire marshal and police that I caused it. That I was playing with matches. You were a fabulous mother. And let's not forget the men. The uncles who'd hang around for a few days. And they'd look at me. I was eight the first time one of those bastards touched me. And where were you? Too drunk to stop it. Too drunk to care. Too drunk to give a shit about your only child.'

'Lies. You make stuff up. You always did that. Always told lies. I don't know what I ever did to deserve this treatment. I'm an old woman, locked away by a daughter who doesn't care. I was a good mother, Leona. Lots of people have worse. I had worse.'

'Fine. I'll put that on your tombstone. Here lies Karen Krawsinska, there were worse mothers.' She shook her head. 'Why do I even bother. I'm glad to see you're doing well. I'm sorry you're unhappy with your one-point-five-million-dollar prison, but no, there will be no Manhattan apartment. And here's the thing, Mother, everything you have hinges on your discretion. Should I find that you've done anything to disparage me, or should you again give an interview, this prison will be gone. No condo, no housekeepers, no weekly booze and cigarette delivery. So take some Ubers and see if you can get laid. I'm beyond caring, and no, none of the hell you put me through as a child was a lie. I remember it all. And I wish I didn't.' She turned to Dalton. 'We're leaving.'

'Sure.' He put his tumbler into the sink and walked to his grandmother. He kissed her on the cheek. 'You be good,' he said.

'I always am. Visit me without her. We didn't even get a chance to talk about your latest video. It's wonderful, baby. You should pursue your music full time. You have a talent. It's a pity to waste it.'

'I love you, Grandma.'

'Love you, too, baby boy.'

'Dalton,' Leona said. 'Let's go.'

He rolled his eyes.

'Do it,' Karen urged.

'She hates it when I do.'

'I know. Do it for me.' Karen smiled, he saw a glint in her eyes.

He glanced at his mother who clearly wanted out. He lowered his voice, and in a pitch-perfect imitation of Leona Lang whispered, 'Dalton, let's go.'

Karen grinned and clapped her hands. 'Love it. Love you.' And she gave him a second sloppy kiss.

'Got to go,' he said, still in Leona's voice.

She beamed at him, but as the screen door shut behind her she shouted, 'Whatever Leona wants, Leona gets.'

EIGHT

Frank's head spun with *what ifs*, on a Friday that seemed like it had no beginning or end. And now, here he was, seated on a stainless-steel workbench in the Brookline PD's forensic IT lab next to Brody who three hours back had turned into Sean. *But why am I really here? I can't go to jail. I can't get locked up. Not again.*

He'd been asked to help unlock Jackson's computer and to serve as a technical consultant on its scientific contents. *But why am I really here?*

Gabe, the balding computer guy, had started with the admission. 'We haven't made it past the log-in screen. Any chance you know his pass code?'

'It's HarveyKillsJackson,' and Bingo, the screen booted up with Jackson's last words, an email to him, with an ultimatum, and a motive for Frank to murder his mentor front and center for all to read.

Dear Frank:

It pains me to be your stumbling block. Yet, through the lens of my decades I see what you cannot or will not. Your research has ramifications far beyond your purely altruistic aims. Yes, I believe you could save those children. But at what cost? That's the rub and until you can address it in a manner that assuages my concerns I see us and you at a crucial point. For me to continue to offer my support I would like you to consider formally terminating your current research. Perhaps develop a new project that focuses on one of the many rich and related topics. I believe for someone as brilliant as you, this should not be difficult. However, should you not decide to terminate your current efforts

'This was the fight you'd told me about,' Sean, then still Detective Brody, had said.

'Yeah. Either I switched up my work, found a new sponsor, or packed my bags.'

'No idea being an egghead was so hard,' Detective Brody said with a smile.

'He never finished it.'

'It helps confirms the time of death, not long after you left.'

'This is interesting,' Gabe said.

'What?' Sean asked.

'About a third of the emails in his history came from dark web servers.'

'Then I'm surprised they're still there,' Frank said, finding it hard to breathe. 'They delete themselves after they're read.'

'You know about this stuff?' Gabe asked.

'Jackson was obsessed with privacy. I'm surprised he hung onto these.'

'Who's Blue E?' Sean asked, as he leaned into the screen. His shoulder brushed Frank's.

'No clue,' Frank said, but what was on the screen raised strange possibilities. Not so much from the content, which was about manipulating DNA in live organisms – essentially his work – but how it was signed by Jackson. '*Yours always.*'

'Here's another one from . . . I'm assuming a her. February of this year. Is she talking about you?' Sean asked.

Frank read the brief message.

J –

Theory is wonderful, but at some point becomes masturbatory. When Dr G progresses off the page and into the lab, or more importantly, into the nucleus, then we've moved forward. Has this happened? Will this happen? My inquiring mind wants to know.

Blue E

'He had a girlfriend?' Sean asked.

'No. At least, not that I knew of. He was married and widowed.'

'And you knew him well.'

'I thought I did.'

'Thing about homicide,' Sean said, 'turns out a lot of the time people aren't who we thought they were.'

Now, three hours later and slogging through hundreds of emails, Frank wondered, *Why aren't I a suspect? Or I am, and this is how they do it? Soften me up with beautiful hazel eyes, and a wonderful smile . . . and he's smart, and funny, and great. I'm crushing on the guy who's about to arrest me.* And sitting so close made it impossible to avoid shoulder grazes, and the accidental bump of feet or knees below the table.

'Earth to Doctor Frank,' Sean said.

'Am I a suspect?' He blurted. 'Is that why I'm here?'

'No. You're not,' Sean said. He paused and met Frank's gaze. Frank didn't flinch or blink. He was confused, from the tingle in his toes to the whirl in his gut, to the hammer of his pulse in his ears. *What is going on? I think I might puke. So uncool. And that's what you're worried about?* 'I've not told you everything. I can't and probably shouldn't. But we found the jewelry that was taken. It was pawned by a drug addict name of Brian Baker. Thirty-two, with an extensive arrest history. We tracked him down.'

'And he confessed?'

'He was dead,' Sean said. 'Got his hands on what was probably fentanyl-laced dope and he OD'ed.'

Frank felt like he'd been punched. 'And that's that. I should have stayed later. I should have . . .'

'Stop,' Sean said. 'You can't undo the past. He still had a few pieces of Ruth Atlas's jewelry. It would have been enough for a conviction.'

'If he were alive,' Frank said, gazing into Sean's eyes. It was awkward but comforting and even wonderful in the midst of another awful thing in his life. *And this is where I turn into a twelve-year-old with a crush and make an idiot of myself.* 'So why are we doing this?'

'To be thorough, Frank. You said some interesting things about Jackson. They all checked out. People feared him. Hated him. Didn't feel bad that he'd been murdered. A couple said they weren't surprised. I was sort of shocked.' Sean broke eye contact. 'Not what I expected about an academic.'

'You made a conclusion before evaluating all possibilities,' Frank said.

'Yes, professor. That's why we're here, looking at all the ways Jackson insulted and attacked his peers. A bruised ego or destroyed career has been motive for many murders. Not to mention the financial side. When he went after something, he took no prisoners.'

And there's that smile. A, is it possible he's gay? B, is it possible he's into me? And C, I always get this shit wrong. 'That was Jackson. A one-man army against big pharma. And thank you for taking this seriously.'

'You're welcome. In my job ninety percent of the time things are what they seem, but you never know when the other ten percent will hit. Parts of this case seem too tidy. It gets my spidey-sense tingling. Did you know that the cost for the average cancer patient from diagnosis to death is over a million bucks?'

'I did. It's a massive money-making industry. And most of it's crap. It enraged Jackson.'

'And it seems like your work with those telomeres . . . Can I ask you something?'

Frank was struck by the sincerity in Sean's tone. 'Sure.'

'I pulled your article, *A Theoretical Argument for Extension of the Hayflick Limit*. Took me a couple times to get the gist. If I understood it, you're proposing a process that can reverse tumor growth and potentially extend life. This is why you've got all these drug companies blowing up your phone, correct?'

'Yes.'

'OK.' Sean paused, and returned to the last Blue E letter. 'So, is it just theory? I know you said it was, but . . .'

Frank said nothing.

'Frank?'

He felt trapped. Here was the heart of what had pissed off Jackson and what if Detective Brody . . . Sean, wasn't who he seemed. *What if he's connected to a drug company? What if this is a different sort of trap? One that comes with beautiful eyes. It wouldn't be the first time.* Since he'd published the article Sean referenced, on three occasions he'd had curious meet-cutes with exceptionally handsome men. Two had progressed to dates, both cut short over dinner when the conversation shifted to his work and pitches from pharmaceutical giants. 'Is this part of the investigation?'

'Not really, but you got to admit, this is fascinating stuff. You don't have to tell me.'

'I can't.'

'And you just did.'

'Tell me you're not a secret agent for a drug company.' Frank tried to make it sound like a joke. It didn't.

'I'm not.'

'I did a small study with tumorous Norwegian rats,' he blurted.

'What happened to the rats?'

Frank faced Sean, Jackson's object lesson about Leona Krawsinska screamed in his head. 'I shouldn't tell you this.'

'I won't repeat it.'

'They got better.'

'No more tumors?'

'Not a one.'

'And you know that because . . . when the study was over you sacrificed the animals.'

'I did.'

'Why?'

'To perform thorough dissections on all the major organs. I needed to see if in fact the infusion I'd given them had been taken up into all nucleated cells. And . . .'

'And what?'

'People started to notice that my rats acted different from other rats.'

'Go on.'

'Smarter, bigger, on more than one occasion Grace and I came into the lab to find they'd figured out how to unlock their cages.'

'You terminated the study before people asked uncomfortable questions?'

'Yes.'

'That must have been hard. I mean, no fan of rats, but they sound kind of fun.' Sean looked at him hard. 'Did you kill all of them?'

Frank started. He hadn't told Sean about Caesar and Lavinia, the two he'd saved from the post-study massacre and dissection. 'You ask good questions, Detective.'

'It's my job.'

Frank's cell buzzed. He felt sick to his stomach. *I shouldn't have told him any of this. What have I done?*

'Speaking of,' Sean said. 'You going to get that?'

Frank glanced at the screen. It was Grace. He nodded.

'Let me give you some privacy.'

Frank watched as Sean walked to the other side of the narrow room, *stop checking out his ass . . . is that why you told him? Nice ass.* 'Hey Grace.'

'Where are you? I've sent you like ten texts. Aren't you planning to do rounds at the hospital this afternoon? And you know we have a game at four.'

'I'm at the Brookline police department.'

'Oh shit, Frank. What do you need?'

'It's good . . . at least I think it's good. I'm helping the detective go through Jackson's files. Like a consultant.'

'Be careful.'

'He said it was a robbery and that the guy who did it pawned some of Ruth's stuff, and then overdosed.'

'Then why go through Jackson's files?'

'Sean said it's to be thorough.'

'Sean?'

'Yeah, the detective.'

'First names . . . he cute?'

'Very.'

'Wedding ring?'

'No.'

'Gay?'

'Can't tell.'

'You into him?'

Silence.

'OK, nerd boy,' Grace said. 'Do something.'

'Like?'

'Ask him for coffee.'

'He already brought me some.'

'God, for someone with your IQ you are the dumbest person I know.'

'Thank you.'

'Ask him out for coffee.'

'He's looking over here. And it's already two thirty.' *How did it get to be so late?* 'I got to go.'

'Do something. And if you're going to make it to the game on time, you're going to have to do it fast.'

'Right,' and he disconnected. Grace's instructions rang in his head. But any way he ran the script he couldn't make *'you want to go out for coffee?'* sound right. Sweat trickled down the back of his neck, and with every step Sean took towards him, the saliva drained from his mouth. He swallowed. 'Sean, I got to go.' *And this is where he pulls out the cuffs.*

'I hadn't realized how long I'd kept you. Sorry about that.'

'Don't be.' Frank grabbed his knapsack from under the table, hoisted it over one shoulder. He stood but miscalculated the distance between them, and nearly clipped Sean's chin as he stood. He backed away and tripped on a chair leg.

Sean reflexively grabbed him by his shoulders to steady him. Frank's pulse raced. He berated himself for his utter lack of cool. With his five-inch height advantage he looked down into Sean's clear cool gaze.

'You OK, big guy?'

'I'm a clutz.' He didn't back away and Sean didn't loosen his hold.

'You're allowed.' He let go. 'I didn't ask how Killer and the bird are doing?'

'My place is too small for a four-hundred-pound tortoise. And I've already gotten complaints from the downstairs neighbor about Harvey's swearing.' *Ask him for coffee. Ask him for coffee.*

'Not to mention Caesar and Lavinia.'

'Who are they? Cats? Dogs? Norwegian Rats?'

Frank started.

'Right,' Sean said. 'And that's when you were saved by the bell. You don't have to tell me if you don't want . . . but I'm thinking Caesar and Lavinia aren't your average rats.'

'They're not.' Frank's thoughts spun hard and fast. *If he's read my work, what else does he know?*

'I'd like to hear it,' Sean said.

Was that an invitation . . . or an interrogation? 'If you need more help with Jackson's computer . . .' Frank offered as the moment slipped away. *He's probably not gay. The odds are small. Even if he were, someone this smart and good looking, he's got someone. How could he not? And does he know about my mother? About me? About my shit luck with guys?*

'Naah, you've been more than generous with your time. But I'll call if we get stuck. Chances are good that when we get the rest of the forensics back on the dead junkie, I'll close it out.'

'Right.' Frank slipped his other arm though the backpack. 'You play baseball?'

'Not since college, why?'

'That's where I'm headed. It's a LGBTQ team, but it's not a requirement,' he added. 'And we're always down a player or two. No uniforms. We do have jerseys.' *Shut up.* 'We're The

Nimble Nerds, mostly lab rats and researchers.' He held his breath and forced himself not to look away. He couldn't read Sean's response.

'Wish I could, but it's one of my long days. Some other time, maybe.' His smile didn't waver, he didn't break gaze.

'Right.' The moment was gone. Time to go. He headed towards the door.

'You taking the bus?' Sean asked.

Frank looked down. 'It's not far. I was planning to run.'

'To Cambridge?'

'Yeah. I run. It clears my head. There's a science to it, actually.' He stopped himself from launching into all the neuro-transmitters, endogenous opioids, and growth factors that get released during intense exercise and how that stimulates increased synaptic connections and density.

'Got it, and Frank . . .'

'Yeah?'

'Thanks again, and have a good game.' His gaze was intense.

'But something else.'

'Yes?'

'Be careful, Frank. If even a quarter of what you hinted at in your study is true, or if it's not, and people think it's true, you've got something with serious value. Be careful.'

'You too.' *What the hell did I just say? What the fuck is wrong with me?* And before he could turn into a bigger moron, he headed out.

NINE

L eona stared up through the magnifying lens into the distorted eyes of her plastic surgeon, Dr Ramon.
She tried to read his expression and wondered how much Botox it had taken to give his forehead its porcelain-smooth surface. Not a line, not a wrinkle. She avoided her own reflection, magnified and brutally lit in two cantilevered mirrors on either side of the doctor's head. *I hate this.* So she focused on

her own forehead, just injected and tried to feel her skin. Nothing, just a sea of numb.

'It's time, Leona.' He pulled out a black marker.

Get that fucking thing away from my face.

'Nothing drastic . . . not yet.' Without asking her permission, he deftly traced potential incisions under her eyes, chin, neck. 'Unless you want to.' His touch felt feather light on the chemically-frozen planes of her skin.

She forced her gaze onto the magnified horrorshow of her marked-up face. She tried to remember when it had turned from being her best friend, to this . . . problems everywhere. Like a work of art left out in acid rain. Her mother had not been wrong about how she'd used her beauty. And yes, if she owed Karen anything, it was that. But now . . . 'I'm not ready for surgery. I need to think about this. But tell me what you'd recommend. And be specific.'

An hour later, Leona drove up to her Greenwich estate and took calls. The two-hour drive, traffic depending, was never wasted. She dispensed with a driver, as trust was a problem. Other than Dalton, no one was privy to her plans. And even with him, it was need-to-know. She was demoralized, *nothing to be done for it . . . at least not yet.*

Now on the line was Lydia Finch, VP of marketing, a typical UNICO executive: hungry, ambitious, and aware that jobs in Leona's executive suite were two-to-five-year stopping points. Do well and bounce up and out to something better; fall on Leona's bad side and kiss your career goodbye.

She listened to Lydia's crisp summation. As she rattled off the highlights of the new campaigns for UNICO's top selling drugs: Primepop – for erectile dysfunction, Grenadavir – an antiviral for hepatitis C that cost over a thousand dollars a pill and sixty grand for the full course, Renepicide B – a chemo-therapeutic infusion agent with recent FDA approval for multiple malignancies, and Serpamaline for anxiety and depression. And as Lydia talked, mock-ups of ad campaigns flashed across Leona's dashboard monitor.

'Haggard. Get someone younger,' she said, critiquing the actress sprawled dishabille on a bed for the Primepop ad, then hazarded a glance in the rearview mirror at her own forehead. Ramon was right, Botox and collagen were no longer enough.

'And for Grenadavir we're no longer the only hep C drug in the race. We need a famous face. Someone hip from the sixties. Send the message that if you can remember the sixties you weren't a part of them. I want marching in rallies, tie dye, dancing naked in the rain, someone passing a joint.'

'Got it,' Lydia said. 'It's cool to be infected. Shows you were relevant, that you cared.'

'Exactly. See who's still alive from Woodstock . . . one of those wispy folk singers. We could purchase rights to a song, get them to sing it. Happy scenes of ex-hippie baby boomers running through fields of poppies . . . with grand-kids and a dog trailing behind . . .'

'Done and done,' Lydia said. 'The insurance companies hate it.'

'Of course they do,' Leona said. 'It's sixty grand out of their pockets and into ours. And with a ninety-eight-percent cure rate, they can't deny their members. So . . . go big. Throw three million dollars on the table and see who grabs for it. Go as high as five, for a Woodstock headliner.'

'I'm on it.'

Leona turned off on the Greenwich ramp. Yes, clear objectives. Either Lydia would bring in a virus-riddled A-lister, or she'd be replaced. 'And Renepicide . . . the numbers suck.'

There was silence.

'Spit it out.'

'Bad spin from the lawsuits.'

'So? Spin it back.' Annoyed, she glanced at the monitor. 'Lydia, these layouts suck. Shaved heads and cancer wards? We're supposed to give people hope. These are fucking funereal. Who did them?'

'Wells and Freeman.'

'Dump them. I don't want to ever see depressing shit like this with UNICO on it. You need to screen this shit. It makes me question your judgment . . . your taste.'

'Won't happen again.'

'Better not. Got to go.' She ended the call, 'Gate,' she said, and turned onto a street of estates, each one different, some with sweeping expanses of glass, others built at the end of the nineteenth century for captains of industry, those on the right, with unobstructed views of Long Island Sound and eight-digit price tags. Hers, at the cul-de-sac's end on a promontory with two-hundred-seventy-degree water views, was unrivaled.

Her hand-forged gates opened onto a beech lined cobblestone drive. Left stood a blooming orchard of mature peach, pear, nectarine, and heirloom apple trees. To the right a Carrera marble turn-of-the-century Greco-Roman three-story masterpiece with panoramic views.

She got out and breathed in salt air, then gave herself a moment to take in the sounds of surf, gulls, bees in the orchard, and her golden retriever's excited barks. She tried to feel the spring sun against her frozen brow but couldn't. And as she pictured Dr Ramon's black pen, her mood sank. *That is not going to happen.* Her pulse quickened, because she knew, like her beauty, time was not on her side. And like chiding one of her employees, or even Dalton, she berated herself for inaction. *Make this fucking happen. You need this and you need it now.*

She headed out back as her golden retriever, Rex III, danced at the outer edge of his electric fence.

Careless of her cream Prada suit, she braced for his inevitable tongue bath. With a click of her keyring she brought down the invisible fence, and woman and dog embraced. 'Love you, love you, love you,' she cooed into the silky softness of his neck. 'Enough,' and she pushed him down to where he could lick only her hand. She stroked his broad head. 'Such a good boy.' And the two walked back towards a pier built on boulders craned in by the house's original robber baron owner. At its end, surrounded by water deep enough to moor a yacht, was a weathered marble cupola plucked from an ancient Italian estate. She sat and petted Rex. 'Who's a good boy?' She pulled out a disposable burner phone from her bag and a rawhide dog treat from a bin beneath her chair. She fed Rex a chewy and punched in a number.

With her free hand, she massaged Rex's favorite behind-the-ear spot, waited, and her call was answered on the third ring.

'Yes?' A man's voice.

Leona savored the view and pictured the lead attorney in a

large class-action suit against UNICO and Renepicide. She'd
endured two four-hour depositions and learned more than she'd
revealed. Including that the case rested on testimony and illegally
obtained evidence from Renepicide's lead researcher, an
annoying little man fired years back when he tried to block the
release of the drug. *I should have done it then.* 'Dr Malcom
Bender. He drinks. Make it look like an accident, an embarrassing one.'

'Collateral damage?'

'Yes.' *Dead and discredited.* She stroked Rex's neck and back.
'Consider it done.'

Leona met Rex's adoring gaze. *Still perfect.* 'Double if it's
within twenty-four hours.'

'Double it is.'

The line went dead. She held Rex firm with her left hand,
and with the muscle memory from high school and college
basketball, she hurled the phone. It splashed and sank into the
depths of the Sound. Rex barked and strained, clearly wanting
both the swim and the game of fetch. *An ender to Doctor
Bender,* she mused.

But then she felt something soft and fleshy on Rex's right
rear haunch. She pulled back his fur. Her spirits plummeted – a
tumor, not the soft squishy fat ones that could easily be removed,
but a malignancy. 'Ah, too bad boy. I thought it might be you.'

'Come on.' She picked up a well-chewed tennis ball hidden
under a flowerpot and to Rex's delight rocketed it towards the
house. Sadness welled, but she stopped it. *He won't really die.*
She'd have him euthanized once his replacement, Rex IV, with
several embryos on standby, was ready. *This next one will be
the one.* She watched her beautiful Rex, and thought about Dr
Frank Garfield. *How long will your magic keep the next one
alive?* And more importantly, *keep me alive?* As a scientist,
albeit out of the lab for decades, Garfield's work obsessed her.
While a generation separated them, he'd effectively picked up
where she'd stopped. *But had I known . . . and how does he
do it? What's the trick, Dr Garfield? Did Jackson know?*

Rex bounded back with the spittle-soaked ball. He dropped
it by her feet and nudged it with his nose. She threw it again
and headed towards the back porch. Her thoughts were a torrent

of anxiety. *What if Dalton can't convince him? What if Jackson was wrong about the process? What if it's a fake? If he's a fake?* But she'd read the study and knew that Jackson would never have allowed his name to go on anything inaccurate. It was maddening. To know that Garfield had unraveled the key to something amazing, real life extension, and with it the tantalizing possibility of a return to youth. Something she desperately needed. She thought, *what if Dalton can't bring him in? What then? And her back-up, Jackson . . . no longer an option. And how the fuck did that happen?*

As Rex returned, she knew Garfield was her only shot, others would figure things out but that would be years down the line, years she did not have. 'Whatever it takes.' And speaking to her rapt canine audience, she added, 'Everyone wants something. Garfield wants to heal the children, to be Jesus Christ. Good for him. And I will make that happen. He will make the sick, well. He will give me back my youth, my beauty. And after . . . crosses to bear.'

TEN

Preoccupied, Frank watched from the bench as the pitcher, a Harvard biophysicist, over-spun a curve ball and walked Dirk Carver. They were two down in the first, and Frank, might, or might not make it to bat in this inning. But his thoughts weren't on the game.

'The cop,' Grace said, from her spot on his right. 'Tell me.' She had her cap on backwards, and her *Nimble Nerds* T-shirt had fresh stains from a fudgsicle.

'What do you want to know? He hasn't arrested me.'

'You said, he's cute and no wedding ring. Did you ask him out?'

This was pure Grace. The only person on the planet, whom he knew without doubt, had his back. A week ago Jackson had been mostly in that category. But even he, after years of mentorship, still gave Frank unconditional respect . . . but not support.

'His name is Sean Brody. I have not yet Binged or Googled him. Around our age. Good looking. Objectively, out of my league. But I asked him to the game. Told him we were a mostly LBGTQ team. He said he couldn't, but maybe some other time.'

'Ouch. That's vague. A for effort. But, Frank, your romantic life may now have to be taken off life support and declared dead. Forget him being out of your league, you're not even playing.'

'People in glass houses, Grace . . .' he said, not wanting to rehash his romantic misadventures. Which he chalked up to a simple equation. His work and patients took precedence, and if he subtracted out the recent drug-company moles, the only two guys he'd fallen for had both run off after he'd told them a fraction of his story. There really was no slick way around, 'yeah, my Mom killed my Dad, tried to kill me, and is locked up – hopefully for life – in a hospital for the criminally insane. Oh, and she still wants me dead. And . . . when I was a kid I was in a few nut houses myself. But I'm fine, really, sort of . . .' After the last one, Dean, bolted and accused him of lying and keeping things from him, it seemed like a no win to even try. Now, he looked at Grace, short, cute, blonde and curvy. While he'd always known he was gay, they had nonetheless shared a few fumbling adolescent make-out sessions, which ended with laughter and the recognition that theirs was not a romantic connection.

'Point taken. But my dating problems are your fault.'

'How's that?' He lowered his voice, not wanting their business overheard by their notoriously gabby teammates. But even more, an uncomfortable tingle, like being watched. It was hard to shake, and since Jackson's death it had been like background noise. Which he knew, based on experience, could blossom into full-bore paranoia.

'I have you and my dad as templates for what a guy can be. Dad is bedrock who in fifty years of marriage has loved my mom, supported me . . . you, and my sisters. And then I have you.'

'And I mess up your love life . . . how?'

'Frank, you are thick. Brilliant, but—'

'I know. Give me the remedial and no big words.'

She jabbed him with her elbow.

'Ow.'

'You're my perfect guy, Frank. That's the problem. You listen to me, don't pull any competitive bullshit or get upset that I'm smart and can make a lot of money. You're my best friend, have never betrayed me . . . and you're gay.'

'There is that.'

'It pisses me off.'

'I've never hidden it from you. And we did try.'

'Doesn't matter, and don't remind me. I did not need to know you had a crush on Cory Johnson in the seventh grade.'

'I wanted you to know.'

'We all had crushes on Cory . . . he was dreamy, and that's not the point . . . it's just, why can't I find a version of you who's straight?'

'You can do better than me, Grace. If you didn't have chocolate on your shirt, you're quite attractive. But maybe you shouldn't play on a gay team.'

'I have to,' she said. 'Someone has to look after my best friend. And I'm tired of guys hitting on me because I'm pretty. Pretty fades.'

'That's how it works. Law of attraction.' He pictured Sean and chided himself for the memory of his ass walking away. *It's hormones. You're gay, horny, and he's hot. Get over it.*

'I know, and it sucks.'

The crack of a ball meeting the bat. And they watched Jane Brettford get a solid base hit. Dirk advanced to second.

'You're up,' Grace said.

'Right,' he strode to the plate, made a few practice swings. His legs felt good and loose from the earlier run from the Brookline PD. Though for the first few miles of that he'd not been able to clear Sean from his head. *Did I make an idiot of myself by asking him to play, or by saying it was a gay team?* But other stuff intruded. Jackson's murder, a horrible sense of freefall, of not knowing what the hell he was doing, and where he was supposed to go with his work. Jackson couldn't have been clearer. *And he's gone, and you've got no sponsor . . . at least no one you can trust. And why did you tell Sean about Caesar and Lavinia?*

Distracted, he made eye contact with the pitcher. He gripped
the bat and focused. He found comfort in, *keep your eye on the
ball*.

The first pitch came in hard and fast, he swung and missed.
'Strike one.'

He adjusted, then thought. *What the hell am I doing here?*
Pitch two was low.

'One ball, one strike.'

Pitch three was a gift. *Eye on the ball*, and that awesome
feel of the bat's sweet spot as it connected. It was good.
His feet dug hard. He rounded first. *What am I doing? Tenure
track means something . . . Or does it?*

Oblivious to the other team's frantic efforts to field the ball,
he pumped hard and rounded second and then third. He heard
cheers as Dirk, and then Jane, scored. He glanced back to see
an outfielder fumble. He sprinted home.

Surrounded by teammates his head buzzed. If he couldn't
make it stop, it would overwhelm him. *What am I doing here?*
Panic, never far from the surface, clawed at him.

'Fuck, that's a hard act to follow,' Grace griped as the players
resumed the game.

'Eye on the ball.' He forced a smile and practiced a breathing
technique his shrink had taught him. *What am I doing? If I
don't have my work, if I don't have Jackson.* But what helped
was thinking about Jen Owens and the kids on that ward. *That's
the point. They're the point.* Problem was getting his research
to where it could make a real difference. But the truth crushed
him. *It's too late for her, for any of them.* It would take full-
scale studies, and that was money. Big money, which no matter
its source, came with strings. Jackson knew that. And Frank
too had seen colleagues get sucked into the pharma industry
where they lost all control of their research.

And then his psychotic mother's voice rang in his head. *'Son
of Satan. Dance with the devil you know or the one with the
pretty bow.'* He gripped the bench.

Shut up. It was always like this, when he was at his most
jangled, dear old mom, Candace, crawled into his head. Not really
a voice, but snippets from his childhood, and the court case that
ended in her being deemed not guilty by reason of mental defect

for the murder of his father and attempted murder of him when he was eight. But that was just the tip of a childhood no one should have to endure.

'You should never have been born,' she hissed.

Shut up. Shut up. Shut up.

'Should have drowned you in the bath. Should have bashed in your skull with a ballpeen hammer.'

His cell rang. Reflexively, he went to reject the call, but looked at the screen. It clicked to voice mail. He put it to his ear.

'Hi Doctor Garfield, this is Cameron Causeway with Frick and Braxton. I'm calling on behalf of Jones-Ehrlichman Pharmaceuticals. We have a unique opportunity that seems like a perfect fit for you. They're most eager to set up a meeting, and I was hoping—'

With his finger poised over delete, Frank did something rare. 'This is Frank Garfield.' He took the call.

ELEVEN

With his *Little Brother* earpiece in place and the powerful receiver in his briefcase Dalton focused on Frank and his gal pal. Earlier in the day he'd told the UNICO recruiter assigned to Frank that he was canned. He'd made zero headway, and the last thing Dalton needed was Mother's wrath. Yes, if you want something done right, do it yourself.

He assessed the options. Through shades, he watched as Frank got up, batted and hit a home run. Then as the lanky scientist rounded the bases and was embraced by his band of teammates, he smiled. He pondered what that must be like, to be part of a team. To have people care for you and cheer you on. His years at NYU's Tisch School of the Arts had given him a taste of that. Being part of a theatre production, performing, albeit mostly with parents and classmates in the audience, the applause, the rush of adrenalin. Leona, of course, never came.

'And what's this?' he muttered, as Frank took the call from one of UNICO's competitors. *Uh oh, Mother will not like that.* He thought of Grandma Karen's, *'whatever Leona wants, Leona gets.' And that's the truth, shit. And you don't have much time. Someone will land this tall fish and it best be you.*

From his shadowed vantage point in the bleachers, he mulled the data. Frank had the hots for the detective investigating Atlas's murder. Pride surged at how well he'd played that and that Leona had no clue that he'd been the triggerman. *She seemed upset.* The fly in that ointment and his current unrest, *Did I kill my biological father? And why did she never tell me about Atlas?*

His thoughts churned, bouncing from Leona back to the detective. It wasn't concern that she might learn the facts of Atlas's murder, but something else. *Interesting.* The past few weeks studying Frank Garfield had given him a sense of ownership. He pondered this. *Do you find Garfield attractive? Are you jealous?*

Dalton's fluid sexuality was not a thing he questioned. Women he found delicious, with their soft curves, and the ease with which they gave themselves to him . . . Men, the few he'd dallied with in college, were another matter. There, it was less about the physical and more a battle for domination. Who would submit? He now stared at Frank's back, broad shoulders, narrow waist, and compared him to Grace. She was delectable, like a ripe blonde peach. And a key component to the Garfield challenge. He pictured the both of them naked, one on either side of him.

Then as one dull inning droned into the next, Dalton listened and scribbled verses in his notebook. Over the years, he'd filled dozens. Nothing fancy. Some he'd go back and work into songs. His most-recent YouTube video had nearly gone viral, with twenty-thousand hits, over a hundred comments, sixty-two shares, though several had been his own to Facebook, Twitter, and Instagram. Almost enough to get him noticed. Though if he'd had Mother's connections and money, it could have happened a dozen times over. But that did not fall under what Leona wants. *What I want doesn't matter. It never has. It never will with her.*

'*Am I Oedipus?*' he wrote at the top of a fresh page.

As he scribbled out the day's emotions, his thoughts flowed. '*When did I become Mother's Renfield? Why does the blood of two fathers stain my waking dreams? Who stole my silver chalice? What ransom will they need?*'

Words spilled forth along with memories. As he listened to the easy back-and-forth between Frank and his Grace, he mused. *Where are my friends?*

The answer was clear. *You have none. You are the man who walks alone.* And then he launched into free verse.

Where are my friends, Leona? Where are my companions of youth? Little red-headed Peter when I was ten, what were his faults? You listed them all. Too poor, not our kind. And don't get me started on the gingers. You called him a throwback and a mutant.

You can do better, Dalton she'd say, try again.

Amy in seventh grade. Dark hair and doe eyes. You summed her up fast and summed her up well. For a fat girl, not bad, but the apple and the tree do not fall far. Look at her dad, passed out on the couch, look at the mom, haggard by thirty-three.

You can do better, Dalton she'd say. Try again.

By ninth grade, he'd stopped bringing home potential friends. And when he'd get invited for sleepovers they were accompanied by Leona's interrogations, and then character assassinations of his prospective hosts and their families. *She didn't and doesn't want me to have friends.*

As his thoughts roamed he took inventory of the people in his life. It was mother and Grandma Karen. The Lang cousins, Rebecca, Kendra, and James, children of his Aunt Joan and Uncle Bennett, they'd been a part of his life before Dad's death. But after . . . Well, he'd attended Becca's wedding two years back. Leona had declined the invite. 'They're jealous of what we have, Dalton. I have no intention of going, but will of course send a gift. It's the only reason they invite us.'

Where are my friends, Leona? Who will love me?

With pen poised, he stopped. The answer was too painful, but as a true artist, he had to go there. *I have no one. I have only blood and water on a shower floor. I have another man, an older one, crumpled on the floor.*

But then a sixth-inning conversation between Frank and Grace pulled him from his reverie.

'Her review is soon, isn't it?' Grace asked, all humor gone from her tone.

'Next week.'

'I'll go with you.'

'No need. I'll be bad company,' Frank said.

'I don't care. And I don't understand why they put you through this every six months.'

Dalton knew what they were talking about. Perhaps the most interesting aspect of Dr Frank Garfield, his curious origins and that his mother had bashed out his father's brains with a hammer and had tried to do the same to Frank. *We have things in common, you and me.*

'I have to.'

'I know, it's just . . .' Grace said.

'They're well intended,' he interrupted her, 'but they miss the central problem with my mother.'

'Which is?'

'She's smarter than all of them; the doctors, the social workers. She knows how to keep her crazy hidden. If I don't go, there's no telling what they'll do.'

'They wouldn't let her out?'

'Yes, they would. And that's why I go . . . and we're out.'

Dalton also followed the game as The Nimble Nerds got their third out on a simple fly ball, and Grace and Frank headed towards their positions at first and second base. He studied them. Frank, tall, dark-haired, good-looking albeit with scruff and a fourteen-dollar haircut with long wavy bangs, which back in the eighties were a thing. And Grace, five-two, curvy and blonde, though Leona would savage her features one after the other. There was an ease to the two of them together, no pretense, no holding back. *What is that like? To have friends? Real friends.*

Leona would call him naïve. I'm the only one who truly loves you, she'd say.

'Right,' he muttered. *Head in the game.* And as he had nights earlier, when he'd killed Atlas, he calculated the equation of Frank Garfield. Only now was not the time for murder, but for casting bait, hooking, and then reeling in this fish. He weighed the variables, the pretty best friend, the dying children, and his mother's insistence that Garfield had something she needed. But into the mix, he allowed the possibility for something else. *Maybe Mother always gets what she wants.* He stared at Frank, gawky, poetic, and from angles, beautiful. *But maybe, just maybe, I get something I want.*

TWELVE

F rank stared at the Persian carpet in Dr Aaron Stein's cozy office in the university mental health clinic. His thoughts swam with badness. It began with Jen Owen's latest MRI, progressed to the neurologic decline in five-year-old Lakeesha Thomas, as her astrocytoma now spread to her visual cortex, and to a sick sense since Jackson's murder. *But this started before that. So why aren't I doing something to save them? Because you can't. Not true. You can, you have to figure how. You know how.*

'Put words to your feelings,' Stein urged.

He looked up at his bearded and bespectacled therapist. 'Hollow, empty, sad. But that's not it . . . not all.' He checked out the color of Stein's socks, having been disturbed in a session a decade ago that one had been black and the other blue. Today, they matched . . . *thank God.*

'I'm sorry about Jackson. I know he was important to you.'

'To lots of people. But yeah, he's been my faculty advisor since I was twenty-two. He helped me write my first grant, got me through my thesis and lots of papers.' *So why couldn't you have done what he asked. Change directions. Do something else.* 'I've been with him almost as long as I've been with you.'

'Did you go to the funeral?'

'It was a memorial service on Saturday. He wanted to be cremated and hated funerals. People said nice things.'

'And you? Did you speak?'

'I didn't. And most who did were full of shit. The dean could not stand Jackson. He made it sound like they were chums. It stank.'

'Jackson liked to stir the pot. The dean was being political.'

Frank nodded. His gaze caught on an arabesque in the rug, symmetry and chaos. 'It's like DNA.'

'What is?'

'Everything. People think it's order and structure. But when you really look, it's a frenzy. Apparent anarchy, but it's not.'

'What is it?'

'God . . . and the devil, too. One brings order and the other chaos. Nothing happens without cause.' He sensed Stein's interest intensify, a shift in posture, an eyebrow raise.

'You've come a long way, Frank. You know that, don't you?'

'Thanks . . . but she's still in here . . . I hear her sometimes.'

'Your mother.'

'Yeah. Me and Norman Bates. I push her back. I couldn't when I was a kid. Your rug helps. DNA helps. Baseball helps. Jackson helped . . . and that's another thing, his murder can't have been a robbery.'

'What if it was?'

Frank met Stein's gaze. 'It is what it is, right? Accept and move on. His murder makes no sense. Sure, he had stuff that someone could sell, but it's like going to the Museum of Fine Arts to commit a robbery and taking the donation box.'

Stein nodded, 'What else, Frank? You've got stuff going on in there. Big stuff and you don't have to be a psychologist to see it.'

'Everything. Like, what am I doing here?' He caught a flash of concern cross Stein's face. 'No. I'm not suicidal, haven't been for years. I stayed at MIT to work with Jackson, he was helping me figure it out. It was my name on that last grant . . . with his, so it's not like anyone's going to kick me out. At least not right away. But I can't see how I'm going to get the funding I need without becoming some giant drug-company whore.'

'So Jackson's killer murdered your work as well?'

'If I let it. Jackson wanted me to shift directions.'

'Because?'

'He thought I was headed down a dangerous road. Something that could be twisted into . . . I don't know what. Although he did. And maybe I do too.'

'You work on the stress response and its effects on the DNA?' Stein asked.

'Yes . . . I'm trying to alter the natural course. At this point everyone knows that the more bad things that happen to you when you're young, the shorter your life expectancy. In the lab, under the electron microscope, this translates to shorter telomeres.'

'Which means what?'

'That the biological clock is older than the person. The DNA has lost the configuration of youth, and diseases of both the body and mind, increase.' Frank paused, caught on a thought. 'Age is relative. We say you don't look your age, or man she's really aged bad. Numeric age is irrelevant. Cellular age is everything.'

'Interesting. I've read several of your articles. The last one on the stress response was mind blowing.'

Frank started. Stein checking on his work outside of their fifty-minute sessions, felt discordant. It made him think of Sean, and with that came a pang of regret that he'd never hear from him again. 'Jackson didn't want me to publish that.'

'Really? You'd not mentioned that. What reason did he give?'

'That some drug company would see potential in what I'm doing and sweep me off to their evil world.'

'You've had a lot of offers,' Stein said.

'True. And since that paper came out, my phone hasn't stopped.'

'It's important stuff, Frank. You don't need a PhD to see that. You're onto a central question of existence. What causes us to get ill, to age, and to die? What you're investigating in the lab, I work with in my office. The fallout of trauma. Although for me it's mostly about the mind and less the body.'

'It's a mistake to separate them.'

'You're not alone in that belief,' Stein said. 'But back to you and your life after Jackson Atlas.'

'I took Killer and Harvey.'

'Jackson's pets.'

'Yeah, my place is too small.' And he'd never told Stein about Caesar and Lavinia, how he'd crossed a line . . . several actually, including one of the most basic rules of animal research – don't name test subjects.

'From what you've told me, it's too small for you.'

'It's easy to manage. It was . . . Killer eats twenty pounds a day.' He stared down. 'I feel lost, Dr Stein. Outside of Grace . . . I don't have extra people in my life. My family, what's left of them, is for shit. I loved my grandparents, but they're gone. I know you're here to help me figure stuff on my own, but this time I need advice. Can you do that?'

'Of course,' he said without hesitation.

'What should I do?'

Stein paused. He smiled.

'What's funny?'

'I was going to flip it around on you.' He mimicked himself, 'What do you think you should do? It's a reflex. But you asked for advice. So here it is, Jackson's death, and I am sorry for your loss, Frank, but it's created a hole filled with opportunity. You don't see that yet, but it's true. You've worked hard to get yourself where you are today, and I'm not talking about your papers and your prowess as a researcher or how good you are with your patients.'

'I'm not as big a head case. And no meds.'

'Correct . . . and no meds, though—'

'Don't. Not happening. Out with the advice. What kind of opportunity?'

'No crystal ball here, but I'm sitting with an articulate, brilliant, and quirky thirty-two-year-old man, who has achieved great things and overcome a brutal childhood. I know how hard you work to hold it all together. The voices, the flashbacks, the nightmares, all of it. But what I'm going to suggest goes opposite to your instincts. But you're strong enough. So here goes, rather than walling off and shutting out, allow stuff to happen.'

'Like how?'

'Easy. You've learned how to figure out your emotions. When we first met those were a foreign county. Here's the deal, when you catch yourself avoiding something, ask one question, "is this a real threat?" If the answer is yes, then step away, but if the answer is no, or even neutral, do it. You get what I'm saying?'

'Like, pick up the phone when my mother calls from the nut house? Even though I have a restraining order and she's not supposed to have my number?'

Stein chuckled, 'Start easier, but that's the idea. If fear tells you to go left, go right.'

'Ignore fear? Isn't it there for a reason?'

'Absolutely, but in your case, it takes over when it's not needed. It's what causes your panic attacks, and the anxiety that makes you afraid to leave the house some days. Fear and anxiety want to keep you in a tiny prison cell, which is now filled with a giant tortoise. But you hold the key. Turn the lock, Frank. Push back. Do it consistently. Over and over and over. Maybe you won't slay the dragon, but you'll kick it out of your way. And then you'll be able to move on with your life.'

THIRTEEN

Stein's words echoed as Frank left the health center where he'd come since he was a seventeen-year-old undergrad. He headed towards the subway, not wanting to arrive at the hospital in a soaking sweat. His mind raced. He pictured Sean's hazel eyes – *probably not gay, probably not interested. He seemed sincere about me not being a suspect . . . and the Dean sounded sincere about Jackson. People lie. You didn't kill Jackson. And that matters, how? Well, if he's gay he's got a boyfriend . . . or a husband. And why do I feel guilty about Jackson. Did I have something to do with it? It was a robbery. What if it wasn't? And Sean's smile, the way he looked at me. And I'm what, twelve? It's a crush, it's hormones, get over it. Or . . .* He thought of Stein's suggestion, *Start easier.* He pulled out his cell and looked through the history of calls, almost all unanswered.

Then a prickle at the back of his neck. *Don't turn back. There's no real danger . . . other than they're going to kick me*

*out of here when I can't land enough grant money, and Jen will
be dead; they'll all be dead, when I could have done something
and didn't. I can't let that happen. Yeah? How you going to
stop it?*

Again, the sense of being watched. *Don't look back. Don't*
– he stopped and turned around. His gaze landed on a black
BMW as it pulled into a parking space. The driver's door opened.

*I should run. But if you do, they'll just run after you. Face
the fear. Maybe it's not so bad.* A young, dark-haired man in
an immaculate suit and shades emerged. *Not a cop. Unless he's
FBI . . . no, that suit is too good. FBI with family money, maybe
secret service. Great hair. How do people get it to stay like
that?*

The man approached and from thirty feet away called, 'Dr
Garfield?' He didn't wait for Frank's reply. 'I'm Dalton Lang
with UNICO. I was hoping—'

Despite Stein's advice, Frank turned away. *Another fucking
recruiter. I shouldn't have answered that call. Stein was wrong.
Pimps and whores. And they send hot male recruiters because
they know I'm gay. Pimps and whores.*

'Dr Garfield,' the man shouted after him. 'Seriously? Some
basic civility would be appreciated here. I've driven two hundred
miles to see you.'

What's the harm in talking? Like a Greek chorus inside his
head, *'pimps and whores'. I'm not a whore.* He wanted to run.
If someone chases you, you should run. He swallowed and felt
the need to be somewhere else, anywhere else. To lock himself
in the lab or be with the kids on the ward. Adrenalin surged.
His pulse quickened. *You can control this.* He slowed his breath
and focused on the feel of his feet against his shoes and how
his weight passed into the earth below.

He stayed like that, and used what he'd learned in two decades
of therapy about how to abort a panic attack. Running wouldn't
help, it would leave him winded and gasping for air. But worse
were the flashbacks, and a dread that something horrible was
about to happen. With his back turned, he listened to the hand-
stitched-leather-shoed approach of Dalton Lang from UNICO.

'I told that recruiter I wasn't interested.' *Lang . . .
UNICO. Their CEO is Leona Lang. She has a PhD . . . from*

MIT. Fuck me. How did I not see this? He replayed his final argument with Jackson. The student his mentor had slept with who'd gone to the dark side. Not that she just worked for the pharma industry and that she'd used research she'd stolen. Leona Lang was THE industry. *Not possible.*

'Are you related to Leona Krawsinska?' Frank asked.

'She's my mother. That's her maiden name.'

What the fuck? This is no coincidence. Stein's advice now seemed too simple. How can you know if there's a tiger in the room, when you don't know what a tiger looks like? He turned and faced Lang.

But that made it worse. The guy removed his dark glasses and Frank got the impact of the most beautiful man he'd ever seen face to face. The planes of his face appeared sculpted, from the high cheekbones to his strong jaw, but it was his eyes, a vivid sapphire, ringed in black lashes. They stared at him. He smiled, and Frank remembered what Jackson had said about Leona, *'the most beautiful girl I'd ever met.' Like mother like son.* As his panic eased, Frank felt a different wave of emotion. He felt trapped in Dalton's gaze. 'I told your recruiter I'm not interested.'

'I know.' Dalton moved closer, barely five feet between them. 'Let me take you to lunch. Your work is far too important for a recruiter. At least talk with me.'

Frank felt frozen. He and Jackson had joked about how the more they rejected the advances of the drug companies, the better-looking the recruiters got. Dalton Lang, like a model out of a magazine, brought this to a new level. 'I like Indian,' Frank blurted.

'Me too. You have a favorite place?'

A simple question, but his gut was on high alert. Too handsome Dalton Lang, son of too-beautiful Leona, was here to sell something . . . something Frank wanted no part of. Jackson had warned him, and he'd seen colleagues, the best of the best, get sucked in. *Pimps and whores.*

'Dr Garfield?'

Frank cracked his neck and tried to clear his head. 'On second thoughts, skip the restaurant. You're here to make a pitch, right? You've got five minutes and then I need to be places.' He pulled out his cell and set the timer.

Dalton grinned and dimples popped. 'A man after my own heart.' He stepped in closer and lowered his voice. 'So here goes. Vice President of Research and Development for UNICO. You know who we are. My mother, Leona Lang, is CEO. We're offering a five-year, million a year, contract with structured bonuses at signing and every six months. Vesting after three months.'

Frank smelled the spice of Lang's cologne. The deep timber of his voice seemed to give his words layers of meaning and spoke more of a bedroom and less of a lab. His brilliant gaze and dazzling smile were a genetic anomaly where God had decided to see how far he could push masculine beauty.

'You have the wrong guy.' Frank stepped back and nearly tripped on the heel of his sneaker.

With cobra like speed, Dalton shot a hand forward to steady him. 'I don't have the wrong guy.' His hand lingered on Frank's shoulder as he rattled off the titles of Frank's recent articles, *Multi-Generational Implications of Protracted Stress on Longevity, Correlates of Adverse Childhood Experiences and Telomere Length, Implications of Elevated Telomerase in Hepatocellular Carcinoma*. And my favorite, *A Theoretical Argument for Extension of the Hayflick Limit*. Seriously, why not just title that one, *How to Live Forever*? Is it just theory, Dr Garfield?'

Frank shrugged off Dalton's hand and stepped back. He swallowed, shook his head and thought of Sean . . . *Detective Sean, who might still arrest me.*

Dalton ran a hand through his hair and squinted into the sun. 'Our recruiter said you were a flat-out no, and . . . your work is too important to be buried here, Dr Garfield. You've got to know that.'

'I'm a researcher, and a pediatrician, not an executive, Mr Lang. I have no interest in anything outside the lab and the wards.'

'Understood. That's where we want you. Where you need to be. I get that. But the right labs with the right equipment, working on the right projects, with actual patients, children and families who need your help. The VP title we'd give you, head of R&D is unimportant, the day-to-day business hassle will go to someone else . . . unless you want it. It's what you're destined for and what we need to support.'

'Which you'd own.'

'Yes. True. We're a Fortune Five Hundred Corporation, and I didn't even get a chance to tell you about the stock options, though I suspect you don't care about those.' He paused. 'Look, I'm throwing a lot at you out of the blue. So rather than come up with an answer now, can I offer you a dinner meeting with myself and my mother?'

Jackson's Leona. 'When?'

'Tonight.'

Everything inside of him screamed no. But didn't something have to change? He took Stein's advice and went opposite to his churning gut. 'OK.' He broke from Dalton's gaze. And before the beautiful Mr Lang could say more, he walked away. His head filled with the intensity of those rare eyes.

'Don't you want to know when and where?'

Frank stopped, but didn't turn back. 'You know who I am, what I do, and where to find me at two o'clock on a Tuesday, getting me to dinner shouldn't be hard.'

'Right.'

Frank resisted the urge to get another helping of Dalton's smile. Instead, he glanced down at his cell. Two minutes left on the timer. *Pimps and whores* . . . And with a nod to Stein's advice, *No harm in hearing what they have to say.* He rejected his earlier decision to take the subway and started to jog and then to run.

Dalton watched Frank flee. *Good, but no slam dunk.* He thought of his fishing metaphor, and as Garfield ran, probably all the way to the hospital to do rounds on his dying children, Dalton visualized his line being let out. The fish, thinking it was free would exhaust itself prior to being reeled in, and then: scaled, gutted, filleted, and served.

He glanced around at the students and faculty and their hive-like activity. He'd loved his years at NYU's school of the arts. But in hindsight, a cruel joke that Leona had consented to let him go, thinking his artistic passions would run their course. Which only made things more painful. Still, what he'd learned was not wasted. He thought of what separated good artists from great. He'd learned it had to do with holding nothing back, of throwing your whole self into the work, no matter the cost. It's what he did with his prose and his lyrics, and when he sang and posted videos, he wanted the viewer to be able to stare deep inside and taste his desolation. Though what they saw, and what Garfield saw, rarely went below the surface. He hated that. *Yes, Frank is the fish, but what does that make me? Am I fisherman or just bait?* It wouldn't be the first time his mother had traded on his looks. While he should have been disgusted at the prospect of being pimped out, there was something about Frank, from his awkward stance, to the way his hair flopped into his eyes, to his devotion to his work and more importantly, to the children he treated. *He's a solid guy. And we're going to fuck him over.*

Disgusted, he returned to his car, pulled out his notepad and angrily jotted lines of acid prose. He stuffed it back into his briefcase and called Leona.

'Yes? What is it?'

Her tone was brusque. *And nice to hear from you too, Mother.* 'He agreed to dinner.'

'Good, when and where?'

'Tonight. I've reserved suites at the Taj. I'll order a private dining room. He likes Indian.'

'What made him change his mind?'

As if you don't know. 'I was persuasive. But the real hook is those kids.'

'Whatever it takes, Dalton.'

'Yes Mother.' And he hung up.

FOURTEEN

Leona lay back on the Taj's sumptuous sheets as waves of pleasure mounted. This one was good, talented. Through hooded eyes, she watched the top of his curly blond head between her legs. *I can't remember his name . . . Jerod, Jacob, not Jesus, but a J, aren't they all? . . . Jeffrey.* 'That feels wonderful, Jeffrey,' she gasped and bit her bottom lip, using the pain to hold back the inevitable release. She rode the surges as his nimble tongue pushed her higher. *So good.* Her thoughts drifted and for a bit she imagined herself young, free, and beautiful, and that this Jeffrey wasn't just another eager-to-please underling, one interchangeable with the next.

He looked up at her, his lips plump and swollen from their efforts. She suppressed a giggle. *Like a puppy dog, lick lick lick.*

'Good?' he asked.

Give the dog a bone. 'Very.' And not wanting this to become a conversation, which would invariably center on how to get ahead . . . she drifted and closed her eyes. *So good.*

An orgasm rolled through her body, her toes curled. Even her hair follicles spasmed with something like joy. *So good.*

Jeffrey, twenty-seven and without an ounce of fat on his swimmer's body, flopped beside her on the pillows. 'You are so lovely.'

For a few seconds, she languished in content, his words, and the voluptuous joy of being in bed with a handsome young man.

'You have plans for tonight?' he asked.

'Yes.' *Please don't talk. Give me a little longer. Don't ruin it.*

'And they don't include me.'

'Business.'

'I know,' he said with the hint of a sulk. He rolled on his side and stared at her. 'It's always business, isn't it?'

And now the tit for tat. With a sigh, she pulled the sheets up and covered herself. She tried not to think of how he saw her, judged her. She thought of Dr Ramon who had plans for more than her face, her breasts, her butt, her thighs.

'It's always work,' she said, then schooled her expression into a pleasant smile. She wanted to have another go or two with this talented Jeffrey, but sensed the tipping point had come, where the cost and expectation exceeded his service. She tried to recall his stats, Boston based, part of UNICO's army of thousands of drug detailers. She'd noticed him at an auditorium

style orientation session. California surfer looks in a navy suit.
Yummy, both dressed and un.

'You ever think about a week off? Maybe an island . . .' His
voice trailed off.

She searched his words for irony. *Could he find me beautiful?*
'Tempting.'

Disappointment crossed his face. 'But unlikely.'

'It is.' *Give the dog a bone.* 'I will think about it.'

'Good . . . and now I should go, right?'

'Yes, I have meetings.' Glad he seemed appeased, so perhaps
this particular good time could be had again.

'Right.'

She felt relief, desire, and something else, as young
Jeffrey slid from bed and retrieved his clothes. 'OK if I grab a
quick shower?'

'Of course.' She followed him with her eyes, tracing the taper
from broad shoulders to his narrow waist, firm ass and long
legs. And once she heard the water, she pushed back the sheet
and belted on a plush white Terri robe, heading to the living
room that overlooked the Boston Gardens and the Commons
beyond. Through the glass she could both look out on the city
and see the reflection of steam and Jeffrey's silhouette in the
shower. *How nice. He left the door open. He's not stupid. He'll
go far . . . if he doesn't push.* She made a mental note to goose
his career. A simple phone call . . . not from her, but Dalton,
to the Boston head of marketing. Give young Jeffrey a larger
territory, make him a manager. She gazed on the split show,
Boston at night, and hunky Jeffrey soaping up. But there were
many Jeffries and Jennifers, Jerods and Ashleys, her army of
young and beautiful sales reps. Their targets: physicians,
advanced practice nurses, and physician assistants, anyone who
could write a prescription for a UNICO product. Battalions of
millennials with degrees in poly-sci, psychology, literature,
English, all a hundred thousand or more in debt with degrees
barely worth their faux parchment.

She drank in the afterglow, and followed Jeffrey's naked
progress from the shower, to the reverse striptease of his yellow
bikini briefs to his blue button-down shirt, suit and tie. It
reignited a tingle in her belly, and for the briefest of moments

she considered a second round. *No, that would make him impossible.*

He crossed to her spot in front of the window, leaned down and kissed her on the cheek. 'Call me,' he said, but did not push.

'I will.' She watched as he headed out. The kiss on her cheek burned, *like I'm his fucking grandmother*, worse than a punch. When she turned back to the window, she saw her own reflection. The compare and contrast between her and golden Jeffrey was harsh. *Lines everywhere. It's just the lighting. No it isn't. It didn't do it to him.* Her buzz dissipated in the reality of her reflection. *Beauty is power.* He knew it. She knew it. He had it and she did not.

She leaned forward and grabbed her laptop and booted up. *First things first.* She logged on to her secure hotspot, and entered a password for a dark-net browser. She typed in Dr Malcolm Bender – *traitor, let's see what happens to whistle blowers.* She was rewarded with pages of news feeds. *How sad.* With a blood alcohol level three times the legal limit the ex-UNICO oncology researcher had crashed his Mercedes into a busload of children. The images were fabulous and gruesome. He had not worn a seatbelt and gone through the windshield. Color photos of tearful kids being led away from the mangled remains of a man who thought he could snitch his way to a multi-million-dollar payout. 'And that's what you get.'

She toggled to her email and hit the attachments Dalton had assembled on Garfield. The man was a mix of damaged goods and brilliance. *What do you want, Dr Garfield?* Unlike Jeffrey whose ambitions were tattooed on his forehead, Garfield was subtle. *And this may be my last chance.* With her phone on speaker she dialed Dalton. 'Where is Garfield's mother?'

'Croton Forensic Hospital, it's near Katonah,' Dalton said.

'Why did she kill his father and try to kill him?'

'Delusions. She thought Frank was going to grow up to be Satan. Wanted to do the world a favor, by killing him before that could happen . . . and she was pregnant at the time.'

'What happened to the baby.'

'She self-aborted in prison, but I don't have the details on how, not something the warden was eager to release. Then transferred to Croton, copped an insanity plea, and has been there since.'

Leona toggled through PDFs about the stabbing death of Garfield's father, Edwin Garfield, MD. 'Apples and trees . . . How crazy is he?'

'He's intense, driven. Invested in those kids at St Mary's. Sees a psychologist at the university health center and has for more than a decade. On no psych meds. Raised by his paternal grandparents, both now dead. They brought him to a lot of shrinks, and he got locked up a few times on psych wards, but nothing since twelve. I scanned the records.' He directed her to a file labeled *FG Behavioral Health*.

Leona clicked on it. It was a psychiatric evaluation of ten-year-old Francis Xavier Garfield. 'Interesting, sent to an emergency room after he trashed his classroom. Smashed some windows and threw a chair at a teacher.'

'Keep going,' Dalton said.

'Let's see . . . they shot him up with drugs and got his grand-parents to sign him into Beekman Lodge in Massachusetts. You never said he had money.'

'He doesn't and they didn't, but they did have good insurance. His grandfather was a lifer with the postal service. Second generation Italian Americans.'

She read on. 'Early onset psychosis, and post-traumatic-stress, rule out Asperger's, rule out schizophrenia. They had him on a bucket-load of medications, risperidone, haloperidol, Ativan . . . and the episodes continued. Had him in restraints . . . at ten, really? Someone did not like this child.'

'They couldn't get him under control. They kept him at Beekman for nine months.'

'And then?'

He directed her to another PDF. 'Grandparents had him discharged. The doctor disagreed and tried to stop them. At discharge the diagnoses were schizophrenia and autism.'

She scanned handwritten notes from the psychiatrist.

Appears to be responding to internal stimuli, but denies hearing voices. Oppositional and participates only in school-based activities where he excels. Isolative and no meaningful social

*connections on the milieu or with staff. Consistently asks to
leave.*

*When directly asked about his mother, he either dissociates,
or becomes mute. Similarly, when asked about the events that
led to this hospitalization he is uncooperative. Makes minimal
eye contact and seems oblivious to social cues. Left alone he
reads for hours, excessively and obsessively, and will cease only
when repeatedly directed to do so.*

She jumped over pages of laboratory results, including an
MRI scan of his brain, which was read as normal. 'This is
interesting.'

'What?' Dalton asked.

'You read the psychological testing?'

'Yes. What catches your eye other than his IQ is monstrous?'
Dalton asked.

'195, yeah that's up there. And no surprise. But whoever did
this report . . . a Dr Jillian Grossman, she disagreed with the
psychiatrist. Her summation is interesting.'

*Frank is an intense and brilliant child who has suffered over-
whelming trauma that has left him with typical and extreme
psychological symptoms, all of which can be traced to what he
experienced both on the night of his father's murder, and during
a prodromal period when he was left alone in the custody of a
mother who was psychotic and abusive. It is this combination
of years of verbal, emotional, and possibly physical abuse,
coupled with the horrific events that led to his father's death
and his mother's current incarceration that have led to
Frank's current symptoms. These are: Extreme dissociative
episodes, which appear to be triggered by either real or
perceived cues from earlier traumas. During these episodes,
Frank loses all sense of control, and blacks out. He has limited
recall after these events which last from a few seconds to hours.
He clearly suffers with symptoms of both depression and anxiety,
much of which he relates to his current hospitalization.*

Leona chuckled.

'What's funny?'

She read on. 'I can only imagine how this went over with his shrink.'

As to the diagnosis of autism, based on his poor eye contact, social avoidance, and intense interest in reading anything and everything, this appears to be related to issues of impaired trust, self-preservation, and escapism from his current situation, which he finds painful and frightening. Throughout this evaluation, Frank was engaged and forthcoming and made a good effort on all the administered tests, displayed an interest, commensurate with his IQ, but well beyond his numeric years. There is no evidence of a true psychotic process, or of schizophrenic illness.

'And the psychiatrist just ignored that?' Dalton said.

'Pretty much, went with the diagnoses he wanted on the discharge.'

'After that,' Dalton said, 'one more brief hospitalization at a community hospital for ten days, a couple emergency room evaluations for similar school meltdowns, but all outpatient treatment.'

Leona pulled up random files and sifted through the data. 'Bat-shit crazy mother who wanted to kill him.' She thought of her own mother.

'Still does,' Dalton added.

'You have her records? From Croton?'

'Of course. Would you like them?'

'You have to ask?' Again, impressed with Dalton's resourcefulness. *Tell him.* But she didn't. 'And no boyfriend?'

'He's got a crush on the detective assigned to the Jackson Atlas case.'

'Useable?'

'Possibly, but not bankable. Sean Brody, Brookline PD. Thirty-two, nice to look at, clean record. Could be gay. Probably not. Although . . .' he chuckled.

'Share.'

'That's poor Frank's dilemma. Gay, but clueless. Is he or isn't he? Does he like me? Pathetic, but cute. I'll send you what I've got on the detective.'

'My bet, you figure him out before Frank.'

'That's a sucker bet.'

'Should make for an interesting dinner.'

'If he shows.'

'If he doesn't,' she said, 'we track him down. His work matters . . . a lot. I need him and it now.'

'Understood. Atlas's murder rattled him, and now I think we've got the right bait.'

'The kids? You said he has a Christ complex.'

'Yes. That's what deepened the split between him and Atlas. He thinks he can save them, and Atlas told him not to.'

'I hope you're right. I'm trusting you on this.' And then she did the thing that took effort. 'This is good, Dalton. I'm proud of you.'

Silence on the line. 'Thank you, that means a lot.'

Best to leave it there. But she couldn't, 'Now if you'd only ditch that silly music stuff and those videos, this is what you're meant for.'

'Right. Eight o'clock it is.' And he hung up.

FIFTEEN

uck! Will I ever learn? Dalton seethed as he stared out at the million-dollar view of the Boston Gardens after dark. Fairy light reflections rippled on the lake, colors muted to grays, black, and white. Seated at the linen-covered table, he swigged craft beer and fought back the bitter pill that his life was not his own. *I am Renfield. I am Mother's Renfield . . . not bad, maybe a song title. Or just shorten it to Renfield.*

He sank back and surveyed the private dining room in the penthouse of the Taj he'd arranged. *It's good.* Lux Indian silks festooned the walls and ceiling. Candles birthed soft shadows, and aromas of tamarind, cinnamon, turmeric and other spices softened his senses. *Frank likes Indian . . . I'll give him Indian.* The only thing left to chance . . . the big thing. *Will he show? And what will she do if he doesn't?*

He turned his head at the sound of a door. *Mother. Too bad it wasn't Frank. Might be nice to get some time alone with him.*

'This is beautiful,' she said. 'A bit gaudy for my taste. I assume it's deliberate.'

'Of course.'

'Should I have worn a sari?'

'Overkill.'

She looked back at the red-and-black uniformed host who'd escorted her in. 'Single malt, neat.' And then to Dalton. 'Where's Garfield and what does he drink?'

'Not here, and he likes bourbon, though not a big drinker.' He held her gaze and observed the shifts in her expression, near-imperceptible quivers beneath a Botox mask. If he'd been a regular employee his ass would have just been canned. Like Medusa, stare too long and you're dead.

'Shit,' she said. 'I'm tired of this. Did you do *everything* to get him here?'

'Short of a blow job, yes.'

'Don't be crude . . . Would that have worked?'

'No.'

Her expression softened. 'Should we hunt him down on the streets of Cambridge.'

'Tranquilizer darts and a net?' he offered.

'You look handsome, Dalton.'

Her compliment set him on edge. Could she know he'd tried on four shirts before returning to a soft white button-down? But then he'd obsessed over how many buttons to open. Where was the line between professional, casual . . . slut? Or that he'd spent thirty minutes gelling and then ungelling his hair? Finally settling for something unpolished and in step with Dr Garfield's unruly mop. 'You too.'

'That's nice of you, but we don't lie to one another. Correct?'

If only that were true. 'You do look good,' *for your age.* Her fitted green Chanel suit softened at the neck by a triple strand of pearls, that caught the candlelight and distracted from the wrinkled mesh beneath her jaw.

The waiter returned with her drink, accompanied by a flustered maître d'.

'Excuse me Mr Lang, Doctor Lang, I have a young man at the front desk who says he has a meeting with you.'

'And?' Dalton stood.

'He didn't come dressed and refuses the jacket we have for these occasions. He's quite loud. I don't know if I should call the police or . . .'

Are you fucking kidding me? Dalton bolted from the table and headed towards the elevator. He suppressed the urge to punch the maître d' and wondered if he was a different species from the morons who populated the planet. *I could not have been clearer.* Hours earlier he'd alerted the desk staff to their guest, complete with photographs he'd taken of Frank so they wouldn't fuck it up. *And she'll blame me for this.*

He tried to calm himself as the elevator stopped and started. Each second increased the likelihood that Garfield would say this wasn't worth the hassle, and leave. *And this is where the fish breaks the line.*

The doors swished open. Dalton scanned the meant-to-impress space with its marble-inlaid floors, gilt-edged paneling, and wrought-iron grand staircase. He spotted Frank's back, he was headed towards the revolving doors. He ran. 'Dr Garfield. Frank.' *Is he ignoring me?* 'Frank.' He shouted, but he'd already pushed into the door.

Dalton followed, rapped on the glass.

Frank turned, and stumbled as the door clipped him on the heels.

'Frank.' Dalton watched as he steadied himself, looked out at the street, back at him, and then pushed to keep going around and return to the lobby.

A lump caught in Dalton's throat. *Too fucking close.* His pulse pounded in his ears as he came out next to Frank in the lobby. Words would not come, which was strange.

'I'm here,' Frank said.

He looks pissed and . . . crazy. Dalton did a fast reappraisal of the man he'd had under surveillance for the past six weeks. 'I'm sorry, Dr Garfield.'

'You didn't tell me I needed a jacket,' Frank said, his gaze fixed on Dalton.

'You don't.' He wondered if Frank had given any thought to

his leather bomber jacket, olive cargo pants, worn red sneakers, and blue button-down. But after six-weeks of surveillance he knew the answer. No. 'I screwed up,' Dalton said.

'Everyone does,' Frank said. 'But I'm not dressed for this place. Didn't this use to be The Ritz?'

'Yeah. And you look fine,' and Dalton did something he'd not intended. He showed his hand . . . at least a part of it. 'I rented a dining room on the penthouse so we can talk. We're having Indian. Really good Indian.'

Frank smiled back. 'I love Indian, and I told you that. You did this for me.' His gaze narrowed as he scrutinized Dalton.

'I did.' Dalton found it hard to breathe.

'And your mother is here?'

'She's waiting.'

Frank rocked back on the heels of his runners.

Dalton sensed his conflict to stay or to go. *What can I do? There has to be something.*

'Lamb?' Frank asked.

'Rogan josh, on the bone.' Weeks of preparation had led to this. *Why does he matter so much to her? . . . to me?* He knew this was Frank's favorite dish, that he and Grace Lewis ate Indian at least once a week, and one or both would order the rogan josh.

'You've put a lot of thought into this.' Frank's gaze didn't waver. 'I don't trust you . . . but I love lamb. I want to meet your mother. I have questions for her.'

'Good,' Dalton said, though that last bit rang sour. 'Let's get you past the guards.' He fought the impulse to grab Frank's arm, and waited for him to follow. They rode up in silence. *Come into my web said the spider to the fly.*

As they exited, Frank asked, 'What is this costing you?'

'A few thousand,' Dalton said. 'Maybe ten.'

'Right. Good to know,' and Frank followed him.

Is it too much? Dalton wondered, as he opened the door onto the lush Mughal-themed room.

Leona rose, smiled, and extended her hand. 'Doctor Garfield, thank you so much for agreeing to meet. I hope you don't mind but I took the liberty to order you a bourbon, but if you don't drink or would rather something else . . .'

Frank ignored her extended hand. He stopped two feet from the table and stared at her.

Leona's smile didn't falter, as seconds stretched into a minute. She let her hand drop.

Dalton, by the door, watched and wondered *what is he thinking? What are his first impressions?*

Frank broke the silence, 'I can see it.'

'What's that?' Leona asked.

'Jackson said you were the most beautiful girl he'd ever seen. Your face is frozen now . . . Botox?'

'Yes, sadly time will have its way.'

'Did you care for him?' Frank asked, not moving to the tumbler of bourbon, and assortment of samosas, fritters, and steamed breads.

'I did . . . a lot.'

'OK then.' He glanced back at Dalton. 'I'll stay.'

'I'm glad.'

'I'm not agreeing to anything.'

'We're just here to talk.' Leona said.

Frank sat, picked up the bourbon and sniffed. 'Ten thousand for one meal.' He sipped. 'And you're both staying here?'

'Yes,' Dalton said.

Frank swirled his liquor. His gaze fell on the treats. He reached for a chickpea and onion fritter and said, 'Tell me about Jackson,' popping it into his mouth.

'What do you want to know?' Leona asked. 'Like you, he was my PhD supervisor. And then years later I wanted him to work with us. Like yours, his work broke new ground.'

'You recruited him for UNICO?'

'I tried.' She smiled. 'Jackson was not having it.'

'You hurt him,' Frank said.

'I did. He told you about that?'

'Yes.'

'Interesting,' Dalton said, wanting to ease the tension, and aware that Leona did not know that he knew about her affair. 'Something you haven't told me, Mother?'

'I was young, and we got too close. I should have known better. He certainly should have known better. But there you have it. Things happen.'

'He wanted to leave his wife and marry you,' Frank said.

'He was in love with me,' Leona said. 'Or who he thought I was. We would never have worked. I knew that, he didn't. I ended it, before it could destroy his career and his marriage. You never met Ruth, she was a lovely woman and more than anything I regret the pain our stupidity caused her.'

'You walked away from your research,' Frank said. 'You might have been the first to correctly identify that DNA leader sequences had purpose. Why wouldn't you follow that up?'

'Who says I haven't?'

A knock, and the waiter entered with a cart laden with polished brass tureens. He arranged them one by one on the table, removed the lids and announced the contents, then left an ornate tantalus with three crystal decanters labeled: Maker's Mark Bourbon, Islay Single Malt Scotch, Gray Goose Vodka.

Once he left, she continued, 'Dr Garfield . . . may I call you Frank?'

'Sure.'

'And Leona works for me . . . I knew that academia was not me. I won't bore you with the parts you know. The competition for grants, equipment, lab space. The constant jockeying for promotion. Being female made it worse. The glass ceiling is real. Then and now.'

'So you married Lionel Lang.'

She stiffened. 'You don't pull punches. Yes, I did.'

'And now you're the CEO of UNICO.'

'Yes, I am. And I'm sitting in the penthouse of a beautiful hotel, with the single-most important researcher on the planet, though I'm not certain you're aware of that. But you do know . . . I assume, that the work you said I walked away from is connected to yours.' She risked a smile. 'Is it fair now to ask about your work, and see if we can come to a meeting of minds?'

Frank assembled rice and fall-off-the-bone braised lamb onto a torn-off piece of Naan, folded it and bit down. 'Delicious.' He looked up from his food. 'You've done your homework.'

Dalton nodded. 'Yeah, it's a bit much, isn't it?' He gave a

half-smile that on YouTube and Insta might garner a few thousand thumbs up, and swooning comments.

'You think?' Frank said. 'But I'm here, so let's flip it around. Let me see what you know . . . or think you know.' He looked to Leona, 'Specifically, what is it about my work that interests you?'

'You're at the cutting edge of genetics, Frank.'

'Epigenetics,' he corrected, 'but you knew that.'

'Yes, epigenetics. Which evolved from the abject failure of my generation and our belief that sequencing the DNA would unravel the mysteries of the body, how and why we get sick, all of it.'

'Yes,' Frank said. 'It was too simplistic. You got the sequence but no answers. At least not the ones we need. You wanted *War and Peace* but got *Dick and Jane.* Do you ever notice how if someone repeats a lie over and over, it sounds like the truth?'

'Sure,' Dalton said, entranced by the change in Frank's demeanor. 'Look at the Trump administration. Anything that veers from his twisted version of reality must be fake news.'

'Right, they're not big on science and reality. But that's what happened with genetics and a lot of that early work. People came to wrong conclusions. Which makes me a little critical about how you didn't pursue your hypotheses on leader sequences. For decades they called it genetic garbage, and then you came with your thesis and laid down possibilities of their true purpose. Or at least some part of it.'

'It wasn't time,' she said almost sadly. 'You can't imagine the pushback I got. But now . . . here you are.'

'They were idiots,' Frank said. He glanced at Dalton. Their gazes connected. 'DNA holds the face of God, the layers of complexity that cause it to bend and conform are miraculous . . . There is no garbage, and there are answers. This is where epigenetics begins, and it's connected to everything.'

'What answers have you found?' Dalton asked. He leaned closer and noted how Frank swallowed hard and ran a hand threw his tangled bangs. *Fish is on the hook. Reel him in.* He refilled Frank's bourbon.

'You're trying to get me drunk.' Frank broke the connection.

He looked from his half-eaten shank of lamb, to Leona, and then back to Dalton. 'You think because I'm gay and awkward that your looks will . . . How far would you go, Dalton?'

'Far as you want.' But as the words left his mouth, he knew he'd miscalculated.

'Pimps and whores.' Frank pushed back from the table.

Leona interceded. 'What I want to hear is where your research is headed. What it is you—'

Frank stood. He tossed back the bourbon and winced. 'We're done. I may not know my next move, but it's not with the two of you.'

Dalton felt him slip away. He stood and pulled his ace. 'And the little girl on 8C? Jennifer Owens.'

'How the fuck do you know about her?'

Dalton was startled but did not back down. 'Jen Owens. Disseminated small cell, stage 4. And 8D Carter Jeffries with an undifferentiated sarcoma. Or Lakeesha Thomas with an inoperable astrocytoma spreading through her brain, not expected to see her sixth birthday and likely blind within the month.'

'How the hell do you know this? You shouldn't know any of this?'

'Frank . . . Dr Garfield,' Dalton said. 'In the big picture, Mother and I don't matter. Your work does. That you can't see the next step forward is a great problem and not just for you . . . but for those children. So forget what I just said, I misjudged you. I'm sorry. I can be an idiot . . . but just so you know, you're not that awkward.' His words spilled out fast. 'Here's the big difference between us, we have no hesitation or doubts about the importance of your work. More than that,' he locked gazes with Frank, 'we can take it and you from the lab into clinical trials with those children . . . now. Not a year from now, not after Jennifer and Carter and Lakeesha are dead and buried, but now.'

'No. You're lying,' Frank said. 'No one gets approval that fast. No one. None of those kids has more than a few months.'

'Wrong. We can. And we will. The bigger question Frank, is what will it take for you to stop jacking off and make this happen? Not a year from now, or two, or three, or ten, but now.

Not with some theoretical future children, but with your current patients, who between all of them, don't have even a year.'

Frank looked from Dalton to Leona. He appeared confused. 'But that's not why you want my work. It's not for those kids.'

Leona nodded. 'You're right.' She too stood. 'It doesn't have to be one or the other. It can be both.'

'No. Say what you've got to say. Two minutes.'

'The other obvious application is life extension,' Leona said. 'There, the questions are how much? How long?'

He stared at Leona, his gaze narrowed. 'You want to live forever.'

'Who wouldn't? If you're in decent health. So how far can you push it?'

'Don't know,' Frank admitted. 'It's going to depend on the person and their telomere age.'

Dalton watched the space between Frank and Leona. He now realized that she had something he did not . . . scientific credibility.

'For someone like you, in good health, maybe an extra ten years, maybe a hundred, maybe more. It's unknowable . . . without studies.'

Leona let out a slow breath. 'That's what I needed to hear.' She looked to Dalton. 'What would someone give for another hundred years?'

'What wouldn't they?'

'Frank,' Leona said. 'The question is what will it take to get you to work with us? You tell me and I will make it happen. If it's fast-tracking a human study with those terminally ill children, we'll have you in a lab with everything you need by the end of the month. June one at the latest, possibly sooner.'

Silence.

Dalton knew that Mother had just tossed out their best ploy. It would be those kids . . . or nothing.

'Thank you for the bourbon and the lamb,' Frank said to Leona, and then to Dalton, 'and the offer to fuck me.' Without another word, he grabbed his jacket from the back of his chair, and left.

SIXTEEN

The late April night held a warm chill and oblivious to the dangers of walking the Commons after dark, Frank needed air. He pictured Jackson. Again, that weird lost-limb feel. The person he needed to talk to was gone. Worse, the background buzz in his head, made it hard to think. *Don't focus on it. It makes it worse.* Walking helped and talking, if he did it loud enough, muffled the crazy. 'What am I supposed to do?' he said loudly.

A pair of late-night joggers glanced and then sprinted past.

'Jackson would say no.' He replayed their conversation. 'She said she'd tried to recruit him. I wonder what she offered.' His thoughts bounced to handsome Dalton, *'Whatever you want.'* He snorted, knowing exactly what Jackson would say, *'Pimps and whores.'* He'd say they're in it for the money. 'Pimps and whores.' But then they brought up, 'Jen . . . Carter, Lakeesha.' Young faces scrolled through his mind. Most of them now dead . . . and not easy deaths. 'Children shouldn't have to suffer . . . They said they could get me into human trials within a month. Impossible. What if it's not? What if . . .' As he lapped the Commons, time slipped away.

A heavy-set man in a shiny red jogging suit approached and intruded, 'You got a light?'

'I don't smoke.'

'Neither do I. You looking for company?'

'Yeah,' Frank said. *Good idea.* He pulled out his cell.

Perplexed, the man watched.

'Grace.'

'Frank, it's two in the morning.'

'I know. I need to talk.'

'Where are you?'

He glanced up. 'The Tremont Street side of the Commons.'

'By yourself?'

'Yeah.'

'Call an Uber and get over here. Can you do that?'

'I'm not a child.'

'I know, Frank, but you're peculiar. And we peculiar folk need to watch out for each other. Get out of there. It's not safe.' He headed towards the street.

'Where you going?' the guy asked. 'I thought you wanted to, you know . . .'

Frank looked at him and realized what was being asked and offered. 'No thanks.'

He walked away. The man followed. 'Then give me your wallet and your phone.' And he pulled out a switchblade.

Frank responded reflexively. He grabbed the man's wrist and jabbed his forefinger up and back into the release point. His pulse raced. Then a flashback of his mother's deadly rampage flooded his mind. He heard his father's shouts, *'Get out of the house, Frank. Run!'* His mother's rants a muddle of bible verse. *'Child of Satan, I abjure thee to hell.'*

The man shrieked and fell to his knees. The knife dropped to the ground.

Frank kicked it into the bushes, but didn't release his grip; he increased the pressure and twisted the guy's wrist up and back to near breaking.

'Let go of me, you psycho!' the man shrieked. 'Help! He's killing me.'

A patrol car, parked on Tremont, flashed its lights and cruised towards them. A window slid down and a blinding white light illuminated them. 'What's going on?' An officer exited the car, and clicked open his holster.

Frank startled, aware that he'd just lost track of the past few moments. He relaxed his grip but held on.

'He attacked me.' The man on the ground shouted. 'He's psycho.'

'Let go of him,' the officer said. 'Then take two steps back and keep your hands where I can see them.'

Frank complied . . . barely; his thoughts in freefall. He focused on the feel of his feet and his breath. *I watch my breath come in. I watch my breath go out.* A mantra learned decades ago. It helped . . . some. But the flashback, fueled by the attack and the glint of killer steel in the night, would not stop. Only back then it had been a hammer, smeared red with blood.

'Be careful,' the downed man cried, 'he has a knife.'

'Officer,' Dalton Lang suddenly emerged in the flood of a streetlight, 'I saw the whole thing. Doctor Garfield,' emphasis on doctor, 'was attacked by that man. He was defending himself.'

'IDs, now!' the officer ordered. And to Dalton, 'And you are?' He reached for his ID.

The attacker bolted into the park.

The officer shook his head. 'Great. You two get out of here,' and he gave pursuit with his partner trailing in the cruiser.

'You followed me,' Frank stated. He felt a sharp pain in his chest. *I watch my breath come in. I watch my breath go out.*

'Yes. And with reason.'

'What reason?'

'You didn't say yes at dinner.' Dalton smiled and raised a hand. 'To coming to work with us, nothing more, and again I apologize for being an idiot.'

'I said no.'

'True, sort of, kind of.' Dalton dropped the smile. 'So what will it take for you to say yes? I know it's not money. But seeing your work come to fruition has to mean something.'

Frank said nothing. He looked from Dalton towards the flashing lights of the cruiser, now deep in the Commons.

It was a good question. *What do I want?* The answer came fast. It was Jen's voice as she reassured her parents that a six-year-old dying from monster tumors was OK. It wasn't. Or four-year-old Carter whose sarcoma had already cost him a leg and would soon end his life. Or Lakeesha, or Ben, or . . . 'Your mother said she could get me into human trials within a month. How?'

'The children,' Dalton said. 'If you could do any study, you'd start with the kids you're seeing at St Mary's, correct?'

'Yes.'

'Would it have to be there?'

'No, but I'd want to offer the kids . . . their families, the option.'

'You have a protocol ready?'

Frank nodded. Something in Dalton's gaze held him, an intensity, a sincerity. 'Yes, a simple one. Treatment as usual as the placebo arm vs my compound.' He stopped himself from saying more. Yes it was a compound, but in fact was more of a process. No one needed to know that.

'You wouldn't need big numbers to show an effect,' Dalton said. 'If even a couple kids separated from the treatment-as-usual arm of the study, we'd get you fast-tracked into a large stage-two trial.'

He's not kidding. Possibility, and hope surged. He imagined Jackson's protest, but also knew that his mentor had railed against the crushing weight and petty in-fights of academia that slowed research to a glacial pace. Even Jackson might be tempted by what Dalton and his mother offered. *But it's not just lamb and bourbon. Pimps and whores.* 'What's in it for you?'

'Are you kidding? I'm no scientist, but I see the ramifications.'

'Dalton. Just tell me. What's in it for you and your mother?'

'Those hundred years, she wants them. And Frank, if you say yes, I promise you that it won't be a month. Jen Owens doesn't have that long.'

Frank grimaced. 'She doesn't. And how the fuck do you know about her?'

'Because for the past six weeks, I've had you under surveillance. And Mother has tracked your progress much longer.'

'Right,' Frank said, having read hundreds of Jackson's emails with Sean, and seen a steady thread between his dead mentor and the mysterious writer, who he now knew was Leona Lang.

'Yes.' Dalton closed the space, inches now separated them. 'UNICO has facilities that we will put at your disposal. You say yes, and I say tomorrow. We've got a spread in Connecticut you won't believe. We can house the families and get you all the equipment and lab support you want. Even a farm next door where the kids can play with the animals, horses, sheep, llamas. We have our own research review board for whom getting your study FDA approved will be their only priority. We . . . I personally will pull in every favor, of which we are owed many. But here's the deal, Frank, you have to say yes. You have to sign a contract that will give you what you want and a whole lot more. You can save Jen. You can save all of them.'

Frank's cell rang. Grace's number flashed. 'I'm supposed to be somewhere.'

Dalton nodded, 'True. You are supposed to be somewhere. In your own lab, running a study with kids and families who through no fault of their own, got dealt shit hands.'

This was horrible manipulation, beyond anything Frank had ever experienced. But the offer . . . and this surge of excitement. Like waking from a coma. He stared at Dalton who was everything Jackson loathed. Slick, too handsome, with truckloads of money and research shortcuts, even willing to jump into bed to seal a deal, and then just as quickly twisting to offer something wonderful and game changing. His thoughts raced as he weighed the proposal. Jen's face appeared in his mind's eye, her quirky expression as she stated the things no one else would. And it wasn't just her, but all the dead children he'd cared for and couldn't save. Like an army of translucent skinned baby birds. They haunted him. *I can do this. And what's the worst they can do? Make an infusion to extend life? Not what I'd intended . . . not so bad.*

'I'll do it.'

'Good.' Dalton extended a hand.

Frank paused. Stared at Dalton's perfectly groomed nails, and long fingers. Jackson and his own crazy mother wailed in his thoughts: *Pimps and whores. I abjure thee Satan.*

He took Dalton's hand. As he did, Dalton gripped tight and pulled him in to a kiss. His lips mashed against Frank's as his tongue sought entry.

'What the fuck, Dalton?' Frank pushed back hard. 'Does everyone just fall into bed with you?'

Dalton stumbled. A speck of blood blossomed on his lower lip. 'I misread, again . . . sorry.'

'You did,' Frank said. 'And please stop.'

'Understood.'

'Good.'

'Did I just screw the deal?' Dalton asked.

'No, but stop trying to screw me.'

Dalton extended his hand a second time. 'Do over?'

Frank hesitated. 'What the hell am I getting into?' But the thought of putting his theory into practice and maybe preventing Jen's death was too strong. *I can save her. I can save all of them.* 'Yes.' He took Dalton's hand and shook. 'I'm in.'

SEVENTEEN

Frank drove the dreaded route to upstate New York's Croton Forensic Hospital. He'd come twice a year since he was nine, when his mother, Candace, had been admitted under a not-guilty-by-reason-of-mental-defect plea for his father's murder. At first, in the company of his grandparents, Ida and Henry, who shielded him from the worst of it. Then just Grandpa Henry, and for the last ten years, alone. He had to, because if he didn't, some well-intended pro-bono lawyer would turn the lock and let her out. So twice a year he faced his worst fear with a single goal; *she never leaves.*

He drove past the barb-wired perimeter, turned down the drive, and as he walked from his car – a 2012 maroon and black Honda Element – he collected items from his pockets, wallet, keys, Chapstick, cell phone.

He dropped them along with a bulging Manilla envelope, the type without a metal closure, into a plastic bin and walked through the detector. He stood motionless as a guard patted him down and leafed through the envelope. Another scanned a computer log to verify that he was expected.

'Conference room C?' Frank asked.

'Yes.' The guard replied. 'You know your way?'

'I do.'

'They're running late. You can wait in the chairs outside until the judge is ready.'

He nodded, 'Sure.' He walked the dingy hall and sat on a bolted-down oak bench. He was not alone. His mother's social worker smiled, 'Hi Frank.'

He said nothing. Forty-five minutes later the door opened and a group exited including a distraught older couple. The woman was in tears. 'They don't understand.' She turned back. Her husband urged her forward.

'We'll get a lawyer,' he said. 'We'll find a way.'

'They don't understand. How can they think he'll be all right? That he won't . . .'

Frank gripped his envelope. As he listened to the drama he faced his greatest fear. *That could be me.*

A clerk now stood in the doorway and called out. 'Garfield hearing.'

Frank, the social worker, a doctor in a lab coat with his name across the pocket, a woman in a navy skirt suit, and two others filed in.

Frank took his usual seat at the oval table across from the probate judge, a woman in her fifties. She presided and to her right a clerk typed on his laptop.

As two guards escorted his mother into the room, Frank kept his gaze fixed on the table. Rather than look at her he listened to the shuffle of her feet. The voice in his head stirred. *You come from my brain, you are only thoughts.* It would not quiet. Worse, images, sounds and raw fear from the night she killed his father and came after him, roared to life. Like a dentist's drill hitting a nerve. *Do not freak out. Not here. I watch my breath come in. I watch my breath go out.* He stared at the table and counted the whorls in the wood. It didn't help. He smelled her crazy and the ramble of her thoughts. Because although the horrible thing had happened when he was eight, he'd endured a whole childhood of her delusions and abuse. *Don't look at her.*

The clerk read off the case. 'Candace Garfield, found not guilty by reason of mental defect for the murder of her husband Dr Edwin Garfield and attempted murder of her son Francis Xavier Garfield committed to Croton Forensic Hospital on April fourth 1994.'

When Grandpa Henry was alive it had been less awful, but now it was just him and an envelope of insanity. He sat motionless as one by one a state psychologist, the social worker, and a patient advocate testified. The judge addressed his mother. 'Ms Garfield, do you understand what we're doing here today?'

'Yes, this is my semi-annual evaluation.'

'Do you know the function of this evaluation?'

'It's to see if I can be safely discharged to a less-restrictive setting, like a group home or supervised apartment.'

'Correct.'

Her voice made it hard to breathe. So normal. So convincing.

'And how have you been doing?' the judge asked.

'Well, thank you.' Candace replied. 'I take my medications religiously. I haven't heard a voice in years. And it's so good to see my son, who never visits me. Though I understand, Frank.'

He felt her gaze, but would not look.

'I'm so sorry for what I did,' she continued. 'You have no idea.'

Her words burned; he'd heard them before. All lies. The only remorse she felt, was that she'd not murdered him too.

The judge turned to the social worker and doctors and reviewed the treatment plans for any signs of troublesome or dangerous behavior. In the past six months there had been none reported.

The patient advocate, an attorney with a legal rights project, spoke, 'Your honor, based on Ms Garfield's exemplary progress I strongly advocate that a release plan be put forward.'

Frank looked up.

Finally, he glanced at his mother. Her graying hair was long and tied up in bun. Instead of hospital pajamas, they'd let her dress in street clothes. Their gazes met, and beneath the veneer of normalcy he saw that thing in her eyes. The hint of a smile formed on her lips.

The judge spoke, 'Unless there's testimony to the contrary, I agree. It's time to draft a release plan.'

Not breaking his gaze from his mother, he spoke, 'I have something to say.'

Her smile vanished.

'Go ahead,' the judge said.

Frank emptied the contents of his stuffed envelope onto the table. Inside were dozens of hand-written letters. 'Six months ago, at the last one of these, my mother's mailing privileges were restored. I don't know how she got my address.' He looked at the social worker, and then at the doctors, it likely had been one of them. 'The restraining order that's been in effect since I was nine has never been revoked. And she's been writing me . . . as you can see, a lot. I've kept the envelopes so you can verify when they were sent. Here's one from last week.' He picked it up and read it.

Child of Satan:
Number your days. Count the seals as they dissemble and
shatter. One, two, three, my avenging arms will reach for
you. Four, five, six, your rancid blood will stain the floor,
seven, eight, nine, salvation will be mine. From the father's
seed that polluted me. To the vile taint of his demon
progeny. Back to hell, back to hell. I will send you back
to hell . . .

He read on, needing to readjust the page into the light, turning
one hand-written side to the next. The letters tight and small,
like she'd tried to conserve on size to get it all down.

'Demon!' his mother screamed. And before the guards could
stop her, she leapt across the table and launched herself at Frank.

Just as with Tuesday's early a.m. mugger, Frank fended her
off. Years of training, mostly Aikido, held her back. Even so,
she savagely raked her nails across his forearm and then his
cheek.

An alarm sounded. The room filled with guards. She did not
go down easy. Her fingers, like talons, slashed and drew blood.

'You must die,' she shrieked. 'Don't you see? We are not
free as you walk the earth. You must be put down. Dog! Devil!
I abjure thee Satan, back to hell, back to hell! Back to hell!'

Winded and bloody Frank stood with his back to a wall as
she was restrained. Two guards on each limb as they strapped
her to a gurney with padded leather straps.

The doctor ordered a powerful tranquilizer.

Candace screamed and sobbed. 'You know not what you do.
He is Satan given flesh.'

A male nurse entered with a drawn-up syringe.

'No!' Candace writhed. 'You mustn't weaken me. I am God's
true purpose. I am his flaming sword.'

A second nurse pulled down her pants as two guards twisted
her up enough for needle nurse to get a clear shot at her buttock.

They were brutal and efficient. As the drug went in, Candace
gasped and prayed. Her words shuddered forth. 'The Lord is
my shepherd. I shall not want. I shall seek vengeance. It is mine
sayeth the Lord. The angels weep as Devils . . .'

She lost speed and clarity.

'Another ten milligrams of Haldol and two of Ativan,' the doctor gasped.

'Got it.' From his lab-coat the nurse produced a second pre-filled syringe.

'He maketh me to lie with demons, so that I may give flesh, and then destroy that flesh.'

And then she was out.

Frank stared at her. Her mouth hung open. She snored. He looked from her face to her hands, now bound tight by buckled leather straps. Her fingernails were filthy. *She's a germaphobe.* He felt a trickle of blood on his cheek where she'd scratched him. *Even here. Fuck!* He spoke through a clenched jaw and turned to the judge. 'My mother has a fixed delusion. She believes that she gave birth to a child of the devil . . . me. It's why she killed my father and tried to kill me when I was eight. Nothing has changed. Other than she's learned to hide her delusions. And just because she's insane does not make her stupid. If you ever release her, her single aim will be to find me and to kill me.'

'Point made, young man,' the judge said as they rolled Candace out. 'Candace Garfield remains at Croton. A release plan is premature. We will re-evaluate in six months.' She glanced at Frank. 'We should also curtail her mail privileges.'

'No, don't. She fooled her treatment team. Let her write.' He turned to the doctor and tried to keep his voice neutral, while rage burned. 'I need alcohol, wipes, and bandages. Please culture whatever is under my mother's fingernails and instruct anyone who's been scratched by her to get their wounds cleansed immediately . . . and thoroughly.'

'You don't think . . .' the psychiatrist stammered. His face blanched as he realized how deeply he'd been duped. And worse, the danger they'd all been exposed to.

Frank's shoulders sagged. *This will never fucking end.* He tried to remember all the doctors and psychologists he'd faced through the years. Each one greener than the next, thinking they had the key to unmake Candace Garfield's crazy. In the past he'd argue with them, and worked to hammer home the point. But now, he just wanted to wipe off whatever poison she'd just tried to infect him with. 'I need to wash these cuts, now. Your staff needs to do the same.'

'Right.'

A nurse led him to a staff bathroom and gave him alcohol wipes, a bottle of peroxide, cotton swabs, and several packages of an iodine compound. 'Thanks.' He locked the door and examined his face – his right cheek had three tracks of drying blood where she'd landed her strike. Nothing needed sutures, but she'd broken the skin. He wondered how long she'd planned it. Possibly since the last six-month review. He unwrapped a sterile cotton pad, blotted it against his wounds, resealed the bloody cloth in its original package, and put it in his pocket. He mused, *if this doesn't kill me, it should get me through the next one of these.* He had no faith that the Croton doctor would do as he'd asked. And knowing his mother, at the first possible instant, she'd scrub the evidence.

For ten minutes he sterilized, and pried each of his wounds open to ensure that the soap, the iodine, and the peroxide worked. He reflected on what just happened. 'Sometimes Dr Stein,' he said aloud, 'there really is a tiger in the room. And that's my problem. How the fuck do you know?'

He retrieved his belongings from the guards, and walked back towards his car. He glanced at his cell; he'd missed several calls. One was from Grace checking up on him. There was another from a number he didn't recognize, they'd left a voice message. He clicked on it.

'Hi Frank, it's Leona Lang. Dalton filled me in on last night's yes and a handshake. I'm so pleased. We're both working like mad to make certain you don't regret it. To be fair, I've not been this excited about a project in . . . well, in a long time. Call me when you get this. We're getting the Hollow Hills facility in Litchfield cleared out for you. It would be best for you to come up, check it out, and whatever you want and need we will get . . . Seriously, anything.'

Frank stopped and stared back at the maximum-security hospital. He pressed the *return call* icon. He expected voicemail, but Leona picked up.

'Hi Frank. Please tell me it's still a yes.'

'If you can make good on what your son promised.' His words rambled in his head. He heard them like they were being spoken by someone else. Someone whose mother hadn't just tried to kill him . . . again. 'A human trial with terminally ill children. The ones at St Mary's.'

'Not a problem. Though the study design with non-heterogeneous tumors will raise eyebrows.'

'It'll work,' he said. He thought of Jen, Ben . . . Lakeesha. 'But a month is too long to wait.'

'Understood. Let me give you the address so you can tour the facility. It's spectacular and we can rent as many additional homes as necessary for the families. We'll foot the whole thing. Hell, Dalton even cut a deal with the neighboring farm for equine therapy. Whatever you need Frank. Just think of me as Santa.'

He parroted something his mother said when he was four and was told there'd be no Christmas or presents. 'That's an anagram for Satan.'

'I'm aware. There's something dead wrong about that fat man breaking into all those homes. And why mothers let their children sit on a strange old man's lap at malls, seems . . . But I digress. We are going to do great things you and me. You will make a huge difference in those children's lives. And I'm honored to be a part of it. And seriously Frank, whatever you need, ask and it's yours. If you get any pushback, you will have both my and Dalton's direct lines. I certainly understand the time crunch. Those children don't have time. We will make this happen. You do your part and we'll do ours.'

Frank typed the Connecticut address into his phone and hung up.

His cell rang again. He was about to ignore it, *probably another recruiter*, but he was on a roll with Dr Stein's do the opposite thing, so he picked up.

'Frank?' A man's voice.

'Yes, who is this?'

'It's Sean. Sean Brody.'

'Yes?'

'You just called me,' Sean said. 'I was returning it.'

'I didn't.' Frank checked his cell's memory.

'Maybe you butt dialed. Regardless, when's your next game?'

'Thursday, unless it's raining. Or . . .' *I'm no longer at MIT. I think I just quit my job. What have I done?*

'What about coffee?' Sean asked.

'This about Jackson?' Frank asked.

'No. We've got that tied up. Like I said, it was a robbery and the guy who fenced the jewelry OD'ed, probably fentanyl, but can't say for sure till the final toxicology comes back. That seems to be the motive, money for drugs. Though I'm still pulling at the threads you raised. Something doesn't fit. You were right. A lot of people hated Jackson, and why am I rambling on like this? So, coffee?'

'Like a date?' Frank asked, having misjudged similar situations in the past.

'Yeah, like that.'

Bonus points for Dr Stein. 'Yes.' And not used to good things happening to him, he thought of Leona's promise to give him everything he wanted. *'Think of me as Santa.'*

'What are you doing now?' Sean asked.

Frank sorted through possible replies. From finishing up with my psychotic and homicidal mother to getting set to make a huge change in my life. 'I just accepted a new job and am going to check out my lab.'

'That's a big deal. One of those recruiters finally get through to you?'

'Offer I couldn't refuse.'

'You want company? I'm off today.'

'It's in Connecticut and right now I'm in Croton New York.'

There was silence. 'You still there?' Frank asked.

'Yeah. I don't mind the drive, unless you don't want the tag-along.'

He gave Sean the address for UNICOs Hollow Hill Labs.

'See you in a couple hours,' Sean said.

'Yeah,' Frank managed, and hung up. He stood in the parking lot, cell phone in one hand, keys in the other. In the space of minutes, he'd been assaulted by his mother, set on a new career trajectory, and made a date. *What the fuck just happened?*

His cheek tingled and two male robins in a beach-rose bramble fluttered around a drab female. He watched them, the contrast of their bright orange chests and the pink flowers, which someone had bothered to plant outside a hospital for the criminally insane. *Is this really happening?* He looked at the address for the Litchfield facility. Pressed on it, and listened to Siri say, 'OK, navigation started. Proceed to the highlighted road.'

He got in the Element and turned the key. *I'm really going to do this. They don't have to die . . . if it works.* He pictured Caesar and Lavinia, they were rats not children. It worked for them, but . . .

He drove off, and once on the highway voice-dialed Grace. 'How did it go?' she asked.

'Bad . . . good, they're not letting her out. I'll explain later. How do you feel about leaving Cambridge and coming to work with me in Connecticut?'

'When?'

'Now.'

'Start talking.'

EIGHTEEN

Frank slowed as he approached the gates of the Hollow Hills address. Parked on the side was a black Jeep Wrangler and . . . Sean. In jeans and flannel shirt. *So out of my league.* His chest tightened as Sean waved and jogged towards him.

'They won't let me in without you,' he said, as Frank rolled down his window.

'Get in.' As an uncontrollable smile at seeing Sean ripped open his mother's handiwork, he popped the locks on the passenger door.

'Big day,' Sean remarked. 'What happened to your face? Scratch marks? Heavy date?'

'Long story and no,' Frank said, not wanting to start things with an explanation of his crap childhood that led up to the crap morning at Croton.

'I've got time. You OK? Looks like those just happened.'

'I'm OK, and . . .'

'And you don't want to talk about it. Well then,' Sean said, 'I can take a little mystery, you did wash those out? The stuff under people's fingernails you would not believe.'

'I would,' Frank said, not wanting to voice his suspicion that they'd been a murder attempt by his mother. 'Hey, I'm a doctor, I disinfected the hell out of them.' He drove up to the guard station and pulled out his wallet. Sean did the same.

'You're on the list, Dr Garfield,' he said to Frank. 'You're not.'

'He's with me.' Frank wondered if that carried weight.

'Let me check.' The guard, whose nametag identified him as Brett Condon, vanished into his steel-barred hut.

'Good security,' Sean remarked. 'Gates, ten-foot fences. Razor wire, not what you expect for Connecticut, but nice . . . welcoming. And hear that hum? They're electrified.'

The guard returned with plastic badges, one had Frank's picture and name, and the other said VISITOR. 'You're good to go. Wear this at all times,' he said to Sean. And then to Frank, 'Yours lets you in everywhere.' He passed him a small black binder. 'If there's anything you need, all the numbers are here.' He opened the front page to display a laminated card of extensions. 'And on behalf of UNICO, Doctor Garfield, let me be the first to welcome you aboard.'

'Thanks,' he stared at the guard's tag, 'Brett.'

'You're welcome. I hope you like it here. Don't know much of what goes on inside, but for my part, sitting out in this beautiful country forty hours a week and catching a paycheck . . . no complaints.'

'Right.' Frank, feeling at sea, took the binder, passed it to Sean, and waved back at now-friendly Brett.

'Welcome to Stepford,' Sean said, as they rode down a winding two-lane road. 'They've got acreage.'

'And fences, and lots of privacy,' Frank added. They crested a hill and got the long view of a gleaming Brutalist cement, steel, and glass structure that sprouted strangely from the rolling wooded hills.

'Nervous?' Sean asked.

'Yeah, lots happening.'

'It is,' Sean said. 'And I'm probably not helping things.'

Frank slowed the Element and looked at Sean. He epitomized the all-American guy, *so out of my league.* And Dalton's question from the other night, *Why don't you have someone?* Not the first time he'd been asked. And at thirty-two, not an easy answer. Sure there'd been guys interested, but the couple times he'd let down his guard and given a prospective boyfriend his sad history, or worse, a taste of the shit that ran between his ears, they'd not stuck around. *He doesn't need to know any of that . . . he's a cop . . . he'll find out.* 'I'm glad you're here.'

'I hope that's true, cause I'm glad to be here,' he smiled.

Frank's gut went soft. 'Good.' He remembered something Stein had told him. *'No one can see the crazy in your head. The only way they find out is if you tell them.'* He wondered, when, and if that time came with Sean, how long he'd stick around.

Without further talk Frank pulled into a circular covered drive made of free-form bronze-patinated arches that cascaded from the building's roof to the ground.

'Very Downtown Abbey,' Sean quipped, as a row of UNICO employees in various uniforms assembled to welcome them.

'Yeah, a lot to take in.' And it was, all of it – the enormity of what he'd agreed to, the beautiful man next to him, his mother's attack . . . *don't think . . . just breathe.*

As they got out of the car, a balding man in his forties approached. 'Dr Garfield, we are so happy to have you here. I'm Melvin Carter, Program Officer for Hollow Hills. Would you and your guest like to use the facilities before we start? Some water? Coffee? Something stronger?'

'I'm good.' He looked to Sean.

'Same.'

The tour started with a rapid meet-and-greet the employees. Everyone from maintenance, to the technicians in charge of the different laboratories, then onto ivy-league PhD researchers who seemed less happy to see him.

'Melvin.' Frank reached into this pocket. 'You have a micro-biology lab that can culture a sample?'

'Of course,' he looked over the employees who had broken ranks and milled about in the bright spring day, 'Lynette.'

A young woman with a ponytail in scrubs and a lab-coat came over. 'What's up?'

Frank pulled out the package with the cotton swab folded into its wrapper. 'Can you culture this and tell me what grows?'

'Easy peasy,' she said with a smile. 'Anything else?'

'No, just let me know everything that grows at twenty-four, forty-eight, and seventy-two hours.' He scanned her nametag, Lynette Halpern, PhD.

'Both aerobes and anaerobes? I'll check for spores, as well. I mean, if you want.'

He nodded, glad that she'd asked, and that she knew her job, having initially assumed – incorrectly – she was some lab grunt. 'Thanks.'

'If it grows anything, do you also want antibiotic sensitivities?'

'Good thought. And yes, please.'

'And if there's anything else, don't hesitate.' She pulled a card from her lab-coat pocket. 'If you don't hear from me, this is the best number.' And off she went with the proof of whatever his mother had attempted.

Sean watched. 'And that was about?'

Frank could not find the words. 'Can I say nothing?'

'As opposed to lying?'

'Yeah.'

'Sure,' Sean said, his tone disappointed.

It was a discordant note, and Frank knew it. He hated lies and liars. He knew that Jackson would have been disgusted by today's turn of events. *Pimps and whores . . . which am I?* And he'd already lied to Sean about his parents, going for the simple one his Grandpa Harry told him was OK, *'Just say they both died when you were young. Your truth is too much for strangers and acquaintances.' And is that what Sean is? And a detective. What if he already knows? And what if this isn't a date . . . then why is he here?*

'Gentlemen.' Melvin beckoned them towards the glass doors. 'Let's see what's what?'

Sean whispered, 'And here we go from Downtown Abbey to Willy Wonka.'

Frank blinked as they entered the three-story vaulted foyer. Light streamed and refracted into rainbows that danced around the soaring interior with its potted citrus trees, some in bloom with scented white flowers, and others, tricked by the building's endless summer were laden with out-of-season grapefruits, limes, and Meyer lemons.

'Wow. Not what I'm used to,' Frank commented, comparing this architectural pastiche to the dingy, cramped, and hotly contested lab space in Cambridge.

Melvin rattled off a narrative of the building's history. Its famous New Haven architect, its unique features, which allowed the entire facility to be repurposed at nearly a moment's notice. 'Half the walls are modular, but also soundproof. We configured most of the lab space for your arrival. Last night was busy. It's not often we get marching orders from Dr Lang herself. It's so exciting.'

'And the existing labs? The work being done . . .' Frank asked.

Melvin lowered his voice, 'Some of the grumpier hands you shook. We had to do several relocations to give your work priority. But Dr Lang was explicit, nothing is to be held back. So please, if there's something you need, ask. I'm serious about that. You ask, and we'll find it.'

'I have some pets I need to bring and accommodate.'

'I've been told; I'm quite excited about the Galapagos tortoise. I will personally insure we have perfect accommodations for everyone,' and to Sean, 'including guests. I had some ideas that with the children spending so much time here, perhaps we could bring your tortoise and the parrot here.' He gestured to the atrium.

'Nice thought,' Frank said. 'But those kids have all been through horrible chemo. None of them have immune systems that can handle anything.'

'Understood,' Melvin said. 'I was thinking plexiglass and this room is equipped with reverse airflow. Less a petting zoo and more of a habitat exhibit.'

Frank thought of Jen, Ben, Lakeesha, Tara . . . 'That could work. Harvey swears.'

'So I heard; we can do things to muffle the sound, maybe a water feature. You also have a pair of pet rats, or so I was led to believe.'

'Yes, they'll stay with me.'

'I could easily—'

'No,' Frank interrupted him. Something about all the Lang's knowledge of his menagerie tripped his paranoia. Caesar and Lavinia might prove too much of a temptation for Leona's inquisitive mind. 'They stay with me.'

'No problem.'

'You guys have thought of everything,' Sean said, as they rode up in a glass elevator that offered views of the indoor citrus orchard below and the Litchfield hills beyond.

'We try,' Melvin said. 'Dr Lang was clear. She's immensely interested in this project.'

As they were shown not one, but two sparkling new high-speed DNA sequencers, an electron microscope with higher resolution than anything at MIT, Frank's excitement grew. *Sweet Jesus, it's all here. Everything I need.* The realization that he was about to take theory and make it flesh pressed in on him. Without Jackson, he saw no downside. *Why was he so against this?*

He noted the building was all arranged around the lush atrium. Then, as they exited an odorless rodent lab, fitted out with floor-to-ceiling cages, he saw a flurry of activity below as two BMWs pulled up. Leona exited the white one, and Dalton, the black.

'You guys make yourselves at home,' Melvin said with a nervous edge. He motioned them towards an employee lounge that overlooked the atrium. 'I'll be right back.'

'The famous Langs,' Sean said.

'Not the best date,' Frank said and then thought. *If that's what this is.*

'You're doing OK,' Sean said. 'And the glass elevator . . . like I said, Willy Wonka with rats and microscopes. But what I don't get . . . and maybe on a first date you don't go there, but . . . just a few days ago you wouldn't even take a call from these guys and now . . .'

Frank looked from the Lang's three-stories below, back to Sean. 'I think I can make a difference in some children's lives. Possibly a big difference.'

'That's a good thing. Those kids you treat at St Mary's?'

'Yeah. It's just—'

'Strings attached.'

'I'm not sure where to find them,' Frank admitted. 'Look at all this. It's perfect, but kind of too much.'

Sean now focused on Dalton and Leona thirty feet below as they chatted with some UNICO staff who had stayed to enjoy the outdoors. 'The dragon lady and her pup.' Sean mused aloud. 'Strings are another way to think of motive. What's in it for them? Answer that, and you'll see the strings a mile away.'

'Life extension,' Frank said, and immediately wished he hadn't.

'Seriously? Your telomere stuff.'

'Maybe.'

'For how long?'

Frank thought of Cesar and Lavinia, twice as old as average Norwegian rats, and randy as adolescents even though he'd spayed and neutered them. 'A long time.'

Sean's tone turned serious. 'How many people know this, Frank?'

'Grace, me . . . now you. Jackson.'

'And them.'

'Yes, although . . .'

'What?'

'They don't have proof. Neither do you. You just have my word.'

'And once they have proof?'

'You ask a lot of questions.'

'You interest me.'

'Like a perp?'

'Like a hot, super-smart guy who's sitting on a game changer and doesn't know if he's just made the best, or worst, decision of his life,' Sean said.

Dalton looked up at them and waved.

'We've been spotted,' Sean said. 'You didn't mention that the pup is an underwear model.'

'He's aware,' Frank said, as Leona and Dalton headed towards the elevators.

'Do I have competition?'

'For what?'

'Good answer,' Sean said.

'I just missed something.'

'Don't sweat it. When do you get to work with your kids?'

'Soon, that's the deal . . . Hopefully this week.'

'Huh? Isn't that kind of fast? Don't you have to get approvals and . . . I don't know, not a researcher here, but I'm thinking . . .'

'It is fast. But they said they could and would do it.' His voice trailed. 'Said they could pull strings.'

'Something starting to smell funny?' Sean asked.

Their conversation was halted by the elevator doors and Melvin's animated voice. 'Been showing around our new R&D director. Everyone is super excited.'

Leona, in a deep plum suit, was all smiles as she walked past Melvin. 'Frank, and Detective Brody.' She took in the scratches on Frank's face. 'Do you need antibiotic cream?'

'I've got some, but thank you.'

Dalton smiled. 'Not even one day into a new venture and we've got bloodshed and the police.'

Frank watched Sean's gaze narrow.

'No,' Sean said. 'It's a date.'

'Sadly,' Leona said, 'it's got to be a working one. And Frank, not to get off on the wrong foot, anyone you bring into this facility needs security clearance.'

'I can disappear,' Sean said.

'Please don't,' Frank said.

'No need,' Leona said. 'I got a call from the gate. It's fine. Done.' She waved her hands and turned to Melvin, 'How far did you get?'

'Pretty much showed him what there was to see.'

'Excellent.' And then to Frank. 'You have everything you need?'

'I think so. Those sequencers are amazing, and the administration is a simple infusion.'

'Just intravenous?' she asked.

'Yes, but slow,' he said.

'How slow?'

He paused and studied her. He remembered that last talk with Jackson. He'd said she was the most brilliant student he'd mentored. And here she was, decades out of the lab, asking the right questions. He glanced from her, to Melvin, to Sean, Dalton and the milling employees among the citrus below. 'It's like Velcro,' he said.

'Your telomere compound?' Leona asked.

'Yes, it attaches to the ends of DNA.'

'Fascinating . . . and once it does, it pulls everything into a tighter configuration.'

'Yes, exactly.'

'And because the telomeres have a sequence which is preserved through most of evolution you don't have to worry about compatibility.'

'Correct.'

'Isn't that something,' she said with a sense of awe. 'That the most-important discoveries are the most elegant and simple ones.'

'True.'

'But,' she added, 'until we make this thing happen in humans, it's still just theory. What about dialysis machines?' she asked.

'I hadn't thought of that,' Frank said. 'It's not a bad idea. And . . . it's actually a really good one. We could do a slow infusion over four hours to insure a consistent rate, essentially bathe them in the compound. The goal is to get every nucleated cell in the body to incorporate the compound.'

'But there's a trick, isn't there?' Leona said. 'That's why no one has beaten you to this. You've figured out a way to have not only the cell take up a complex molecule, but also to get it into the nucleus.'

'Yes.'

'And?' she asked. 'What's the trick?'

'Let's make sure it works first.'

'Fine.' The corner of her lips twitched as if she'd tasted something gone sour. 'So dialysis machines it is. We'll retrofit them however you'd like.' She turned to Melvin. 'Get eight dialysis machines, make them kid friendly.'

'The first experiment is just with six,' Frank said.

'Something always breaks,' Leona said. 'Make it ten, Melvin.'

'Of course, Dr Lang.'

'Anything else, Frank?' She looked him in the eyes. 'Anything at all?'

'No, I think you've got this covered.'

'Excellent. Now we've got a few places lined up for you. I hope you like one.'

'For?'

'Your house. You didn't think we'd lock you in the lab. And I don't know about you, but I love to look at properties. Problem is, I tend to buy them.'

They piled into Leona's car, Frank and Sean in back, Dalton in front. She first took them to a condominium complex a quarter mile from Hollow Hills that would also house the six test children and their parents.

'These are so much better than my place in Brookline,' Sean said, as they walked through one gleaming marble back-splashed kitchen after the next.

'No comparison,' Frank said, having handed over the keys to his tiny apartment, and given clear instructions on how Killer, Harvey, Caesar and Lavinia were to be handled and transported.

'I'm so glad you recruited Dr Lewis,' Leona said. 'If you see something you think would suit her, we might as well go ahead and lease it.'

'I didn't say I had,' Frank said.

A quick look passed between Leona and Dalton. 'You didn't did you?' she said. 'I just assumed.'

'You assumed correct,' Frank said, as he tried to remember what he might have told the Langs about Grace. *I didn't tell them anything . . .*

From the condos it was on to a series of beautiful colonials, many eighteenth century when Litchfield was Connecticut's capital. 'I tasked the handlers with ensuring that all details were managed,' Leona said, as they walked through a property off the town green.

'Handlers?' Frank asked.

'Subject navigators. We have a lot of variables to control, and in a study with only six subjects, I thought it best to attach a handler to each of the children and their families.'

'To do what?'

'Whatever you need them to do. Make sure they're where

they need to be when they need to be there. You've never done a study with human subjects, Frank. I've overseen many. A lot can go wrong. This is too important to risk any screw-ups.'

It was during a tour of a spacious modern home with long views over the hills that he found himself alone with Sean in a walk-in closet. 'Bet you regret coming up here.'

'You'd lose that bet.' Sean said, 'But if you're getting a new house, I want one thing.'

'What's that?'

Sean closed the space between them. He gripped Frank's hand and drew him close. 'May I?' he asked, his breath hot against Frank's lips.

'Yes.'

They kissed.

Sean pulled back slightly. His voice deep, 'That's what I want.' They kissed again.

'You like this house?' Frank asked.

'Good closet.' Sean pressed Frank back against the wall.

'It is.' Frank pushed into him, his hands around Sean's broad back.

A throat-clearing noise intruded.

'I'd say get a room,' Dalton remarked, 'but seems like you've got one.'

'This place will do,' Frank managed. He didn't break gazes with Sean. 'It's got nice closets.'

'Good,' Dalton said. 'I'll have the paperwork drawn up. It comes furnished, but we can bring in a decorator and get it more to your taste.' He fixed on Sean, his expression unreadable. 'We've got a few more things to go over . . . we'll be down in the kitchen.'

As soon as he left, Sean stole another lingering kiss. 'This is an excellent date, Frank. But I don't trust either one of them . . . especially Dalton.'

Dusk fell as the details were hammered out around a butcher block table. It was clear that Leona intended to make good on her Santa promise of everything Frank needed to bring his research to fruition.

'The biggest question, Frank,' Leona said, 'is how fast can you produce your telomere compound? That is the rate-limiting step, correct?'

'With the sequencers I just saw, it won't take long. It's basic, followed by a couple additional steps. Grace and I should be good to go in a couple days, three tops. You've got everything else I need at Hollow Hill, and I'll use your dialysis suggestion. But . . .'

'But what?' she asked.

'I can't just leave my other patients, and I've got my classes, and—'

'Dalton.'

'On it, Mother. Frank, we've got you covered. We'll make a donation to the hospital to more than cover any inconvenience, and MIT will piss and moan and throw some poor doctoral student in to cover your classes. The tortoise, the bird, and your rats are in transit as we speak. We've got this.'

Sean looked at Dalton. 'You sure know a lot about Frank.'

'Of course, we do,' Leona said. 'And if you're going to be a part of this, we'll know a lot about you as well, Detective Brody.'

'Big business,' Sean said.

'Yes. Big business, big money, and Frank's research has tremendous potential. It's going to save lives.'

'I get that. And you're the lucky ones to sign him.'

'Yes, we are,' she said. 'As apparently . . . so are you.'

NINETEEN

'I don't like this detective,' Leona told Dalton, via car phone as she headed home to Greenwich and he was en route to Manhattan for a bone-dry series of budget meetings.

'Agreed. Still, he could prove useful.' But Dalton heard her unstated directive – Detective Sean Brody is a problem. Fix it.

'In what universe?' she asked.

'The one where I live.'

'Really. You think you can divert him? Frank resisted what you offered.'

'Don't know until I try. Frank is an anomaly. And if not, Mother, people who get in your way are prone to misfortune. Also, he's potential leverage. Which we've little of.' He braked as the traffic slowed and three lanes merged to two for the agonizing stop-and-go entry into Manhattan through the Midtown Tunnel.

'Points taken. So how goes our Frank the Saint Save-the-Children cancer study? You've had three days, where are we?'

'We're good.' He knew that anything less would set her off. 'What I'd not counted on was how quick those families said yes. No hesitation from any of them.'

'They're desperate,' she said. 'It's understandable.'

'It's Garfield. I told them it's his study and they didn't need anything else. Just, "where do we sign?" The man has something, some quality . . .'

'Dalton. What aren't you saying? Do you have a little thing for him? I thought we were done with your boy phase.'

'I like him, he's compelling, something about him draws people in. Which is fascinating considering how little he thinks of himself.'

'Wounded birds,' she offered. 'Never cared for them.' A brief silence. 'We need to move fast. How long before he or the detective catch on?'

'Frank so far has no experience with human studies. Everything looks perfect, and barring a leak, we should get a month, maybe longer. But that month will give us the answers you need, correct?'

'I hope so. I need his telomere compound and the process. Worst scenario we work backwards from the molecule. Though it's risky. Somehow, he's figured the impossible. And all those years with Jackson . . . all that simmering paranoia. Jackson trusted no one.'

'They're set to close his case,' Dalton said.

'A pointless robbery. Trinkets for drugs. And then the moron winds up dead from an overdose. A strange symmetry there.'

'How so?'

'Jackson believed pharma was the root of all evil. In the end, we caused his death.'

Dalton startled. *Does she know?* 'I don't follow. How does a random robbery for drugs have anything to do with pharma . . . with us?'

'Connect the dots, Dalton. Without us there would be no opioid epidemic, or whatever they call it. We created the market for synthetic opioids. Convinced doctors and the whole health-care industry that pain was the fifth vital sign. And shame on them if they didn't dole out the oxies and percocets.' She chuckled. 'I remember when we released Tranxic patches. Potent and non-habit forming . . . at least the first part was true. But doctors believe what they want, especially when delivered by a pretty face with a box of donuts and coffee for the office staff.'

'And now it's cheap fentanyl from China.'

'Yes, and everyone is happy. Except the dead junkie, of course.'

'And Jackson.'

'A waste . . . a sad waste.'

Dalton said nothing. He waited.

'Tidy, too. And as you observed, the murder proved a catalyst for Frank. So regretful *and* a good thing . . . at least for us.'

'Yes,' Dalton said. 'And now on to the main course. You've made a believer of me, Mother. Or maybe he has.'

'Jackson knew,' she sighed. 'It would kill him again to know that he's the one who led me to Frank's potential. But until we pry this potion out of his head and into our hands that's all it is, untapped potential.'

'And an extra hundred years of life. Seems a bit pie in the sky.' He advanced two car lengths and stopped.

'It's not. The best friend, Grace Lewis. All tucked in?'

'Yes. Like those parents, people follow him.'

'Good. A happy Litchfield family out to save the dying children.'

'With a study that will never see the light of day,' Dalton added.

'Pity that. But Frank, for all his brilliance has missed the forest for the trees. Jackson saw that. It's why he wanted Frank to cease and desist. The minute you manipulate the telomere to stabilize the cell, you reset the biological clock. The ramifications are unprecedented.'

'Dying cancer children aren't a bad place to start. Think of the upside for UNICO. A cancer drug that actually works. It would be a first.'

She snorted. 'Not going to happen. Not on my watch . . . and not on yours. The minute his molecule, and whatever process gets it into the nucleus becomes public, the hordes will descend and reproduce it. The Chinese and Russians don't give a shit for patents. Just look at the dozens of fentanyl analogs pouring in. It's not an option. Garfield's telomere compound, if it does what he and we think it does, will not be shared, at least not in the usual way. Your question, what would someone give for an extra hundred years? is the right one. What's the answer? A million? Ten million? A bill stalled in the senate? But cart and horse.'

'Yes,' Dalton said. 'And on the matter of misfortune for our detractors, I see we're out of the woods with Renepicide. They want to settle.'

'No. Not a dime. Their case imploded. With the whistle blower dead and discredited they have nothing. File a countersuit for legal fees and defamation. Break them.'

'Bad luck for him. Bad luck for them.'

'Yes,' she said. 'Bad luck. One more thing, Dalton.'

'Yes, Mother.'

'This study with the telomere compound. I'm adding a test subject. One Frank can't know about.'

'You're certain of this?'

'Very. I can't wait. I need you to make this happen.'

'It's risky. Frank is squirrely enough as is. I don't think this is the time to throw a curve ball.'

'Point taken.'

'If he only produces enough for the six children?' Dalton asked.

'Then one of them gets a placebo,' Leona said.

'And this mystery subject. Do I get to know their name?'

'Don't be coy. You know,' she said.

'Yes, Mother. But are you certain? It could go south, he's

only tried it on rats. I'm not the scientist here, but genetic manipulation seems like a big deal. Like you'd want to know about potential side effects or—'

He heard a sigh.

'Calculated risk,' she said, and ended the call.

TWENTY

F rank blinked as sunlight flooded down through the atrium windows. It bathed citrus trees, six terminally ill children and their parents, half a dozen nurses in Disney-themed scrubs, a Galapagos turtle, and a swearing Macaw. He batted back tears, *this is really happening.* He ticked off the days it had taken to set this stage. Ten. Not even two weeks. *Not possible.*

His cheek tingled and itched from where his mother had clawed him. He'd not been wrong about her intent. The Hollow Hills microbiologist had called him less than twenty-four hours after he'd given her the sample. 'It's fecal, e-coli and some campylobacter pylori, but something else, too. I'll need another twenty-four hours but thought I'd give you the first results.' She'd contacted him twelve hours later. 'There's MRSA in it. And that's not fecal. Quite a cocktail.' He'd thanked her, contacted Croton, and insisted on speaking with their CEO, Colette Stong. She'd been polite, but he felt patronized.

'We all have bacteria under our fingernails,' she'd said.

'Not this mix. I hope you took care of those guards.'

'I'm not at liberty to share that information.'

'Right. This was a murder attempt.'

'That's a stretch, Dr Garfield. But your concerns are noted.'

He touched his cheek and rubbed the thick antibiotic cream, he'd applied four times a day, up and down the wounds. They were healing. But he knew enough not to mess around with MRSA, which once it took hold, earned its reputation as the flesh-eating bacteria.

A tiny hand tugged at his lab-coat pocket. 'Doctor Frank.'

'What's up, Jen.'

'This is nothing.'

'No,' he replied, 'this is everything.'

'No, silly.' Her china blue eyes were wide open, there was mischief in her smile. 'I'm talking about Killer's poopoo.' She settled back into her Barbie-themed pink infusion pod as a nurse wiped her forearm with an alcohol prep.

He marveled at Jen's disregard for the needle. No fuss. Not from the beginning. 'It's just my body,' she'd told him months back when she'd been in the midst of a brutal, and ultimately futile, round of chemo. *It's not really me. I separate me from my body. I hardly feel it. When I die that's what happens. So I'm practicing.*

'OK, what's the deal with Killer's poopoo?' he asked, as the nurse hunted for a usable suitable vein.

'It's got lettuce in it. And it's huge. Not like Harvey's or mine.'

'Every animal poos different,' he said. Hoping the pediatric nurse, who'd been retained for this project, along with five others, lived up to her resumé. He watched as she tied the tourniquet, patted Jennifer's arm to pop a vein, and with a single shot, got the tiny needle in, taped down, and flushed with heparin.

Relieved, he looked up and down the lush space dotted with bright plastic infusion pods, each customized to their occupant. Leona had delivered . . . *'Think of me as Santa.'*

Melvin, the program officer, skirted around a potted tangerine. 'It's good isn't it. Everything is set?'

'Yes, thank you. And where did you find those dialysis units? I didn't know they came in colors.'

Melvin beamed. 'We retrofitted and painted them. Did it over the weekend. They came out well, I think.'

'And now, using the atrium. This is beyond my expectations. And the infusion pods, where did you find them?'

'That was Melanie's doing,' he said giving credit to his assistant. 'She asked each of the kids about their favorite toys and stuff, raided a furniture store, and presto-chango Barbie, dinosaur, and NASCAR infusion pods, all with gel foam mattresses and hypoallergenic. But kids aside, everyone loves our new Killer and Harvey exhibit. Now are you certain everything is set?'

'It is.' *But what if it's not. What if . . .*

'Well, if they've got to be here for four hours, seems the least we could do to try and keep them happy and comfortable. Though your bird . . .'

'Yeah, he swears.'

'But everyone loves the tortoise. Never knew they ate so much, but not a problem. I've got to check on a few things,' Melvin said. 'You have my number. Again, if there's anything you need, get me or Melanie.'

'The two Mels,' Frank said, having in a few short days gotten to appreciate the efficient duo.

'Exactly. And Dr Garfield?'

'Yes.'

'Good luck. I realize this is need-to-know. But I can tell this is big . . . so good luck to you . . . and to them.'

'Thank you.'

Grace, who'd been attending to five-year-old Carter Jeffries with his undifferentiated sarcoma that had already cost him his right leg, joined Frank. 'Excited?'

'Terrified.'

'This space is amazing.'

'I know. No expense spared.'

Jen, nestled in her pink pod, overheard them. 'Can I play with Killer?'

'Not yet,' Grace said. 'But hopefully after. We've got tons of games and videos. It won't be too boring.'

'I know,' she said. 'And this is a lot prettier than St Mary's, and we get to play with the horses, right?'

'Eventually,' Grace said.

Frank gazed out at the western hills. Beyond a manicured lawn, walking paths, and dotted benches and picnic tables for the UNICO employees, was a tree line hemmed with razor-wire-tipped fence. He listened to Grace and Jen, his thoughts distracted. *This is too fast. But it's here. This is happening.*

Like medical rounds at the hospital, he started at one end of the room, and checked in with each of the six: Lakeesha Thomas, Ben Bradley, Carter Jeffries, Jen, Tara James-Morgan, and Logan

Tanner, all with advanced malignancies, all under ten. He smiled and chatted with them and their parents.

He read hope in the adults' eyes. *What if this doesn't work? What if something goes wrong? Why are they trusting me like this?*

'I don't know where she gets it from,' Jen's mother, Marnie came over with a purple juice in a sippy cup. Her eyes were red-rimmed. She glanced at her daughter's catheter, handed her the drink and turned to Frank. 'Can I talk to you in private?'

'Of course.'

'I want to hear,' Jen said.

'It's grown-up stuff, hon.'

'Mommy.'

'I just wanted Dr Garfield to explain the new drug to me again. It doesn't even have a name it's so new.'

Frank nodded. 'It's got what's called a registry number, UB482 and I don't know that I'd call it a drug.' His gaze was fixed on a nurse as she attached an IV tube to Lakeesha's bright red dialysis machine that Melvin's minions had modified. Each child had one, in colors that matched their cozy pods.

Carter Jeffries' parents, Petra and Ken, at the adjacent station overheard. 'OK if we listen in?'

'Sure.'

And from up and down the strange makeshift ward parents flocked around Frank. *They have put so much trust in me. What the fuck am I doing?* He looked at their faces; they ranged from twelve-degrees-beyond exhaustion to emotions he couldn't describe. Some he'd known for more than a year, all of them he'd talked through painful decisions and heart-breaking test results. *What do I say?* 'Thank you for agreeing to participate in this study. I know that you've signed lots of paperwork and had things explained and . . . just thank you. Here goes. UB482 is not a drug, it's a complex molecule that attaches to the ends of the DNA, onto something called telomeres. It makes them longer and keeps them from allowing the DNA to unravel in ways that allow things like tumors to form.'

'How?' Daryl James-Morgan asked. He and his husband Douglas had adopted Tara when she was three. Within a year she'd been diagnosed with a rare leukemia. Their last two years had been a hellish series of life-threatening infections, toxic radiation, and the realization that their dreams for a family and a future with Tara were not to be.

Frank paused. These were smart people who'd been through the wringer. He searched for words that would bring them clarity. It felt like being back at MIT, only there he usually lost half his class. *Do better.* 'Think of our DNA as a recording of everything that makes us us. Recordings can be duplicated. That's what happens inside most cells. But not every part of the DNA can be replicated and that has to do with how it's twisted and folded up. Not every bit is exposed to the machinery that makes copies.'

Heads nodded. 'As we age the telomeres, those bits at the end shorten up and the DNA is no longer in its tightly folded configuration. Parts that should not be reproduced are now exposed and get copied. This is how many illnesses, including tumors, originate.'

'But Jen is so young,' Marnie Owens said.

'I know. All of your children are. And while they have different kinds of cancer the out-of-control cell proliferation all stems back to their DNA and things being copied that shouldn't. UB482 will bind to the end of the telomere, lengthen it, and let their DNA tighten.'

'Like a facelift,' Petra Jeffries offered.

'Good analogy,' Grace said.

'It's never been tried on humans?' a parent asked.

'No.' Frank made eye contact with each of them. 'None of the infusions have started yet. And while you've had this explained, and signed all sorts of things, it's not too late to back out.' He resisted the urge to tell them of the only study he'd conducted with tumorous rats. Data that Jackson had insisted he bury, and this study was what he'd wanted to prevent. But looking at these children and their parents, *Jackson was wrong* . . .

'No,' Marnie Owens said. Her words echoed by the others.

'Then let's begin,' Frank said. Feeling a bit like a master of ceremonies, he unlocked a small red refrigerator which contained six glass ampules of UB482. In the rats the results had been fast and undeniable. *Six children are too many. I should try it with one first.*

'You OK?' Grace whispered.

'No.' Careful to keep his voice below what anyone else could hear. 'Scared. This is too fast. We should have done a large-scale rodent study . . . a primate study.'

Grace placed a hand on his shoulder. 'No, look at them. Frank, how many children have we walked to the grave? None of these kids has time for those studies. Even if this goes south, you've given them hope and an awesome time in a beautiful place with their families. Nothing here is bad. Even Jackson, for all his big pharma paranoia, would have to give you this. But just like you gave them a way to back out . . . this is your last chance. It's your decision. Do we move forward?'

He looked from Grace to the sealed ampules.

'I'm ready for my facelift, Dr Frank,' Jen Owens, who'd overheard his mini lecture, shouted from her pink pod.

It turned into a chant of the parents and the kids. 'Facelift. Facelift. Facelift.'

Frank slapped on gloves as Grace did the same. They grabbed vials and one by one broke the tip, drew up syringes, and introduced a molecule that had never been tested on a human being into bags of fluid that over the next four hours would bathe the cells of six dying children.

TWENTY-ONE

At work in the Brookline PD, Sean completed his report on Jackson Atlas's murder. The perp was Brian Baker, a thirty-two-year-old product of the opioid crisis. It was too familiar. Good family, cheap drugs, crushing addiction. And Brian, who should have had the world on a string broke into neighbors' homes to feed his habit.

Sean should have felt relief as he got set to clear the case off his desk. He didn't. *Straight up, murder for drug money.*

Then a few bags of fentanyl-laced dope, and Brian was another face on someone's *Don't Do Drugs* poster.

'This feels wrong. Why?' His thoughts flew to Frank and their make-out session in the closet. *Like a couple of teenagers with Mom and Dad downstairs.* He felt the distance between them, and like probing an unfilled cavity with his tongue, he thought of all the reasons they wouldn't work. *He's too far away. We have zip in common . . . he could have been a perp. And that's a problem . . . don't shit where you eat. You know better. He's not a perp. He's . . . not like anyone you've ever dated. And he's keeping stuff from me. Big stuff.* Sean, as he did with anyone involved in a homicide had done his research. It was easy to learn about Frank's mother. The sensational murder of his father had made it to the national news cycle. From there piecing together why he was in Croton New York hadn't been difficult. *He lied to me about his parents . . . wouldn't you? Hi, I'm Frank my mother killed my father, tried to kill me, and is locked away in a loony bin.* He stopped. *And what must that have been like? Jesus. What kind of childhood did he have?*

He replayed their whirlwind tour of Litchfield Connecticut. UNICO was throwing big bucks at Frank and his research. As a non-scientist he got the gist, Frank was onto something huge. Its proximity to a murder was discordant. It gnawed at him. He wanted to stamp Atlas's murder closed but couldn't ignore the dead man's tirades against big pharma. Or what Frank had told him about Jackson's one-man crusade to sink popular drugs and those who'd brought them to market. *And Frank.* 'Frank, Frank, Frank.' Billions of dollars in drug company profits seemed a better motive for murder than a few five-dollar bags of fentanyl-laced dope.

'And that's the way it is.' He could not make himself hit send. *And that Lang woman and her son.* Dalton; the guy creeped him out. *Really, is that all?* Heat rose in his cheeks, nerves prickled at the back of his neck. Dalton had easy access to Frank, Sean did not. *Jealous. I'm fucking jealous. And why does he have to be so fucking gorgeous? And why did Frank neglect to mention that? What else hasn't he told me . . . or told the truth.* That last bit rankled. Lies and liars, too much like a day at the office, not what one wants in a boyfriend. *And that's the rub a dub dub. You want him. But what if he's not who he seems? Not the first time you read things wrong.*

He pushed back from his desk and the unsent report. His gaze landed on a just-arrived FedEx package stuffed with UNICO paperwork. Boiler plate documents, confidentiality agreements and attestation statements that anything he was privy to at UNICO, or apparently through his relationship with Frank, could never be divulged. As a cop he couldn't just sign this kind of crap. He'd need to read it and ensure it wasn't forcing him to cross lines he'd sworn to observe.

'Seriously?' He felt manipulated. The message was clear. If he didn't sign they'd put obstacles between him and Frank. *Like a couple hundred miles between Litchfield and Boston. Why there? Why pull him out of Cambridge and MIT?* It stank of abusive relationships, where the over-controlling guy – typically the guy – separated his woman from friends and family.

He pulled out his cell and dialed Frank. His gut clenched, as he remembered all the times Frank reflexively sent calls to voicemail.

'Sean?' Frank's voice.

He exhaled. 'I was expecting voicemail.'

'I saw Brookline PD. Figured it was either you or I was being arrested.'

'Not funny. You know how much shit I'd be in for kissing a perp?'

'I wish you were here,' Frank said.

'Me too.' Sean thought of all the reasons why you weren't supposed to say shit like this after a single date and an especially hot macking session. But there it was. 'What's happening there?'

'Waiting. We're about to hit the forty-eight-hour post-infusion mark. No one's dead.'

'You know you're bad with jokes.'

'I've been told. In a few hours we're going to scan them. It's too early to tell anything, but . . . This shit is boring you.'

'No,' and that was the truth. 'Keep talking. What do you hope to learn from the scans?'

'I know every inch of these children inside and out. Jen even named her tumors. She figured that maybe if they had names and faces she could make friends with them. They're like the seven malignant dwarves. Blinky, Stinky, Jinky, I think one's Drinky because I told her it was filled with fluid.'

'And that's what the scans will tell you. How the dwarves are doing?'

'Yeah, if they've had babies, how big they've gotten.'

'Or how small.'

'Yes . . .' Frank's voice trailed. 'I wish you were here. What are you doing?'

Sean glanced at his screen with the Atlas report ready for his electronic signature. 'About to sign off on Jackson's case.'

'The junkie did it.'

'Looks like.'

'You don't sound a hundred percent.'

'I'm not. You introduced reasonable doubt, and my gut screams that the scene was staged.'

'But no evidence,' Frank conceded.

'Strong motive . . . but right, no evidence to back it.'

'And funny timing,' Frank added.

'You read minds now?'

'Maybe,' Frank said.

'Jackson knew what your research was worth. Where it could lead.'

'He did. He also knew that once I made the compound and tested it there'd be no turning back.'

'Can I ask about that?'

A moment's pause. 'Sure.'

'You obviously just passed that point and have a human trial going. Which, even from where I sit, seems way fast and like the Langs pulled strings. Which, billions of dollars, good on them. But that's not the part that sticks. It's you Frank. You synthesized what sounds like something damn complex, damn fast. Is it the same as what you did with Caesar and Lavinia, and their tragic brethren?'

'That was an awful morning, but yes. I tweaked it slightly, but not much.'

'Next question.'

'Shoot, detective.'

'Who else knew about that study?'

'Grace, Jackson, and no one else.'

'Until you published that article.'

'Yeah, but you read it. It's theory, not test results.'

'The ones you brutally slaughtered, admittedly at Jackson's urging, so you were just following orders . . . which kind of makes it worse, but what did you find when you looked inside their tiny murdered bodies?'

'The tumors were either markedly shrunk or gone.'

'And no one ever saw that actual test data other than you, Jackson, and Grace? And no one else knows about Caesar and Lavinia?'

'No one . . . but you.'

'Obviously the Langs knew . . . know. How?'

'I can guess,' Frank said.

'Spill.'

'Those emails on Jackson's computer, the ones that get mushy. I think they were from Leona Lang. He said she broke his heart. I think they stayed in contact.'

'Hope springs eternal,' Sean remarked, wondering when Frank had made this connection and why he'd not shared it. If true . . . *shit, too many fucking coincidences.*

'From his perspective, but from hers?'

'Hard to say,' Sean admitted. 'But if we look at what's transpired with your . . . talent.' He glanced at the time. *Two hours up, two hours back . . . I can do this.* 'You want company?'

'Yes please.'

'Good. I'll see you in a couple hours.'

They hung up. Sean looked at Jackson's ready-to-sign report. He hit save, didn't sign it, and with more doubt than he'd had ten minutes ago, about Frank, the Langs, and the murder, he grabbed a duffel he'd packed that morning, just in case, and headed out.

TWENTY-TWO

Leona stared up into Dr Ramon's puzzled expression. The plastic surgeon squinted and pushed his glasses to the bridge of his nose. He studied her from different angles. She turned and looked at her magnified reflection. For the first time in years she thought, *not bad . . . not great, but not bad. Better, undeniably better.* She adjusted the angle of her chin, aware of his scrutiny and tickled by his confusion. She catalogued the changes. Subtle, but real. *My chin, less loose skin, the neck, maybe a third fewer of those awful lines.* She raised and lowered her brow. *The furrows aren't so deep. I've not had Botox for more than a week.* The moments of doubt and raw terror she'd experienced during her infusion, she now knew had been worth it. She'd taken a huge risk, but a calculated one.

'What did you do?' he asked.

'Facial Pilates. It's new,' she said.

'Never heard of it.' He sounded dubious. 'But look here, your skin, your chin, under your eyes, everything is tighter. You've been to see someone else, haven't you?'

'Never.'

He ran the back of his forefinger down the angle of her jaw. He crouched lower to examine her throat, as he sought the source of her transformation. 'This is . . . this is not possible. I've warned you about those quacks down in Chinatown. What you think are herbs are laced with horrible things. Yes, you get tighter skin, but you also get liver cancer.'

'I swear, just exercise and diet.' Her spirits soared. *He's not going for the black pen.*

'Hmmm.' He sounded unconvinced. 'Let me see you back in a month, and if you have articles on this facial Pilates shoot me an email.'

'Of course, Doctor.' And feeling pounds lighter and years younger she bid him farewell. She pulled on shades and traipsed out into a brilliant spring day. The visit had lasted half as long as usual. *Free time.* *Let's check on Frank and the kids.* She thought about little Jennifer what's her face, *'I'm ready for my facelift.' And I'm not.* She paused. Ramon hadn't even offered her Botox or to plump her lips and cheeks with collagen. She glimpsed her reflection in Park Avenue windows. *Facial Pilates.* She laughed. 'Even my voice sounds younger.' *Certainly not twenty, but thirty-five, possible.* As she walked a good-looking businessman in a bespoke suit and Gucci tie locked eyes with her. He smiled. She didn't look away. *And when's the last time that happened?*

She wandered across Fifth Avenue and into Central Park. Flowers everywhere. Exuberant, she didn't know where to look first. Each person she passed was a universe of their own, from the homeless man on the bench with his bags and cans to the au pair wheeling someone else's baby. She thought of Dalton, and of his father, his real father – Jackson – a man who without question had adored her. *Would he still love me? Men love the pretty face. He thought he loved me. But did he?*

She checked emails and ran through her phone messages. She pressed on the app for *Eternal Buddies* and was afforded a web-cam view of a two-week-old fuzzball of a golden retriever. On the side she toggled through a catalog of his features; he was indeed a perfect replica of her beloved Rex. A date-stamp in the upper right let her know that she could pick him up, or have him delivered, in six weeks, or sooner if she was prepared to bottle feed, which she was.

She hung up, called her assistant, Patrick, let him know about the imminent arrival of Rex IV. And told him to have Rex III brought to the vet and euthanized, like ripping off a bandage, she wanted it done fast. But a deep sadness, old as the first time she came home from school to find her mother passed out naked with a strange man, threatened to pop her euphoria. 'No you don't. Out with the old and in with the new. You were a good dog. And you won't be really dead, but reborn, and this time . . .' She focused on her new puppy as he tumbled around a red rubber ball, 'Forever.' This one would stay with her. She'd infuse him with Frank's telomere extender and he'd live *twice as long? Three times?* She cooed into her cell, 'We'll be together a long time, you and I.' What had been pure theory days and weeks ago was now all giddy new possibility.

She found a guano-free empty bench, settled, and swiped across to a video surveillance app. She started with the family condos around Hollow Hills, then zipped from patient to patient. For the past three days she'd obsessively checked in on the six children. All still alive, nothing obviously wrong with five of them . . . *it's working. I feel it. Ramon saw it.*

The children, except sad little Jennifer Owens, whose dose she'd stolen for herself, looked well, albeit with shaved heads and skin so thin you could see the difference between the red blood in their arteries and the blue in their veins. *Too soon to tell. They're all alive. They seem healthy. I feel fabulous.* She clicked from bedrooms to kitchens. Observed the parents, who'd had years of practice pretending that everything was fine when it wasn't. She sensed it in their expressions, barely contained. 'They see it.' *They know something is happening.* She paused on an intimate kitchen scene of Daryl and Douglas with Tara. Nothing special, the assembly of a quick lunch in a strange kitchen. She put in an earbud. Douglas bemoaned the fact that there was no smooth peanut butter, while Tara had enthusiastically located a jar of marshmallow fluff. 'That stuff will kill you, sweetie,' Daryl said. But she wasn't having it and insisted on a marshmallow, banana, chunky peanut butter sandwich. *She's got them wrapped around her finger.* Leona couldn't look away, from the gentle touch of the two men as they passed behind the quartz island, to the ease of Daryl delivering Tara's sandwich with a kiss to the top of her head. *Good for her. That child is loved . . . and she's going to get better.* With a pang, she thought of Dalton. There had been no such tenderness between her and Lionel. No butterfly kisses on the top of Dalton's head . . . at least not from her.

'And the good doctor . . .' She scrolled to a folder within the app and found him. *In the lab, of course, with best friend Grace.* She turned up the volume, as they prepared to view MRIs and X-rays.

'OK Buster, why are you so fucking happy?' Grace asked.

Why indeed, Dr Garfield? A memory of Jackson popped to mind. One of his axioms, *'Listen, ask good questions, and don't think you have the answers until you do.'* With that in mind, and alert to her surroundings, she focused on Frank and Grace. A thought intruded – *this is historic. True, but if no one ever learns about it . . . like a tree falling in the woods.* What was potentially the most-important scientific study of the twenty-first century was in process, all below the radar. Four people knew its significance: her, Dalton, Grace, and Frank. *And that's two too many*, she mused . . . *possibly three.*

TWENTY-THREE

G race trailed beside Frank as he pulled up radiology files in the dimly lit viewing room.

'OK, Buster, why so fucking happy?'

'Don't know what you're talking about.'

She turned from a SPECT scan of Ben Bradley's liver she'd just analyzed and looked him dead on. 'You got laid.'

He smiled. 'Not saying a word.'

'Details,' she said.

He grinned.

'Oh fuck you. I don't think I've ever seen you this happy. Where's my mopey best friend? Where's Eeyore? What have you done to him?'

'So that's what this is? Happy? This is really happy. It's scary.'

'Where is he now?'

Frank's smile fell. 'Too tired and back in Brookline. He shouldn't have come up yesterday.'

'Why not?'

'Because now . . . Well, this is interesting.' His focus pulled by a month-old SPECT of Lakeesha Thomas's brain tumor. 'Grace, what do you see?'

'Other than you depriving your best friend of prurient details? This in the setting of the wasteland of her own love life. Selfish, selfish friend.'

'Other than that. And don't talk about yourself in the third person. It's creepy. Look at this.'

She stood beside him and viewed the two SPECT studies, the second obtained just hours ago. She stopped them, rechecked the date and played them a second time. 'Interesting. Really interesting.'

'Tell me what you see?'

'Her astrocytoma is smaller. And there . . .' She put her fingers on the screen and pulled down a calibration app to do a volumetric assessment of the tumor. 'The arm that was going across the corpus callosum, it's just touching it now. Shit . . .'

'What?'

She rechecked the calculation. 'It's shrunk, Frank.'

'By how much?' he asked, not wanting to lead Grace with his own assessment.

'By 22.587 percent. And that's about what I get with Carter's sarcoma. You can barely detect the one on his remaining humerus. A week ago it was over two centimeters.'

'That's two of six.'

Grace pulled up all six scans obtained in the early a.m. It had been something of a marathon, shepherding the sleepy children and the attendant parents through the rigors of SPECT scans. Frank had thought that two days after the infusion was too soon. But Leona had pushed to look for early results . . . and so they had. Her instincts had been spot on.

'Forty-eight hours.' Screens of digitalized data added weight to what the blind eye could see. 'Five of the six show significant improvement. I wish Jackson could see this.'

'Me too,' Grace said, as she ran through each of the children's data. 'The only one who isn't is Jen.'

'Nothing with her,' Frank said, 'if anything Drinky is bigger. Shit! Why isn't it working for her?'

'Maybe it is,' Grace said. 'And maybe . . .'

'Yeah, and maybe pediatric oncology is the worst profession for someone who likes children. Damn.' He stared at Jen's scan, and searched for an improvement. There wasn't any. 'Maybe she got a bad sample.'

'Frank, they all got the same thing.'

'We should check.'

'How?'

She was right. In his almost-paranoid concern over divulging too much too soon to the Langs they'd destroyed anything that might contain a trace of the compound.

'There's got to be a way.'

'You come up with it, and I'll help. So, did Sean say anything about the investigation?' Grace asked.

'Murder by the numbers. It bothers him.' Frank stared at Jen's test results. 'It should have worked, why didn't it? Maybe we didn't give her enough, or the dose was bad, or . . .'

'The whole dead fentanyl junkie random thing?' Grace asked, trying to pull him away from the awful truth about Jen Owens.

'Yeah, and some other stuff. We should dose Jen again.'

'We can't Frank, you know that. Not just that it would screw up the study, which has to be perfect for us to get the go-ahead for a larger trial, but what if her tumors are non-responsive, or worse, accelerated by the compound. You have to let it go, Frank. You have to let the experiment run its course.'

'You mean I have to let her go.' His jaw clenched.

'Maybe, you know this.' She laid a hand on his shoulder. 'What was the other stuff Sean told you about?'

'This . . . all of this.' He shrugged off her hand, turned to the screen, and wiped back a tear. 'He said something that I can't stop thinking about. We wouldn't be here if Jackson were still alive. He was dead set against this. He'd have stopped this.'

'I know.'

'Did you know that he knew Leona Lang when she was a doctoral student?'

'What? I did not. When did you plan to tell me this? You and I don't keep secrets. At least we never did.'

He hesitated. 'Sean told me something that I shouldn't repeat.'

'But you will, because I'm your best friend. The one who—'

'Hid me in your basement when my mother tried to kill me. Yeah, you know how Jackson got passed over for department chair.'

'Thirty years ago. He said it didn't matter.'

'Sean spoke with the dean and found out he came close to getting canned for conduct unbecoming.'

'Please don't tell me he diddled Leona Lang . . . I don't want to hear that. He would have been fifty and she would have been . . .'

'She started undergrad at fifteen, and had her PhD at twenty-two, not quite a record, but close. He told me that she was the most brilliant student he'd ever had.'

Grace looked from the scans to Frank. 'I feel sick. That's one hell of a coincidence. And how old is that Dalton dude? This is just gross.'

'Which is what Sean said, not the gross part, but the here we are working for a woman who nearly got Jackson canned. And . . .'

'Out with it.'

'I helped Sean decipher some of the technical stuff on Jackson's computer.'

'You'd mentioned. And?'

'It included his emails.'

'And?'

'I think he kept in touch with her.'

'Leona?'

'Yeah. He was corresponding with someone who knew a lot about my work, about ways to manipulate DNA in living systems. I think it was her.'

'No name?'

'No, and an untraceable dark-web address.'

'Jackson knew lots of people, what makes you think it was her.'

'Tenderness. He was in love with her. And he talked about my work.'

'All of it.'

'Not in detail. But that last night . . . he made a comparison between her and me. Something about her running away from greatness and me running towards it without realizing the downside.'

'Typical. Men and the one that got away,' Grace said. 'You're, taking Jackson's side. He should have known better. His wife was still alive. Everyone knows you don't fuck your students.' Her focus shifted back to the scan playing on the monitor. A look of concern flashed across her face. 'Holy fuck. You know that funky vascular proliferation on Ben's liver.'

Frank stared over her shoulder. 'Where is it?'

She rotated the image. Double checked to make sure there

was no mistake. 'It ain't there. Check your cell. Suddenly, I'm worried that too much of a good thing, might not be . . . a good thing,' she said.

He did. There were no new messages only a pervy one from Sean that he'd listened to many times. Something about the way he said, 'blow job' created an immediate physiologic reaction. It was fun.

'We have to check on them,' Grace said. 'This is good, but also potentially bad. As in bleeding out bad. No one's called . . .'

'That's a good thing,' Frank said.

'Not necessarily.'

'Equine therapy. I caved under pressure. Told them they could look at the animals but still no touching.'

'Come again.'

'They're at the farm. Shit . . .'

'Exactly,' she said. 'Sudden tumor loss, we could be looking at seizures, bleeds, vascular collapse . . .' She mimicked Jackson's Boston twang. 'Nature hates a vacuum.'

'If anything happened you know we would have been called,' he said.

Grace stopped and stared at him. 'You're Mr Calm in a crisis, I'm liking Sean more and more,' and under her breath, 'and trusting Leona Lang less and less.'

TWENTY-FOUR

'This data is spectacular,' Leona said, as she dropped pancake batter onto the griddle and dotted them with plump blueberries. Her kitchen smelled of coffee and bacon.

Dalton fed the tiny pumpkin-furred puppy from a milk-filled eye dropper. He watched his mother and was filled with memories. Some good, some awful, like finding his father, who he now knew was not his father, naked and dead in the shower. 'When do we pull the plug?' He studied her profile in the morning light that streamed through the windows. *She looks good.* The fifties housewife act was disconcerting. *And where the hell did she get that apron? But I can act as well.*

'We don't pull it. Not with the six children, or rather the five, who will benefit. We buy time. As long as he believes the study is moving forward and legit he'll have purpose and won't—'

'Won't see it coming. I wish there was another way. This has so much potential.'

'There is no other way.' She turned, spatula in hand. 'You do see that?'

'Yes.' *Whatever Leona wants.* 'But there are some pesky unanswered questions about UB482, and by the way, it needs a better name, especially since there is no registered compound with the FDA. And you look good, Mother. Younger. I dig your Donna Reed act.'

'Before my time,' she said. 'I was going for Audrey Hepburn in *Breakfast at Tiffany's.'*

Right, he thought. *That's her goal. Young, pretty, live forever . . . or at least freakishly long.* 'You'll get there. It's been what, five days? You look amazing. Ten years younger, maybe fifteen.'

She checked the underside of a pancake. 'I feel fabulous. And yes, too many unknowns, and I can't . . . couldn't, wait. But now. It's all I think about. How to get this fucking process out of Frank Garfield's head and into something I can replicate. Beyond that we're bumping up against things he doesn't even know. Or hasn't shared. Like what's happening to me. Is this a one-time fix, or will I have to hook myself to an infusion pump every year, month, week, decade? Is the compound stable? Does it degrade? Is it like other biological compounds where you need to be on a schedule, but then the frequency decreases?'

She's stressed he thought as he saw lines pop on her once Botox-frozen brow. Playing with the new puppy, identical to his predecessors, he noted his mother's anxiety; it was unexpected and intense. 'Pity we can't clone ourselves.' *And this is where I find out why she's flipping pancakes. What is it you want from me?*

'Our brains mess that up. All those experiences and memories. The body will be the same but that's where it ends. Little Rex won't be exactly like numbers III, II, or I. I regret the years I spent thinking there'd be a payoff there. Cloning is an answer, but not for humans. At least not beyond replacing a lost child.'

'Or dog.'

'Dalton, unlike you, there were not a lot of bright spots in my childhood. Rex was all I had. I knew he loved me, and if he could have, would have protected me.'

'Not criticizing, Mother. I'm aware that Grandma Karen has issues. But didn't you tell me that in research even dead ends are important.'

'True.' She stacked pancakes and placed a plate before him and one in front of her. Meanwhile, Rex's tail went into hyperdrive as he was rewarded with a chopped crisp of bacon.

'Unanswered questions and timing,' he said. 'This is your breakfast agenda?'

'Yes.' She stared past him, at her reflection in a glass-fronted white shaker cabinet. 'If this turns into a *Flowers for Algernon* scenario I will be pissed. Which is why nothing can happen to Garfield . . . yet. I need this formula. I need to know what makes it work, how long it will work, and we don't have time. I'm convinced that not even Jackson knew the details, and if he did . . . he's dead.'

Difficult as she could be, Dalton savored moments like this. *She needs me. Has no one else to confide in.* 'We have made progress. We know it exists and that it works . . . to an extent. We know he can synthesize it with the equipment at Hollow Hill. We've taped every second he and Grace spent in the lab. You might be able to figure this out with what we have.'

'I've watched the footage. I can't risk it. He's made a Trojan horse that gets his molecule into the cell and then into the nucleus. It's brilliant, elegant, and I don't know how the hell he does it.'

'We apply pressure,' Dalton said. 'He signed a contract; he needs to hand it over.'

'No. Jackson's paranoia is all over him. That approach won't work, just make him dig in.'

'But his gal pal Grace knows.'

'She does, but not the fine details. I'm convinced the miraculous trick is in his head alone. Could Grace figure it out? She's smart. Maybe she could.'

'You cared for Jackson,' Dalton said.

'He was an impossible man, but yes, I did,' she admitted.

'The road not taken,' he said into his coffee. But to watch her squirm, added, 'Wonder if maybe he'd written down the details and it's languishing in that Brookline detective's office, or in their forensics lab.'

'Doubtful,' she said. 'He'd never trust something that important to a computer file. And Frank has followed suit.'

The puppy returned to Leona and then to Dalton in search of bacon. Dalton picked him up, cradled him, and gave him the bottle. 'We've two potential resources for the formula, Frank and Grace.'

'Which is why we need to play this farce out. Only when he's convinced that the compound works and that those children are healed, *and* that we are going to wage a crusade against childhood malignancies and conquer cancer, will he let us go into production. He needs to believe that it's a full court press towards stage-two and three human trials.'

'You know we'd make a fortune with this. Not to mention the PR for UNICO. Think of the before-and-after ads.'

'Yes. And little Rex will get his infusion as soon as possible. But no, and I wonder if we shouldn't take a page from our trio of Frank, Grace, and dead Jackson. We make two copies of the formula. One lives in your brain and one lives in mine. Nothing gets written down. Like a family recipe.'

'Four copies altogether?' he said and forced her to articulate her endgame.

'No, just two. Yours and mine.'

He sopped up the last of his pancakes with syrup. 'It will be quite the *old* family recipe. What's the price for others who want to partake and add some years?'

'It'll cost what I want it to. Maybe money, maybe something else. The price will vary. And by invitation only.'

'And the two existing copies of the formula. Frank and Grace?'

'Accidents happen.'

'They do.' He stood and handed her baby Rex. 'Such a beauty.'

'He is,' she said and cradled him to her cheek. 'Set up a meeting with Frank and Grace to go over the details of a stage-two study. Bring lots of forms and all the human investigations releases and permissions. Some of them should have FDA logos on them.'

'Of course. Pancakes were delicious.'

'Thank you. And Dalton . . .'

'Yes, Mother.'

'When this is over, we should chat about your future. I know you're not happy in your present role. I know you have dreams.'

'And . . .?'

'I'm willing to negotiate. Maybe it's time we both get what we want.'

TWENTY-FIVE

Sean tried to focus on work, but Monday morning or not, all he could think about was Frank, those kids he'd met over the weekend, and . . . *you're falling in love.* Although Frank might write off his zippy tingly feelings to hormones, neurotransmitters, too little sleep and too much sex. If that were it, nice. *Feels great. But more.* He remembered Frank with the children and their parents, his ease and loose-limbed grace. Sean had long ago written off the possibility of a family of his own. Between his crazy hours at work, not having met a suitable guy . . . and the logistics of same-sex adoption or surrogacy, but . . . They'd spent Saturday afternoon with the kids at the Crestview Farm and Petting Zoo, although touching the animals had been forbidden. The children and their parents had warmed to Sean, as if he'd always been a part of the strange extended family that orbited Frank and the study. The Douglas and Daryl duo interrogated him about his feelings for Frank. He smiled at the memory, and how devoted the two men were to each other and their little girl, who had the shit-bad luck of getting cancer. 'He's a good man,' Daryl had said, as Tara and little Ben Bradley took dozens of pictures of a pen of miniature black-and-white goats. 'Don't think he dates much.'

Douglas had interrupted, 'What my husband is trying to say is if you hurt him, we'll kill you.'

'You know I'm a cop,' Sean replied.

'Yeah, and he's the man who's saving our daughter's life.'

Threats aside, that afternoon, and making pizza in Frank's kitchen, followed by sex unlike anything Sean had ever experienced . . . *not just sex. I am falling . . . have fallen in love.* His gaze drifted out the single window in his office.

The kids, except for Jen with her oxygen tank and wheelchair, didn't look sick to him. If it weren't for the bald heads and the wigs that none of the kids still wore by the end of the day, he wouldn't have known. Their parents told him that Frank's drug, or whatever it is, had made a huge and rapid difference. Their excitement and hope were contagious. Right there . . . *it's too fast. Too perfect. Something is not right.*

His thoughts flashed on perfect Dalton Lang. He'd done an online search and stumbled upon his music videos on YouTube, Instagram and a dozen other sites. *What the fuck?* Like he was two people. A UNICO top honcho and a wannabe, what? Musician? The music was OK, though the lyrics seemed contrived, somewhere between emo, goth, and whiny twelve-year-old. There was a stripped-down ballad with a guitar and lots of longing blue-eyed gazes into the camera. *Not half bad.* He searched for physical flaws and came up empty. It rankled.

Dalton had called Frank twice over the weekend, both times Sean had been present and overheard. Obviously, he was checking up on the experiment and the kids. But there was something in his tone, possessive . . . seductive . . . *annoying fuck.*

His fuzzy tingles soured. He raked his hands through his hair and reread the-still-unsent final report on the Jackson Atlas murder. *Shit or get off the pot.* Raised in a family of cops, mostly detectives, Sean often warred between the evidence at hand and his gut. Something stank. The revelation that Leona Lang had an affair with Jackson added discordance with the whole murder for cash for drugs for another dead junkie. And it appeared they kept in touch. *Why? Jackson still had something for her . . . but what was in it for her?* He dug.

He went down to IT and touched base with Gabe Duncan, the expert who'd scoured Atlas's hard drive.

'Nothing was copied, nothing deleted. No fingerprints other than his, but . . .'

'But what, Gabe?'

'Around the time of death there was online activity.'

'He was writing an email to Frank Garfield. We've been over this.'

'Yeah, and so it's probably nothing, but the email was never sent and it was opened a second time.'

'So?'

'Well, usually when people save an email they're still working on it, right? If you open it again you're either going to edit it or send it, or probably both. In this case it was neither. People don't realize but that's less than a two-percent scenario, that you reopen and don't do something with it.'

'This has been studied?' Sean asked.

'Oh yeah, email, IM, texting behavior, Facebook, Instagram, tweeting, SnapChat, it's a whole social cyber sub-specialty.'

'For the two percent who reopen and don't send and/or edit what are they doing?' Sean asked.

'Exactly. And in this case. Who's doing it?'

'And what's going through their head?' Sean added, as he tried to picture the dead junkie and couldn't. 'They want to see more.'

'But know they shouldn't,' Gabe added, 'because they're smart enough to know that every keystroke leaves a trail of metadata.'

'Or maybe Jackson *was* going to edit it and that's when he got shot. You found nothing else?'

'Other than Professor Atlas had trust issues.'

'Based on . . .?'

'Sophisticated encryption. He browsed the dark-net, and knew how to properly delete files. Almost no one does.'

'Great.'

'What's the problem?' Gabe asked.

'You ever have the feeling that you're being played with?'

'In what way?'

'In the way I can close this case now and it'll stay closed. Or, I decide that everything on the surface is bullshit, in which case this isn't a single murder, but somebody set up a junkie to look like a murderer and then fed him some bad dope. In which case, it's a double homicide.'

'Occam's razor,' Gabe replied. 'Ninety-nine percent of the time the simple answer is the right one.'

'And one percent of the time it's not.'

'You have an alternative motive to cash for drugs?'

Sean shook his head, as the crazy possibilities of Frank's work hit home. 'How's this . . . what if I told you I could let you live an extra hundred years . . . good years. What's that worth?'

'If it's not bullshit the question is more like, what isn't it worth? You're talking holy grail stuff. You think something in Atlas's research got him killed?'

'Not his.' *Fuck.* The queasy feeling surged. 'I got to go.' He left Gabe's office and called Frank. *Dead junkie was so much better.*

'Sean.'

'Hey Frank. You got a minute?'

'What's wrong?'

'The Langs. When's the first time you met either one of them?'

Long seconds passed.

'Frank?'

'I'm here. Just needed to think a bit. It's weird, with all that's happened you'd think it would be a long time ago. But it's three weeks. Dalton approached me after . . . my therapy session.'

Therapy? Great. More I don't know. 'Nothing before?'

'Not that I remember and—'

'You've got a photographic memory.'

'Not for everything, but yeah.'

'Clearly they've been tracking you and your research for a while.'

'Yeah. They knew a lot about me and—'

'And what?'

'A lot about Jackson. Which considering the history between him and Leona adds a layer. I still don't understand it.'

'The man was a man, Frank. We've all got clay feet.'

'You don't.'

'I do, and hopefully you stick round long enough to see them.'

'I'm not going anywhere, Sean.'

'Good to know. So how long, based on what they've told you, do you think they've been watching you and your work?'

'I'd not thought about it like that. Figured Leona read my recent articles on telomere stabilization and went from there with literature searches and whatever else they did . . . to figure out where I'd be at two o'clock on a Tuesday.'

'That takes more than a Google search.'

Silence.

'Frank? You still there?'

'Something clicked. The night they had me to dinner at the Taj, Dalton knew about the kids at St Mary's.'

'Doesn't surprise me, you're a pediatric oncologist.'

'He knew specifics, names, diagnoses. That's protected health information.'

'Still not surprised. They dug. And they used your compassion for those kids to reel you in.'

'Great, so now I'm a fish . . . something else.'

'What?'

'Something happened after that dinner. I didn't tell you about it, because, it's kind of embarrassing.'

'I'm listening.'

'I went for a walk and got propositioned, nearly mugged, and nearly arrested.'

'A full evening. Dalton figures into this, how?'

'He followed me, and talked the cop out of arresting me. But he said something about having me under surveillance for six weeks, and his mother having followed my work much longer. But what does that mean? I took it as watched from a distance, or like the way you follow a musician or baseball team.'

'You said he followed you from the restaurant, and the first time he approached you he obviously knew where you'd be.'

'I've got another call coming in.' Frank sounded tense. 'Not good.'

'What's happening?' Sean asked.

'I've got to go.'

'Wait.'

'I can't. Shit.' The line clicked dead.

Sean's Monday morning tingles had morphed into gut-churning dread. The one-percent chance that Jackson's murder was not as it appeared, swelled. He pictured the Langs. Brilliant, ambitious, *how far would they go?* He thought of the kids and their families, Grace, but mostly, Frank. *It's not one percent. And someone, or ones, cold-blooded enough to commit a double murder to get access to Frank's holy grail won't stop until they get it.*

His thoughts raced as that scenario grew. What came next sent him flying out the door and out to his car. *Once they have what they want, their holy grail, what then?* The answer was obvious and horrific. *Eliminate anyone and everyone who knows about it.*

TWENTY-SIX

'I can't. Shit.' Frank stared at the number on his cell. *NY State Croton Hospital.* A sick dread flooded him as he answered it.

'Dr Garfield, this is Dr Harris, your mother's psychiatrist, I'm here with Melanie Strong, Croton's CEO, Jasper Tate your mother's therapist, and FBI agents Clarke and Jones. I need to inform you that at around four a.m. this morning your mother escaped.'

Frank swallowed. 'How?' he calculated the distance from Croton New York to where he currently stood in UNICO's Hollow Hills lab with its expansive windows, high-tech security, and acres of electrified fence. 'How?' he repeated.

'She complained of chest pain around midnight and was transported to Westchester Memorial.'

He was incredulous. 'She faked it.'

Dr Harris continued. 'She killed the guard who escorted her.'

A man's voice came on. 'Dr Garfield, this is agent Jones with the FBI. Where do you think your mother will go?'

'To find me and to kill me. You didn't need me to tell you that. Everyone who works with her knows that's what motivates her. Did Dr Harris tell you about her last attempt? That at her bi-annual review she scratched me and two of the guards.'

'I don't see how a scratch—' the agent started to say.

Frank spoke over him. 'She'd smeared her nailbeds with e-coli, probably from her feces, and methicillin resistant staph aureus, likely from another patient. It was premeditated and showed how she's run circles around the Croton staff for years.' His head spun. He had to warn Grace. He needed to call Sean and tell him to stay away. *And what am I supposed to tell him*, having not yet had the discussion about his family other than to lie that his parents had both died when he was young?

'We can keep you in a safe location until she's apprehended,' the agent said.

'That won't help. You need to understand my mother. Yes, she's psychotic, but with a genius IQ. She won't stop until she finds me, and finishes what she started when I was eight.' He paused. 'She'll know where I am because someone at Croton will have told her. That's how she got my Somerville address. Am I wrong, Dr Harris?'

'Staff were warned not to—'

'Yeah, and we saw how well that worked. And the two guards she scratched?'

'I'm not at liberty to say.'

'Even after I warned you.'

Harris did not respond.

The agent shot more questions and tried to sell the safe house idea. He told Frank there'd be a team of agents on site within twenty minutes.

'I got to go,' Frank said. He looked from the files of data he'd just analyzed out to rolling green hills and a vivid spring day. A cold sweat prickled the back of his neck. *She could be here already. I'm a sitting duck . . .* His words echoed. *'Psychotic with a genius IQ.'* Brutal scenes from his childhood played. His mother's crazed insistence that he was the son of Satan. *I've got to get to Grace. To Sean. The children . . . their families No one is safe.*

Still in his white coat, with a stethoscope popping out of one pocket, and an iPad and hand-written journal in the other, he ran towards the elevators. The building's glass walls taunted him. *Like a giant fishbowl.* Even the elevator was transparent. He passed the guard at the front desk. *I should warn him.* But he didn't. *It's me she wants. It's always been me.* Dr Harris's blunt report, '*She killed the guard who escorted her.*'

Outside, he locked himself in the Element and braced for a phone call he dreaded. He dialed Sean. He tried to play through how he'd tell the man he loved, *and how did that happen?* that not only had he lied about his parents and his entire existence, but that his mother was a psychotic killer whose sole motivation was to murder him.

His pulse raced as he dialed and waited. It went to voice mail. 'Call me, it's important,' was all he managed. His anxiety ratcheted higher. *What if she's already there? What if . . .?* 'Don't come to see me, Sean. I can't explain. But it's not safe.' He hung up.

He dialed Grace.

There was no answer.

He tried again.

Nothing.

He left multiple voice and text messages. *Why isn't she picking up?*

Where will she go first? My house. He thought of his duo of frisky rats. She'd kill them just for the hell of it. *Shit.* He dialed Dalton Lang's cell. He picked up on the second ring.

'We have a problem,' Frank said.

'I'm aware,' Dalton said. 'Your mother. You think she'll come here.'

Frank thought of his earlier conversation with Sean. Of course Dalton knew about his mother. Now was not the time to contemplate how much, how long, and how closely, the Langs had watched him. 'Yes. She'll go wherever she thinks she can get to me.'

'OK. I've informed security, but I hear it in your voice, Frank. That's not going to be enough.'

'She killed a hospital guard early this morning. The FBI offered to put me in a safe house. But they don't understand her. No one near me is safe.'

'What will you do?'

'I don't know.'

'You're safest where you are. I'll triple the security force. Stay put, Frank.'

'Right. Good advice. The kids, their families, you have to warn the staff. You don't know what she's capable of.'

'Understood; I'm on it, Frank. We'll lock down the facility, escort all unessential employees to their homes. Whatever is needed.'

Not reassured, he hung up. *People are going to die.* He thought of his father. Images of him were hard to conjure. *I have to get away from here. She'll go where I go.*

In his car, his thoughts focused on Candace. He knew her better than anyone. *The children. But how could she know about them? About any of this.* His rational mind argued that there was no way she could know his location, or what he was doing. *'Psychotic with a genius IQ. She'll go for Grace. Or she'll go for the children. That's how she'll get to me.'*

He felt disoriented and exposed. He glanced at the clock. Eleven-twelve a.m., Monday morning. By general decree the kids had voted to return to the animal farm. Open and exposed they'd make easy targets.

He felt the venom of his mother's delusions, as clear as if she were next to him. *I abjure thee Satan.* He put the Element in drive and sped towards the Crestview Farm and Petting Zoo. *Get to the kids, get them safe.* Decades of nightmares and flashbacks made it feel both unreal and familiar. *Not a dream. She's come to kill you.* The murdered guard a gruesome reminder that anyone between her and him was in imminent and mortal jeopardy.

TWENTY-SEVEN

Dalton got off the phone with Frank. Candace Garfield's escape was bizarre. *Yes*, he thought, *people escape from mental hospitals.* But as part of his surveillance of Frank Garfield, he'd taken a field trip to Croton Forensic. Had gotten inside by pretending to be a UNICO drug rep, with free goodies for the medical staff. He'd then charmed a young female doctor and a social worker into taking him on a tour of the facility.

He'd separated the social worker from the doctor, told her of his fascination for insane female murderers and asked to meet Candace. She resisted at first. So many rules would be broken. She could get fired. He understood, he commiserated. He took out his wallet and peeled off hundreds, one after the other. He smiled and held her gaze, he'd gauged the interest in her eyes, and fed her possibilities of more . . . not just money. 'Maybe we could meet for a drink sometime.'

It was that same, well-compensated social worker, who had called him at five a.m. with the news of Candace's murderous escape. 'If anyone finds out I've leaked patient information,' she'd said. 'This is such a HIPAA violation.'

'Not to worry. If you hear anything else, anything at all, call me, and five a.m. is just fine.'

Now, he looked out the French windows of his rental cottage on the rolling grounds of Litchfield's Inn at Merryvale. He had near total privacy, his nearest neighbors in equally scenic one and two-story Colonial-style luxury condos hidden by dense copses of trees and well-tended acreage.

Poor Frank. He checked the time on his phone. *She could be anywhere.* But, the escape rankled. It was complex and premeditated. He knew Candace Garfield was highly intelligent and from the episode where she'd attempted to kill Frank with flesh-eating bacteria, she could both plan and act. *But but but. And they waited hours to tell him. Sloppy. But but but. Can this be a coincidence?* Candace Garfield was not the only woman he knew capable of meditated murder.

He dialed his mother.

'Dalton.'

Like a connoisseur with a fine Bordeaux, he let her voice, which he could mimic perfectly, swirl inside his head. He listened for subtleties of tone and intonation. 'Did you hear?' he asked.

'What? What are you talking about?'

Useless. If she knew, she wasn't telling. And, if she were responsible, for whatever reason, she'd chosen to keep it from him. *Two can play.* 'Frank's mother escaped from the forensic hospital. She killed a guard.'

'What? When?'

'Early this morning.'

'Interesting. You notified security?'

'Of course.' His phone buzzed. 'Hold on, it's them.' He switched to the head of security.

'Mr Lang.'

'Yes, George.'

'You told me to tell you if Dr Garfield left. I tried to stop him, but he was insistent he had to go. I didn't think I could go any further.'

And the games begin. 'Of course not. Did he say where he was going?'

'No, sir.'

Moron. 'Did you call the gate-house to at least see which direction he'd gone?'

'No, I'll do that now.'

'Good. Then call me.' He switched back to Mother. 'Frank just bolted. I told him to stay put.'

'He knows she's out. You told him?'

'Not me.' *She thinks I'm an idiot.* 'The hospital contacted him. He's freaking. This place will be swarming with federal agents.'

'Interesting.'

'How so?' He clicked open his briefcase and checked his shiny new Glock, the same model used to kill Atlas. Unconvinced that she hadn't orchestrated Candace's escape.

'She could be our catalyst.'

'Excuse me?' He pocketed his keys.

'An agent that brings about reactions without being changed. Candace Garfield is a constant. But she brings change. You do see there's an opportunity here.'

'Yes.'

'The only caution is we've two copies of the telomere formula. Frank and Grace. Until I have it, one must survive, preferably Frank.'

'Why would either one of them give it up now?' he asked. *And what is keeping that fucking guard?*

'The children, of course. It's always been for the children. He has to know that with a threat of this magnitude it would be wrong to withhold the formula in case . . .'

'He's killed. How do you propose we manage this catalyst? Seems like she's an unstable quantity.'

'Not at all. She's singular in her goal. Kill Frank, he's the son of Satan. It's a simple equation.'

'And once we have the formula . . . It would certainly be tidy.'

'Yes, so our objective is just as clear as hers. The trick is the timing. We have to keep her from Frank until we have the process. Then . . .'

'I'm on it,' he said.

'I'll be there as fast as I can,' she said.

'Good.'

'And Dalton, here's the thing about catalysts, they can be quickened. As long as Frank believes there's another copy of the formula, he won't give it up to either you or me.'

'Yes, understood.' He grasped her subtext. Grace Lewis needed to be removed from the playing field.

'Excellent.'

And she hung up.

Case in hand, he paused at the door. Mother's message was clear . . . and risky. What worried him was the risk of taking out Grace, and Frank's mother completing what she'd started, leaving no copy of the formula. But if he had Grace . . . and she were still alive. Possibly unconscious, maybe locked up and tucked away.

He thought to call her back, but no. Wouldn't that be something, to have the only copy of the thing Mother needed. To take the wheel. *What about you, Dalton? What do you want? What do you really really want?* The answer was clear. *To be in charge. To be the one with the extra life. To be loved by millions. To be adored. To be . . .*

His thoughts bounced bright, a world where Mother was less of a presence. Or better, no presence at all. *Head in the game, boy. It's time to play.*

TWENTY-EIGHT

Frank's short drive from Hollow Hills to the Crestview farm was agony. He left a second jangled message for Sean and practiced what he'd say in person. It helped him focus, but then that sick feeling of being chased by Candace returned. In truth, it had never left, not since he was eight. It was not a question of if she would find him, but when. He put no stock in the FBI's efforts. And those UNICO guards, no matter how prepared, were no match for her unbridled crazy. *She's too smart.*

'My fault,' he muttered. 'I should never have given the hospital my address.' But he had. His thought at the time was better to let her keep writing in case they tried to let her out again. A fatalistic crush bore down on him; unfinished business was about to reach closure.

The phone rang. Sean's face appeared on screen.

'Frank, what's wrong?'

Like the start of a children's story with *Once upon a time*, a tale that he hated, spewed out. His final words, 'She escaped. She killed a guard. She's come to kill me. You can't be near me. No one can.'

'The hell I can't. And you were going to tell me about this, when?'

'Never. I'm strange enough without it.'

'I like your strange. No, fuck it, I love your strange. And I love you, Frank.'

A driver, texting in the car ahead, slowed and swerved towards the curb. Frank accelerated and tried to pass, but as they rounded a curve, a slow-moving hay thresher appeared in the other direction. Frank slammed on the brakes, tried to duck back behind the texting teen, but he miscalculated his speed and the loose-gravel road.

The Element fish-tailed and spun out. He turned the wheel into it, but lost traction. His left front tire clipped a guard rail and that, combined with centripetal force, tipped the vehicle off its two driver-side wheels. He held his breath as the car hung undecided on two tires. The decision was made as the Element slammed into a boulder. It flipped up and over. Strapped in, there was nothing to do but wonder, *is this how I die?*

The car rolled across the road and smashed into a phone pole. With two sharp explosions the airbags deployed front and side. They made it impossible to see, and Frank focused on the movement of the Element as it took its final roll, and landed on its roof.

'What just happened?' Sean asked. His voice was muffled by the bags and adrenalin. 'What's happening?'

Hanging upside down and held in place by his seatbelt Frank felt trapped, breathless, and exposed, a turtle on its back. 'Nothing . . .' He reached back, found the door handle, pressed and pushed. Miraculously it opened. 'I hit a phone pole,' he said, his iPhone clutched in his white-knuckled hand. He undid the belt; blood trickled down his back. He lowered himself to the roof and scrambled out on hands and knees; the flesh of his palms burned on the hot gravel.

'Where are you?' Sean asked.

He looked for anything recognizable. 'Don't know.' The thresher driver headed towards him. He had a phone to his ear.

'Are you hurt?' Sean asked.

'Hey Mister,' the driver shouted, 'you OK? I called 911. Maybe you shouldn't be moving around so much.'

'I don't think anything's broken.' His adrenalin coursed. 'Nothing hurts' . . . *yet*. He heard a siren in the distance and fought the urge to run. He turned and stared at his upside-down Element; totaled. But it had saved his life. *What have I done?* He turned in place. It was a warm, blue-sky beautiful day in the Connecticut countryside. *Where is she?*

'I'm on my way,' Sean said. 'I'll be there in two hours.'

'No. Don't.' Panic took over. 'You can't be near me. You don't understand.' Sirens neared. Flashing lights pulsed around the corner. Frank looked for the car he'd tried to pass. It hadn't even stopped. 'Sean. Sean!' The line was dead.

A volunteer ambulance arrived, followed by two police

cruisers. A black UNICO security SUV pulled in behind followed by a second.

Frank felt his forehead. Pain blossomed across his chest from the triple impact of the steering wheel, seatbelt and airbag. Blood trickled from a cut on the back of his neck. It seeped down and soaked his shirt. A pair of older EMTs with concerned smiles, tried to coax him to a stretcher. 'What's your name, honey?' one asked.

'Frank . . . Garfield.' *That's strange, why couldn't I remember that?*

'OK Frank. Mr Garfield. Sit here, lie back and let's get you to Charlotte Hungerford Hospital.'

'No.'

'Frank, sweetie, you're in shock.'

'No.' He pushed back their hands as they tried to strap him down. He stood on shaky legs. Dazed, he watched as cars slowed to look at the fresh accident.

A pair of cops joined the EMTs. 'What happened? And yes, you should get in the ambulance and be cleared medically.'

'I tried to pass someone. I don't think anything is broken . . . and I'm a doctor.' *Why does that matter?*

'Then you know,' one of the EMTs said, 'that internal injuries may not show up right away. You could have an internal bleed. Your seatbelt could have caused a liver rupture.'

Frank paused, *liver rupture. That's not what you call it.* It was hard to think. Like the accident had rattled his brain to where words that should have come, didn't.

The cops asked to see his license, car insurance, and registration. 'Glove compartment.'

They looked at the upturned car.

'OK for me to get them?' an officer asked.

'Yeah.'

They made him blow into a tube. 'You have to really push until you hear the click.'

He complied. All the time trying to make sense of what had happened. And below the surface, Sean . . . *why didn't I want him to come? He said he loved me. That's a good thing. So why . . .* and then like being in a second collision, reality hit. *She's out . . . she's coming, or is already here.*

Two more SUVs screeched into the accident site. Dark-suited federal agents emerged. Their shoes crunched on the gravel.

'Dr Garfield, are you OK?'

Where is she? He squinted against the sun, his focus pulled by the slow parade of cars, all wanting to look at the upside-down car and the tall dark-haired man with his blood-soaked shirt. One held his focus. The breath left his body as he made eye contact. *How did she get a car? It's a Lexus. Who did she kill for it?*

'That's her!' he shouted. 'That's Candace. That was my mother.'

But the woman, not his mother, smiled and sped away. He focused on the New York license plate and repeated it aloud.

One of the agents caught what he said. Grabbed his partner and chased off in pursuit.

'I can't be here,' he muttered . . . *was that really her?* 'The children. Grace.' *I have to get out of here.* He refused the medics, and signed papers absolving them of blame should he drop dead. A cop handed him a citation for improper passing.

'I'll rip this up,' she said, 'if you get checked out. You're really bleeding.'

'No! No hospitals.' They'd shoot him up with drugs, and he needed his wits. Everything was wrong, and not just the accident or his deranged mother on the loose. Everything.

'Dr Garfield,' one of the UNICO security men said. 'We've been instructed to stay with you. If you don't go to the hospital, which we think you should, Hollow Hills will be the safest.'

'Where are the children and their families?' *I know this.* 'The farm. Crestview, they wanted to see the animals.'

'They're being taken to Hollow Hills.'

'And Grace. Dr Lewis, where is she?'

'I couldn't say. Everyone is being brought to Hollow Hills. It's like a fortress.'

He pictured Grace, not as an adult, but as his seven-year-old best friend neighbor, whose basement he hid in twenty-four years ago. *That's who she'll go for.* He looked at the history on his cell. The last message from her had been hours ago. All his messages had gone to her voice mail. *Shit.* 'No,' he said to the guard. 'We have to find Dr Lewis. That's who she'll go after. She'll do it to get to me.'

'I'm sorry sir . . .'

Before the guard could finish his sentence, Frank spotted keys in the ignition of a UNICO SUV. He made an unsteady dash for it, slammed the door shut, locked it, and seeing double, he floored it.

TWENTY-NINE

In the zone with data, Grace sat at the kitchen table with her laptop. Phones went to voice mail, and nothing short of a fire could distract her from the mystery of Jen Owens's cells. She flipped through analyses of all six of the children's DNA. On five the telomeres were robust and twice as long as prior to the infusion. *But Jen's going to die . . . soon. Why didn't it work for her? Why isn't she getting better?* She thought of Frank and how attached he'd become to Jen. *We have to try again. Maybe she got a bogus dosage. Not possible . . . and we can't . . . can we?*

She imagined what Jackson would say. *'When things don't add up, you've not thoroughly assessed the problem. So, stop trying to solve it. Because you don't know what you're trying to solve. Find the correct question, and then – only then – can you maybe answer it.'*

She sat back, again ignored her phone, 'What am I missing?' She replayed the night in the Hollow Hills laboratory with Frank when they'd produced the six doses. It had taken till dawn. They'd sequenced the nucleotide protein, purified it, coated it with sugars to trick the cells into thinking it was food, and created just enough for six infusions.

Her doorbell rang. Like a hypnotic subject, Grace started.

Through the frosted-glass door panes she saw Dalton Lang's perfect profile. 'What the fuck is he doing here?'

She opened it

'Dalton, what's—'

'Grace, we've got a serious situation. I need you to come with me now.'

'What's happened?'

'Frank's mother escaped from the hospital.'

'Candace! Oh fuck. Where's Frank?' She grabbed her cell and saw his missed messages and texts.

'He's safe. He says you're not. Come with me.'

'Right. Yes. OK.' She looked around at her country chic rental home, she thought to grab her laptop. But Candace Garfield on the loose, meant drop everything and get to safety. *Poor Frank!*

'Hurry,' Dalton urged.

She left it and followed Dalton to his BMW. She heard the locks click as they sped out the drive and onto the road. In the rearview mirror she saw a dark SUV race past and turn into her driveway. *Is that her?*

'Wait, stop!' Her pulse quickened. 'Dalton, stop!' She tried to open her door. It wouldn't. Focused on the unraveling nightmare of Candace Garfield's escape she didn't see Dalton's fist as it connected with surgical efficiency to her left temple. Light exploded across her visual fields. Then piercing pain, like someone drilled through her skull. And then she blacked out.

Without slowing, Dalton placed two fingers into the notch of Grace's carotid. It pulsed. *Good.* He glanced at her, like a sleeping doll, save for the angry red mark that grew across the side of her face where he'd hit her. *Like bruised fruit.*

Using the hands-free, he called Frank.

He picked up after the first ring.

'Frank, good news bad news. The children and their families are accounted for. We even pulled your rats back to Hollow Hill.' He paused for effect. 'We can't find Grace.'

'She doesn't answer her calls when she's working. It's annoying—'

'No Frank. We've been to her house. She's not there. It's not good.'

'I'll find her.'

'Frank, no. You need to stay safe. The children need you. Jennifer needs you.'

'I've got to go.'

Yes, you do. 'Frank, no.'

The line went dead. Dalton thought to call him back, *but no.* He drove for several miles to a property that hugged a curve of the Shepaugh River. He turned right onto a dirt road that led back to an abandoned spread that had once been the obsession of an investment banker who'd harbored fantasies of being a weekend farmer. The three-story house was an impractical modern mess with acute angles that made the rooms impossible for furniture, but that's not where he headed. He drove past a cracked basketball court that had begun to break off at the edges and fall down the ravine towards the river. And past a rotting deck that framed an abandoned pool now home to frogs, bright green algae, and hatching mosquitoes. The car jounced over potholes and rocks as a vine-covered barn came into sight.

He stopped, opened his door and listened. He heard the spring-swollen river in the background, birdsong overhead. He noted a deep loamy smell then searched for signs of human activity. He spotted a few rusted beer cans and a faded foil condom wrapper. But nothing recent. *This will do.*

He popped the trunk and opened a satchel filled with samples of UNICO products. He selected a potent surgical narcotic, grabbed a needle and syringe, and drew up a double dose.

Grace moaned.

'It's OK,' he said. 'Shush. Everything's fine, you had a little accident.'

He opened her door and smiled. She looked confused and then alarmed as he pushed up her sleeve.

'What?' was all she managed, as he efficiently jabbed her bicep and depressed the plunger.

'It's OK, Grace. Everything's fine.' He examined the area where he'd hit her, as redness blossomed . . . *like a flower.* Lyrics popped to mind. *Blood red chrysanthemum on my baby's face.* He crouched beside her as the potent narcotic drew her into a stupor. Her jaw fell slack. She snored.

'Cute . . . and you really are.' He put a finger under her firm chin, the way Mother's used to be . . . *and is again.* He compared the passed-out blonde to Frank. 'Who's not into me . . . which makes no sense. What is that boy's problem?'

'But we've things to do.' He liked the sound of his voice against the backdrop of the woods and the engorged river. He

pulled Grace from the car, was relieved to see she wasn't much
more than a hundred-twenty pounds and gently carried her in
his arms into the barn.

Inside, it was dark and smelled of old dung and hay. His
eyes adjusted and he caught small pools of light through cracks
in the weathered siding. 'Here we go.' He carried her to a spot
near the center of the cavernous structure. With his foot, he
cleared away bits of straw and loose wood and nails and laid
her down. He grabbed his cell phone, flipped on the flashlight
and searched around on the floor. 'There you are.' He grabbed
a brass ring and yanked up on a metal-lined trap door that
revealed a tidy root cellar, or perhaps a previous owner's idea
of a bomb shelter. The insides were surprisingly clean and the
air that brushed his face was cool.

He left his cell on the floor to illuminate the interior, and
trying not to injure her further, he lowered her like a rag doll
into the cellar, closed the hatch, found a piece of two-by-four
and pushed it through the brass ring. He tested to see if it would
hold. It did. *Blood red chrysanthemum on my baby's cheek.
Sleeping like an angel in a hollow deep.*

He retrieved his phone and headed back to the car. *Blood red
chrysanthemum why must we weep?* He heard the river and the
chirp of frogs. *Blood red chrysanthemum here now the day of feast.*

He unzipped an outer compartment of his briefcase and grabbed
a burner phone. He dialed Frank. In a well-practiced and perfect
impersonation of his mother, he said, 'Dr Garfield, I'm sorry to
be the one to tell you this.' He paused. 'Grace Lewis was in a
horrible accident.'

'What? What are you saying?'

'The doctors don't know if she'll survive.'

There was dead air over the line.

'Dr Garfield? Frank?' Dalton heard a woman's voice in the
background. 'Frank? Frank?' It sounded like Frank's phone
dropped to the ground. He pressed the cheap cell to his ear.
'Frank?' There was someone with him. She rambled, half talking
and half chanting. Her words sounded garbled. *Latin?*

And he knew. Candace Garfield had found her son. Fascinated,
he listened. She made no sense, her sentences flew fast, muddled
and weird. Then a scraping sound and the line went dead.

He grabbed his iPhone and swiped to a GPS app which had the data for Frank's, Grace's, and his mother's cells. He was at Grace's. *Right.* He now pictured the SUV that pulled in as he'd sped off. He'd been correct that Frank's mother would go for his life-long friend. He'd missed him, and apparently her, by seconds.

Catalyst, indeed.

He sang in a mournful E minor, *Blood red chrysanthemum cruel fate now tears us apart. Blood red chrysanthemum you broke the key to my heart.* He drove off.

THIRTY

'Unclean thing,' Candace Garfield shouted as she emerged through a dense yew hedge outside Grace's.

Frank panicked. He didn't register when his cell dropped or that Leona Lang had just said awful things about Grace. All he saw was his mother, in green hospital scrubs, twigs and dirt tangled in her iron-gray hair, and a black-handled butcher knife with fresh blood on the blade. *Did she kill Grace?* 'Whose blood is that?'

'You'd like to know. Sperm of Satan. Back to hell. Unclean bastard. *Crux Sacra sit mihi lux.*' With knife overhead, she sprinted towards him. 'For a thousand years, burn in the pit.'

Frank knew she was here to kill him. *But this needs to end.* He held his ground, timed her manic advance, and as she neared he feinted back and pivoted to the right.

She ran past, her knife slashed air.

Brutal memories of his father's murder and the frantic run to Grace's, played in his head. Her words, a ramble of English and Latin. The trace of Leona Lang's call. *Is this what happened to Grace? Is that her blood?*

Candace turned. She raised her knife and slashed three signs of the cross. '*Crux Sacra sit mihi lux. Nunquam draco sit mihi dux. Vade Retro Satana!*'

'Are you kidding?' Frank said as a realization hit. 'That's who you think you are?' He'd never understood the source of his mother's delusions. But as she stood with the sun at her back and a bloody knife, he got it. 'You think you're an angel.'

'*Sunt mala quae libas. Ipse venena bibas.*' She came at him a second time, but not as fast. She shuffled, in rubber soled hospital slippers, her knife outstretched like a sword. '*Crux sacra sit mihi lux.*'

'That makes no sense.' He edged back towards the UNICO SUV. 'Are you trying to exorcize me? Or kill me? Which is it Mother?'

'Try to beguile and vex. I will not be swayed.'

'You're crazy. You have schizophrenia. You're mentally ill.'

'Lies.' She shrieked. Her words tumbled fast. 'He came to me in the night and put his unclean thing into me. It spasmed and bore filth. Snakes writhe in the pit. I felt it in me. I wanted to cut you out. But you, but you, but you. Filthy slimy creature, bathed in blood and slime and shit.' She closed the distance with a skipping run. Her mouth contorted with rage, her eyes dark and fixed on him.

'Crazy. Pure crazy. You killed my father. You killed your husband.'

'Satan skin. Put the devil's prick inside of me. Squirming little snake.'

'What kind of angel lets the devil do that?'

'Tricky. Prince of lies.' Her gaze narrowed, she lowered her head and pointed the knife towards his chest. She charged.

Frank turned and ran towards the road.

She pursued. She screamed obscenities mixed with Latin. But years locked up in a forensic hospital, and that she was fifty-seven, left her no match for Frank.

How did this happen? How did they let her out? Grace. Blood on the knife. That's what that phone call was about.

He sprinted hard and tried to think. Sirens neared. He spotted flashing lights in the distance. He chanced a look back. She had stopped in the middle of the road. Half a football field's distance between them. She looked winded but she whipped her head from side to side like a bull set to charge.

Here it comes.

But she just stood her ground, and with legs akimbo and knife raised to the heavens she proclaimed. 'You will die this day, child of darkness. I will send you back to the ooze from which you sprang.'

Between her scrubs, hospital booties, and incoherent ramble, he was mesmerized. In that instant she was no longer the bogeyman of his childhood, but a mentally ill and deranged woman. 'She's sick. This isn't about me.' Wary of the distance between them and of what she would do next, he didn't linger. A police cruiser, followed by a second, and one of the FBI SUVs raced towards him.

He then turned back to see what Candace would do, but she had vanished. 'Crap.' He scanned the quiet neighborhood with its lovely mix of houses, some two and three hundred years old, others built to look like that. *What will she do?*

She'll come for me. But where?

Not wanting to wait for the cops, he doubled back towards Grace's rental. They pulled in behind him as he spotted his cell and scooped it up. Like a berserker he raced through the house. Saw Grace's laptop, but no blood. He heard footsteps behind him, tore out the back, retrieved his stolen SUV, and drove off. *This is not good. Grace, where are you?*

Dread spread through his chest, as events of the last minutes played back. He thought to turn around. Leona Lang's strange phone call replayed in his head. *Where are you?*

Glancing between the road, his cell, and the flashers which now pursued him, he fumbled for Leona's number. He pressed call.

With the phone to his ear and his gaze fixed on the road, time warped. Every turn of the tires seemed eternal.

'Frank?'

'Leona, what happened to Grace?'

'Are you OK?'

'Just answer the question. You called me and said she'd been in an accident. What happened?'

'I didn't call you.'

He slammed on the brakes, and nearly skidded out. 'What the fuck? You did. You said she'd been in an accident and that—'

'It wasn't me, Frank. Someone is playing a not funny joke. Where are you?'

'I don't know. On the road. My mother just tried to kill me.'

'Where?'

'She ran off. She'll try again.'

'Go to Hollow Hills, Frank.'

'No, she'll show up. She's unpredictable. People will get hurt . . . killed.'

'Understood, but it's safest. We can protect you, and the children, and Grace. But we need you in one place . . . and in one piece.'

'Shit!' He looked out as three patrolmen approached. Behind them were two . . . now three, and a fourth cruiser pulling up.

'Doctor Garfield, get out of your vehicle with your hands up.'

'That doesn't sound good,' she said.

'Nothing is.'

'I'll take care of this,' she said. 'Go to Hollow Hills. Do the work you were meant to do. Those children's lives depend on it. If anything were to happen to you right now . . .'

'Understood.'

'Your work is too important. Too many lives are at stake for it to exist only in your head. If something did happen to Grace . . . and to you, this would all be for nothing. All your work . . . like it never existed.'

'You want the process.'

'It's time. It can be just me. Think of those kids . . . If something happened to you.'

'Like almost just did . . . twice. Let me think.'

'No, Frank. That time is over. Get to Hollow Hills. Walk me through the process. We can do it over a secure line. Just you and me.'

'OK.' He was surrounded by a tightening noose of cops. He peered behind them, half expecting to see his knife-wielding mother. *Whose blood was that?* But he saw woods. A squirrel bounded up a tree, and three drawn service revolvers pointed in his direction. 'I've got to go.'

He opened his door, and with the cell above his head, shouted. 'I'm unarmed. And please, someone has to check on Grace Lewis.'

THIRTY-ONE

'What the hell is going on?' Leona said.

Little Rex responded by depositing a saliva-slicked red rubber ball onto her lap. His tail beat a frantic pace. Not minding the slime, she picked it up and rolled it towards a hedge. Her quiet afternoon of mindful contemplation staring at the waves of Long Island Sound and playing with her puppy destroyed by Frank's frantic call. 'What the hell was that? Someone's playing games.'

She knew who. What she didn't know, was why. Since he was five Dalton had displayed a brilliant talent for mimicry. He'd honed it to a razor-sharp proficiency during his years at NYU's theatre program. She considered other possibilities, which included Frank's mental stability, or that a rival pharmaceutical company was making a play for the formula. But no . . . *this is Dalton.*

Rex retrieved his treasure and rocketed back to her. He poked his moist nose and the ball into her hand. She didn't respond. He dropped the ball by her feet. Stepped back and yipped.

'What is he up to?' She picked it up and rolled it a few feet not wanting to risk her new puppy getting too close to the water or the electric fence, which he was too young to understand. 'And he didn't want me to know . . .' She wiped Rex's saliva off her fingers and onto the bench. She stared at her hand, like a stranger's, and the reason she'd holed up at home to buy time for a plausible explanation of her increasingly fantastic transformation. She'd planned on two weeks. Let people think she'd gone to a Swiss clinic for a plastic surgery overhaul. She'd practiced responses to their questions. *'Leona, what did you have done?'*

'Everything.'

She splayed her fingers and rolled them side to side. The fine lines were gone. She stroked her cheek. And ran her fingers through her hair, even that felt different, softer, springier. She sighed. What was on the outside was wonderful, but the best part was how she felt within . . . vibrant, alive . . . young.

Rex ambled back with the ball. She picked it up a final time,
'Sorry boy.' She placed it under a flowerpot, and scooped him
up. His puppy sharp teeth nipped at her fingers as she cradled
him. 'Time to go in my little love. Mother has work to do.' She
headed back towards the house, and with the dog nestled in
one arm she pulled out her cell.

'Dalton,' she said, as his phone clicked to the recorded
message, 'call me.'

Interesting. She knew how dissatisfied Dalton was with his
role of COO. It went beyond his absurd notions of pop star
fame. *But he wouldn't turn against me . . . And if he has . . .
is this the first time?* 'What do you think, Rex? What games is
he playing?'

Her suspicion festered as she settled Rex into his toy-filled
crate in the kitchen and topped up his water and kibble. Dejected,
he stared after her and made high-pitched yelps. 'I don't want
to leave you either, but Dalton has become a pill.'

She got into her car, tapped on the GPS and the Hollow Hills
address. She glanced into the rearview mirror and was startled.
A lovely blonde in her early thirties looked back. She thought
of Frank. He'd know what she'd done, and from there figure
out she'd taken Jen's dose. But with Dalton's games, crazy
Candace Garfield doing God only knew what, she had no choice.
The endgame with Frank Garfield had to be now. This could
not be left to chance, and sadly, could not be left to Dalton.
'What will I do . . . with him?' She thought of Rex and felt a
pang at having to leave him. The maid would take care of him,
but it wasn't that. It was what Rex and his predecessors gave
her, and what Dalton, her mother, her husband, Jackson, never
had. Love, unconditional love. She snuck a glance in the rearview mirror. Luminous blue eyes looked back. *You are young
again.* She put a hand to her belly and a thought took hold, as
a feeling she'd not had in fifteen years, made her stop the car
and race back to the house. *Not possible.*

Once in the bathroom, the impossible was real. *My period.
Which means . . . Not possible. I can't be fertile again . . . but
if I am.* And like exchanging one damaged Rex for the next an
answer of the problem with Dalton, and even more, took hold.
Everything and anything. You can do it all again. She gazed in

the mirror, her beauty and wealth would attract any man she wanted. She chuckled, *or ditch the man . . . they get so clingy, but have a baby . . . hell, have two.*

THIRTY-TWO

Pushing over a hundred with lights and sirens, Sean swore. 'Move, you moron.' He'd tried to call Frank multiple times after he'd crashed his car. No answer. 'Get out of my way,' he shouted at a blue Corolla. Half on the shoulder, he sped past. 'Idiot!'

He muttered, 'Why didn't I stay with him? I should never have left.'

'Right. New relationship, no one likes a clingy boyfriend.'

'And why the fuck didn't he tell me about his crazy mother?'

'Because he likes you and . . . did he say love? Did I say love?'

Little made sense, including this rush of emotions he'd had since meeting Frank. He swerved across the highway for the Farmington exit. 'It was the turtle . . . no tortoise.' He knew that's when it happened, lying on his belly next to Frank in Atlas's backyard looking for a four-hundred-pound Galapagos tortoise.

Please be OK. The awful call when he heard the crash . . . *he said he was OK. Yeah, and that he'd just taken out a phone pole. He could be dead.*

There was that, and the crazy mother, but even before that shit-storm, was the stuff Sean dug up on the Langs and UNICO. Which included the in-the-news death of an ex-employee who'd drunkenly rammed into a school bus and conveniently died . . . while amid a class-action lawsuit against UNICO. As an isolated incident he could write it off to karma. But as Sean had dug through potentially large-payout lawsuits over the past two decades against UNICO a pattern emerged. Dead lawyers, dead witnesses, or witnesses deciding they were wrong and retracting damning statements. One case where the plaintiff's expert was arrested and convicted of pedophilia with his testimony rendered worthless.

'I should have listened to him.' Because when added to the random, maybe not-random murder, of Jackson Atlas and Frank's game-changing research it brought up possibilities. 'Dude is a danger-magnet . . . but they need him, right? They need him alive . . . until they have what they want.'

He glanced at his GPS, where he was a red dot and Frank's cell phone was a blue one. There were still twenty-two-point-four miles between them. *Why hasn't he called back? And where is he going?*

The blue dot was in motion. Sean's GPS rerouted.

He tried to think of reasons why Frank wouldn't answer. *Not good.*

And with the scenic Farmington River to his right, and vibrant green hills on his left, he floored it.

THIRTY-THREE

'You need to stay here, Dr Garfield.' Melvin seemed nervous. Behind him stood the uniformed head of security and three other guards. They effectively blocked the door to his laboratory at Hollow Hills. 'It's for your safety.'

'And if I want to leave?'

'Not recommended.'

'Understood. And if I want to leave?'

'I would talk you out of it.'

'Would you go further?' Frank assessed his chances with Melvin and the guards, who'd made promises to the state troopers that he would not leave the facility.

'Please, Dr Garfield, we're under orders to keep you, the children, their families and everyone safe. Until your mother is found and apprehended, it's too risky.'

That rang true. Little else did.

'If there's anything you need?' Melvin said.

'No. Have they found Dr Lewis . . . Grace?'

'Not yet.'

'The minute they do, please tell me.'

'We're working on it. We have extra security coming in from our Boston and Manhattan facilities. We will find her.'

'What about the police?'

'They said they're doing what they can.'

'What does that mean?' Frank wanted to argue, but he'd been in too many of these situations over the course of his life. Where if he were to say something about Leona Lang calling him and telling him that Grace had been in an accident . . . and then later say she'd never done such a thing. It would not go well. He'd sound delusional, and with mad Mommy Candace amok in the Litchfield hills, people would mix two plus two with the apple doesn't fall far from the tree. 'Then leave me alone,' he said.

'Yes, sir.' Melvin backed out and closed the door behind him.

Frank listened. He heard muffled voices on the other side. *Am I locked in? And what the fuck is going on?*

His cell rang. He looked at the screen, wondered if it was another from Sean, but no, it was an unidentified wireless caller. His vision narrowed, and his breath caught. He picked up.

'Dr Garfield, are you being naughty?' It was that same woman.

'Who the hell is this? Leona?'

'You have work to do, Dr Garfield. I suggest you hop to it.'

'Where's Grace?'

'I told you she was in an accident. Maybe she's dead. She wasn't moving. She could be asleep. It's sometimes hard to know the difference.'

'What do you want?'

'Please. You're not stupid. Make your magic potion, write everything down, and stop being such a princess.'

Frank looked around. He wondered if the guards were still outside the door. *But what would I say. There's a crazy woman on the phone, I think she's kidnapped Grace, and she's got a pitch-perfect imitation of your boss.* 'Let me know she's OK.'

'Frank, you are not positioned to bargain. But I'll tell you a secret. You know your six darling little cancer kids. One of them had her dose stolen.'

'What?'

'It's true, the worst case of candy from a baby I've ever seen.'

'Jen, that's why she's not improving.'

'Yes. Sad. And to sweeten the pot, when you've made your fresh batch of brownies why not give one to little Jen? She doesn't have much time. There, see? Now, there's something for you. And Frank, here's the fun part, everything you say and do, I see. You make your elixir. You do not call your detective, you do not scream for help. If you do, people will die, starting with your gal pal Grace, and then one by one, the kiddos and their loving parents. Are we clear?'

'Yes.'

'Good. Tick tock, Dr Garfield. It's time to make the donuts.' The line went dead.

Frank stared at his phone. He felt trapped. He looked out over the pristine beautiful lab with its stainless work benches, state-of-the-art DNA sequencers, a spectrometer that came with a two million-dollar price tag. *And if something is too good a deal. It probably is. Too late now.*

He stared at the dome cameras on the ceiling. He'd assumed that they were just part of the security. 'You want the telomere process,' he said aloud. Something about the caller's voice, Leona, but maybe it wasn't. *She said not to call Sean . . . but if it wasn't Leona, it seems like she might want to know about it.*

He dialed her number; she answered fast.

'They,' he began, 'she . . . called again, the person pretending to be you.'

'What did they say?'

He wondered if she really didn't know or was this an act. 'That they had Grace. That if I don't write down the formula they'll kill her. She said something else. Something strange.'

'What?'

'That Jen Owens never got her dose, even though I know I administered it. They said it was stolen.'

There was a pause on the line. 'It wasn't me, Frank.'

'On the line? Or are you saying something else?'

'Oh hell. Both, Frank. I took the dose and infused myself.'

'Why? She's going to die. Why would you do that?'

'Make more, Frank. Either way you need to do it. And I know who your caller is.'

'Who?'

'Dalton, who else?'

'Pretending to be you?'

'It's a trick. It was cute when he was five. Now . . . not so cute.'

'And Grace. He threatened to kill her.'

'I'll handle this, Frank. I'll be there in an hour, this will be OK. I will make certain that nothing happens to Grace, or to any of those kids. But don't goad Dalton. You don't know him . . . what he's capable of. When pushed, he is not stable.'

'And what if I decide not to make the telomere compound?'

She sighed. 'End of the day, we all have decisions to make. Yes, I took Jennifer's dose . . . you know she has little time. And Dalton will make good on his threats. Trust me on that. But these are your choices, Frank. I'll be there soon and do what I can.'

Questions queued. 'Dalton said he'd been watching me for weeks. How much and how close?'

'A lot and very. Best not to think about it. He's listening to this. Do what you're going to do, Frank. One way or another we're coming to an end.' She hung up.

Her confession about Jen's dose stunned him, but more than that, there was a weird pathos to it. She didn't need to tell him that, or that her son was unstable and homicidal. Lies on top of lies, and Dalton's surveillance of him for weeks before Jackson's murder. Everything now fit like gears in a clock, or the careful walls of a rat maze.

Dazed, he walked down the long room to the thick glass that overlooked the atrium. Three stories below he saw the children and their families. He wondered what they'd been told about why their day at the Crestview Farm had been cut short and they needed to be brought back to Hollow Hills. Tara James spotted him and waved. He couldn't hear her through the glass. Parents and children alike looked up, smiled and waved. He stepped back as he spotted Jen and her mother. The six-year-old was now wheelchair bound with an oxygen mask strapped to her face. Years of painful experience told him she no longer had weeks, but days, possibly hours.

'Tick tock.' He thought of Leona's confession and Dalton's

masquerade. Both strong-arming him into handing over the formula. He'd come full circle, back to those arguments with Jackson. He knew his formula worked. So did the Langs. It could save dying children. It needed to be studied and developed. Important questions remained. Were the effects permanent? If not, how long until a further infusion is needed? His scientific curiosity was piqued by Leona and the stolen dose. Why? And what were the effects on a healthy adult subject?

He stared out at the high fence that circled Hollow Hills. He thought of his mother and wondered what she'd try next. But something else. Her delusional belief that he was the son of Satan. What if that weren't pure insanity? His telomere compound had wonderful potential, but Jackson had warned of a darker side. If something could heal and prolong life, could it also be used in the opposite direction? It was possible. Horrifying, but possible.

Tick tock.

He looked down at Jen.

'I'll do it,' he said to his hidden audience. He wondered if Dalton understood the science. Leona would. He turned on a sequencer and pulled chemical reagents off the shelves and from a refrigerator. He spoke aloud as if giving a cooking class. 'You start with two parts thymine, one part adenine, and three parts guanine.'

THIRTY-FOUR

Leona let herself in to Dalton's rental at Merryvale. She'd not called ahead, but had no illusions of surprise. On the drive, she'd ruminated over the conversation with Frank. The ball was in play. The Hollow Hills surveillance showed him complying. Now came the not-simple matter of parsing her son's oppositional behavior, getting him back in line, and if that was not possible . . .

She unwrapped a colorful Hermes scarf and checked her reflection in the hall mirror. She touched a finger to her cheek.

Incredible. Only this time, beauty and her brain would not be her only powers. But something greater. Total control over the most-desired commodity on the planet. Youth, and the possibility of a greatly extended lifespan.

A guitar strummed lush cords from the bedroom. She padded towards it. Dalton was singing. She listened to the lyrics.

'Blood red chrysanthemum spread upon my lover's cheek.
Blood red chrysanthemum you took me for a ride.'

She stopped by the entrance to his room. *He's not bad. Good, actually.* She rapped her knuckles against the doorframe.

The music stopped. 'I don't need housekeeping today, just towels.'

'Not housekeeping. It's your mother. Are you decent?'

'What a surprise. And you let yourself in. I don't remember giving you a key.'

'You didn't.' She entered. 'Another video?' She stated the obvious as she took in her son in front of a makeshift green screen with his Gibson, carefully gelled hair, skin-tight black jeans, camcorder, and open laptop. He had a pop rockabilly vibe.

'Yes, and?'

'You sound good.'

'You're here because? I thought you were hiding away from the world until . . .'

'Things change, Dalton.' She stopped and studied him. Tall, model-handsome, good voice, good enough to have done something. *And I wouldn't let him.* 'Do you hate me?'

He cracked his neck and returned her gaze. 'Interesting question.' Seconds stretched. 'No.'

'You don't love me,' she stated, and didn't break gaze, but wondered, *why is he staring . . . right, he hasn't seen me in a few days . . . is it that apparent?*

'Why are you here?' He put the guitar on its stand and headed towards the kitchen.

She followed. *This is how he wants to play this. Fine . . .* 'Grace Lewis is missing. Frank says someone pretending to be me said she'd had an accident.'

'That would be me, of course. But you knew that. Tea?' He poured water into an electric kettle.

'Sure. Why did you do that?'

'Just taking your lead. You said Candace Garfield was a catalyst, I'm helping things along.' He flicked the kettle on. 'Like turning up the flame on a pot set to boil . . . that's a good title. Pot set to boil. Turn up the flame . . . also not bad.' He grabbed a journal off the table and jotted them down.

She weighed his words, and something else, his attitude towards her. What came to mind was contempt. 'Is she alive?'

'Yes. For now. She and Frank are the only two with your magic potion in their heads. I won't mess that up.'

'He's making another batch as we speak,' she said. 'I told him that I took Jennifer's dose.'

'I heard. Interesting.' He looked at her. 'But makes sense. Now you can show up at Hollow Hills and he'll know why you look so . . . refreshed. And you do. You got what you want. You don't look a day over thirty-five. Hell, if you weren't my mother, I'd date you.'

She winced, having done her own assessment as not a day over thirty, at least from certain angles.

'Are you sure he's making the real thing?' Dalton asked. 'It could be a ploy to buy time. Maybe feed his cute detective enough for a warrant. We skate on such thin ice.'

She chuckled. 'This is your mother you're talking to. We'd take care of that, wouldn't we? And besides, he'll give it to little Jen. Once he does that, we'll know it's real.'

'Of course,' Dalton said. 'Saint Francis of Litchfield. That is if *his* mother doesn't kill him first. She is quite determined. In fact, you and she . . .' He chuckled. 'What is it about mothers?'

'Cute.' She made eye contact. 'Dalton. I am getting what I want. And I realize I've not been fair to you. You've done what I've asked. It's your turn. What do you want? What do you really want?'

'Huh. There's a twist. Perhaps the potion has done more than turn back the hands of time. Why this interest in me and what I want?'

'You'll take the potion, as well . . . if you want. Chances are good we'll be around a long time . . . together. I want whatever has poisoned our relationship to get better. I know much of the fault rests with me. I was not the best mother.'

'No arguments here. But you know what I want, what I've always wanted.'

'To be a singer.'

'Singer/songwriter. Yes. Without any of your help I have almost a hundred-thousand followers on Instagram, seventy-eight thousand on Twitter. I maxed out on Facebook years ago. And have two YouTube videos approaching a million hits. Other artists have asked to record my songs. I've always said no.'

'Because of me,' she stated.

'Yes, Grandma Karen put it well. What Leona wants, Leona gets. And if she doesn't, bad things happen.'

'OK then, here's the new deal. We both get what we want. Not only won't I stop you, I'll support you. You sound good, Dalton. I know that. It's why I agreed to you going to NYU. But I thought . . . hoped, it would be something you'd get tired of.'

'It's not. It's who I am. And it makes me sick to see my classmates have careers while I'm—'

'I see that. And I'm sorry for not taking you more seriously. But you've made my last few years at UNICO easier. The sharks are circling. One bad quarter and they'll come for the kill. I want you by my side, but I'll make sure you can do both. Do we have a deal?'

'I'm not certain what's on the table. You help me with my music in exchange for . . . ?'

'No more fighting. No more going behind my back. Maybe even use you and your music in ad campaigns . . . if you wanted.'

He laughed. 'Careful there, I don't know that jingles about erectile dysfunction and ulcerative colitis will help my career.'

'No, but a well-produced anthem and ad campaign for UNICO could.' She weighed the effect her words had on him. He was, after all, a man, and they were predictable. Stroke his ego and make him purr. 'You'll be big. Huge. But we can't ignore what will make this all possible. What exactly did you do with Grace Lewis, and what's the plan?'

'Leverage of course. To make Frank stop farting around and give us the fucking formula.'

'Where is she?'

'In a bomb shelter.'

'You intend to kill her.'

'Yes. Once we have the formula.'

'She has family. There will be an investigation.'

'Mother, this is your son you're talking to. Do you really want the details?'

'No. I'm aware of your skills.' She mulled over this twist; it had merit. As long as Frank thought there was a chance Grace was alive, he'd do as told. 'The detective will be a problem.'

'Yes. Is that a statement or a request?' The kettle whistled.

'The former. I don't want you taking more risks.'

'And then there's Frank,' Dalton said, as he poured boiling water into matching *Welcome to Litchfield* mugs.

'You have something in mind.'

'Yes, actually.'

'Care to share?'

'It's a mousetrap. Grace Lewis is the cheese. Once we have the process, and know that it's correct, Frank will miraculously figure out Grace's location. He'll run to save her.'

'And there'll be an accident.' She sipped her tea.

'Yes. Now about that anthem.'

THIRTY-FIVE

F rank lost time as he went through the familiar – at least to him – synthesis of the telomere compound. As the sequencer popped nucleotides together like beads on a necklace, he'd go to the windows and check on the children and their families. Hours passed and he'd watched as cots were brought in and the sun disappeared with brilliant splashes of orange and pink over the hills. He spoke the steps aloud. It reminded him of MIT and late-night talks with Jackson. He thought about Sean, and hoped he'd done as told and stayed away.

Day dragged into a sleepless night and then early morning, he felt lightheaded. He'd not eaten since . . . hard to remember, at least a day now. Trays were brought by the guards who carefully entered, placed them down, and then exited. The last one who'd come with a pot of coffee and a plate of Danish, commented, 'You need to eat something.'

'I'm fine,' Frank said. The coffee smelled strong. He poured a mug, and then a second, and a third. The sequencer hummed and clicked in the background.

Not long now, he thought, as he worked at the last few steps, the ones that added a sugar coating to the molecule. This was his Trojan horse that tricked the cells into thinking his molecule was food. The inspiration had come to him in a dream over a decade back. It had involved M&M candies. When he'd woken the clarity had hit like lightning.

Now, he thought to call Leona, but figured she and Dalton had been watching him like CNN or FOX election results. 'I need an infusion pump,' he said aloud, 'and someone needs to tell the Owens that Jen will get another dose.' He paused. 'What happens if they refuse?' He shook his head, they wouldn't. Dizziness made him sway. *What have I done?* But he knew. The compound and process were now in the hands of the Langs. Giving it to Jen would be the final proof they'd want . . . *and then what? What are they capable of? Watching me for weeks . . . months. Which means the night Jackson was killed they'd have known . . . Did they kill him? Why?*

Then came a thought. *If Jackson were still alive, would I be here?*

His cell rang. It was Leona.

'Frank, it's best if you tell the Owens yourself. Don't you think?'

'Yes.'

'Good. We'll have her infusion pump and pod sent up to your laboratory. You will administer the solution. I'm aware it will take hours. During that time, you are not to leave, and you are not to say anything about the changed circumstances to anyone. Am I understood?'

'Yes.'

'Good, because Dalton is on a tear. When he gets like this there's nothing I can do. He told me that Grace is alive and safe. I'll work on him, but be clear if he were to suspect you'd betrayed us, or told the Owens, or your detective . . .'

'What happens after the infusion?'

'Business as usual. I put a leash on Dalton, smooth things over with Grace, who will be suitably furious. We figure out what to do with your wonderful compound. We build an ad campaign with children and puppies. We're a pharmaceutical company, Frank. What do you think we do?'

He did not answer. Her words sounded plausible. And he knew they were lies. *Has he already killed her? Grace . . . what have I done?*

'The Owens are being told that you want to speak with them,' she said.

Frank walked over and looked down into the atrium; most of them were still asleep. Blood-red streaks pierced the retreating night sky. He held his breath as Marnie Owens walked to Jen's hospital bed, *like a coffin.* From the distance he couldn't see the rise and fall of the little girl's chest. Marnie's posture was tentative, and for several moments he feared the worst, that she'd died in the night. But then Jen pulled a hand to her oxygen mask and tried to take it off. Her mother helped her to sit, and offered her a sippy cup. Jen pointed up in his direction.

He waved, and forced a smile.

'I've got to go,' he said to Leona.

'Yes, and I'll be watching. Good luck, Frank.'

THIRTY-SIX

Parked on a stretch of abandoned dirt access road that overlooked Hollow Hills, Sean stared at his GPS screen. Around him, daybreak exploded with color. *Red in the morning, sailor take warning.* He glanced at thickening clouds. Rain was not his friend, as it washed away ephemeral clues. His thoughts fixed on a single objective. Find Frank and get him the hell away from the Langs and his murderous mother.

Yesterday afternoon he'd arrived at the gates and been denied access. His calls to Frank had gone unanswered. He could imagine what would happen if he'd attempted a missing-person

report. *New boyfriend won't take your call after the twelfth try
. . . take a hint, Buddy. Is that it? I said I loved him.* Doubt
swelled. *And he said nothing. Fuck! And why didn't he tell me
about his mother? What else hasn't he told me?*

It had been a busy afternoon and overnight. He'd reviewed news
accounts of the horrifying circumstances of Frank's childhood, his
father's murder, and his mother's hospitalization-slash-incarceration
after being found not guilty of first-degree murder by reason of
mental defect. Her escape and murder of a hospital guard thrust
her back in the news. Though not the part about her reappearing
in scenic Litchfield, Connecticut. That he'd gotten from a pair of
FBI agents. He'd spotted their black SUV with the tell-tale plates
and found agents Derrick Clarke and Amelia Jones eating twenty-
dollar burgers in a bistro across from the old jail, which now housed
trendy shops and offices for life coaches and psychotherapists.
He'd introduced himself, shown his shield and told them he was
working on a related homicide in Brookline, the murder of Professor
Jackson Atlas.

The burger was good, but the information they shared made
it hard to swallow. He took notes, exchanged cards, and then
followed the trail of Frank's Monday morning and afternoon.

His mood worsened at the accident site. He'd sheered a
telephone pole in half. The splintered stump gave a stark testa-
ment to the force of impact. Then his gaze caught on a scarred
boulder across the street. He touched the bumper-high gash and
a chunk crumbled beneath his fingers. He reminded himself
that Frank walked away from it; they'd spoken on the phone.
He'd said he was fine . . . *and then he stopped taking my calls.*

From there, he went to the garage where they'd towed Frank's
Element. He flashed his shield and was taken back to the vehicle.
It was totaled, but hopefully had done its job. The damage
further fleshed out the story. The sunken roof – *he fucking rolled
it* – to the crumpled metalwork where it had slammed into the
boulder. To the deeply dented passenger side with wood from
the telephone pole embedded in the trim.

The agents told him about the attack by his mother at Grace's
house. Candace Garfield had still not been found and Grace
Lewis had vanished. They'd been to her home, said it looked
like she'd left in a hurry.

He thanked the agents and went to Grace's rental. The front door was unlocked. 'Anyone home?' Hope surged, but no answer. He went in. Grace's laptop lay open on the kitchen table. The screen had gone black. He hit enter and was met with a password and username page. He thought of Grace, and figured it's not the type of thing he could do fast. He called his IT guy back in Brookline. 'Hey Gabe, anyway I can find the time someone last logged on even if the device is password protected?'

'Sure.'

He followed the instructions and saw she'd last keystroked at 1:02 p.m.

'If you've got time I can get you past the password,' Gabe said.

Sean paused, 'I don't. But thanks.'

He went out front and searched for traces of the assault. It was a gravel drive and there wasn't much . . . just a filthy pink hospital sock with rubber treads. He took a three-hundred-and-sixty-degree survey of his surroundings. The attack could have gone unnoticed, a thick hedge to his left, woods to his right, the house at his back, and a single across-the-street neighbor, with a closed three-door garage and no one at home . . . probably. He walked across and knocked on the front door.

He waited, rang the bell, and knocked again.

He heard footsteps. 'Police.' He pulled out his shield and held it up.

A door cracked open and a teenage boy peered out from the shadows. 'Not from Litchfield.'

'No, Brookline Massachusetts,' Sean said.

The door didn't open further. 'So, what are you doing here?'

Looking for my boyfriend. 'Investigating a murder and a possible attempted homicide that's connected.'

'You mean the crazy lady that tried to kill the guy yesterday?'

'Yes, you saw it?'

'Just the end. I called the cops.'

'What did you see?' Sean asked.

'Lady, with long black-and-white hair, big knife, hospital clothes with those funny slippers. It seemed fake. Like my first thought was they were practicing a play or making a video or something.'

'Then why'd you make the call.'

'It got real. I mean she went for blood. The dude, tall, dark-haired . . . they obviously knew each other but I couldn't hear. Especially not at first cause I had my headset on.'

'What time of day?' Sean asked.

The teen hesitated. 'Maybe one. Maybe a little later.'

'Was anyone else home? Did anyone else see anything?'

'No, both my parents work. I told them about it. Made them nervous. Told me not to open the door to strangers . . . like it's something I would do. But you're a cop, so that's different.'

'Right. What else did you see?'

'After she went for him, I called. I was freaking out. When I came back I saw them running.' He opened the door further and joined Sean on the stoop. He pointed. 'They went that way. It was scary, but he was a lot faster. She stopped by Barnes Road. I guess she figured she wasn't going to catch him. I told the cops all this. But I kept wondering where she went. Did they find her?'

'No, and you're right to keep the door locked.'

'That's fucking sad,' the kid said.

'It is.' Sean looked at the boy, figured his age about thirteen with the first wisps of down on his cheeks, which he'd fashioned into something like sideburns, but not quite. 'Anything else you remember, anything at all? So the guy, Doctor Garfield, he kept running. He didn't have a car?'

'I don't know. There was one in the driveway. A black GMC. When I came back it was gone and there were cops all over the place. Maybe he took it. I don't know.'

'What about the woman renting the place. Did you see her?'

'The little blonde lady with the ponytail. She's cute.'

'She is. Dr Lewis.'

'She told me to call her Grace. But I haven't seen her. She OK?'

Sean paused. 'I don't know. I've been trying to reach her.' He pulled out a card. 'If you see her, tell her to call me.'

'Will do . . . although—'

'Yes?'

'I did see her yesterday, like right before all of this happened.

I wanted to go over after, but there were cops all over the place and I figured I'd just be in the way.'

'What was she doing?'

'She was with some guy. About your height, dark hair . . . looked familiar somehow, like someone you see on TV. You know, one of those perfect people.'

'What kind of car?'

'BMW five series, black, with the sparkles in the paint. At least a hundred grand.'

'She went with him?'

'I guess, I was peeing.' He motioned to a window that overlooked the front of the house. 'And that one's my bedroom,' pointing to another three windows down.

'But the BMW was gone when the attack happened.'

'Yup, just the GMC.'

Sean mulled the new information. The perfect man in the BMW had to be Dalton and the timing, if the kid was accurate, was too close for a coincidence. *What was/is Dalton doing with Grace? Did he have something to do with the attack? Or everything . . . did he orchestrate Candace Garfield's escape?*

'This has been helpful. You got a name?'

'Carlton Grainger. Am I in trouble or anything?'

'Not at all.'

'The guy, is he OK?'

'Don't know.'

'Shit . . . and the crazy lady is still out there. Stuff like this isn't supposed to happen here. That's what my mom says.'

'She's right, but sometimes it does.'

From there, Sean had pieced what came next. Frank retrieved the SUV, was stopped by the cops, and returned to Hollow Hills. Which if he still was in possession of his cell, is where it placed him on the GPS. *Why here? Why not his place? Because he's not calling the shots. The Langs are.*

All of which brought him to his current impasse. Sucking down cold coffee, watching what might have been a romantic sunrise with vivid colors on a cloud-dark sky, and agonizing over his next move. He'd mull one idea, shoot holes in it, and move on to the next. Hours passed, and through binoculars he followed the action at Hollow Hills. Families and kids asleep on cots in the atrium. Frank's laboratory obscured by a trick of the glass. *But he's in there . . . or at least his cell is. And why doesn't he answer? Because he can't . . . or won't.*

A movement in the woods startled him. His first thought was it had to be an animal . . . a big one. *A bear? Or.* An idea formed, he knew it wasn't necessarily a good one. But the FBI were on a manhunt for Candace Garfield, what would be so bad about . . .

He pulled out the business card he'd been given over the good burgers. He called.

'Hey Derrick, it's Sean Brody . . . yeah, I know it's early. Any luck with the Candace Garfield hunt and peck?'

'Leads, some good, some pure crap. You got something?' the agent asked.

'Yeah, and I hope it's not crap, but something's happening at UNICO.'

'Seriously? That place is sealed tight.'

'So was the forensic hospital she AWOL'ed from.'

'Thanks for the info. We'll check it out. What are you doing?'

'Chasing down my own loose ends.'

'The professor homicide?'

'Yeah.' He again heard running in the woods. *What if it is her?* He unsnapped his holster. 'I got to go.' He hung up, and with his service revolver drawn he cracked open the door and got out.

'Who's there?'

Whatever, or whoever, it was changed directions and fled deeper into the woods.

Sean pursued as a first bolt of lightning cracked the sky and rain started to fall.

THIRTY-SEVEN

'What's wrong?' Jen wheezed.

Frank glanced from her to her mother, who had moved to the distant end of the room where she watched the others down in the atrium. *What's not?* he thought.

He moved the gooseneck lamp closer to Jen's tiny arm, and searched it back and front for a usable vein.

'Don't lie to a dying woman,' she said.

'You wouldn't understand.' *I don't understand. Leona Lang stole your dose. Why? And where is she?*

'Try me.'

He looked up from his gloved hand, which wielded a tiny butterfly needle, smaller than he would have liked, but probably the best he'd be able to get in. 'You sure you're only six?' His fingers trembled.

'I know, but you're not OK, Doctor Frank. You're tired and worried. Where's Doctor Grace?'

'She couldn't come,' he lied, and steadied one hand with the other.

'I don't believe you. Did you have a fight?'

'She's not my girlfriend.'

'I know that. You have Sean. He's your boyfriend and a police detective . . . and super cute.' She wheezed and struggled not to cough. 'Where is she? She should be here.'

'I don't know,' he admitted, as he tightened the tourniquet around her wrist. 'Hold still, you're going to feel a pinch.' He held his breath and pierced the skin between her second and third fingers. He loosened the tourniquet, taped down the needle and hooked it to the IV tubing. He started the infusion pump and watched.

'Is it good?' she asked.

'Yeah. But hold as still as you can.'

'How come I get a second dose?'

''Cause you're special.'

'When did you start lying so much?'

He didn't answer. The truth was too awful. A dying child's life-saving medication had been stolen. If he were to even say such a thing, what would happen? How far would the Langs go? Would they kill? Had they?

'Something was wrong with mine, wasn't it? Everyone's getting better but me.'

His cell buzzed. He glanced at the screen. 'I've got to take this, I'll be right back.' He felt his heart pound as he moved to a distant corner of the room. He lowered his voice. 'Hello?'

'Good work.' It was Dalton.

'Nice impersonation of your mother.'

'It's a talent. I have many.'

'Where's Grace?'

'Yes, you kept your end of the bargain. I should do the same.'

Frank waited. His inner alarm told him to do nothing that Dalton said . . . *and if it were just me.*

Marnie Owens moved over to Jen. She stroked her daughter's cheek and sang softly.

'Where is she?' Frank asked.

'And we're certain what you just gave Jen is the good stuff.'

'Yes. Your mother admitted she stole her original dose. Why?'

'You haven't seen her lately. Have you?'

'No.'

'One look and you'll have your answer. It shaved off fifteen years, maybe twenty. Your comment at the Taj about a face-lift for cells was prescient. You, good doctor, have turned back the hands of time.'

'Stop stalling,' Frank said. 'Please, where is she?'

'There is a problem.'

'If you've done anything to hurt her . . .' Panic surged.

'Frank, threats are not your forte. They're also not a good idea, especially when I'm trying to work on a happily ever after.'

'Dalton, you and your mother have what you want. Just tell me where she is, and we'll chalk this up to—'

'Good man. Because while threats don't become you, they are an essential part of mother and me. You know, or at least suspect, our capabilities. Should you, or Grace, or your handsome detective break ranks it would be tragic.'

'Understood.' He didn't believe a word, other than that the peril was real and imminent. 'Her location.'

'Yes, fine, and remember that everything you do, everything she does, we see. Now, in four hours, after the infusion is complete, tell the guards you need to go someplace. I'll make sure they let you. You'll take a company car, get on 202 and head north towards Torrington. You've been there. It's a barn back in the woods.'

'By the Shepaug. We hiked there.'

'Yes.'

Frank shuddered as he again realized how closely he'd been watched.

'There's a dirt access road on the right, it's within a mile of where you flipped your car. If you hit Fern Avenue, you've gone too far. And Frank, not to be a cliché, go alone. If you don't, I'll know, she'll be dead, and it will be your fault.'

THIRTY-EIGHT

D alton hung up.

'Well done,' Leona said. 'And you'll mop up the mess?'

'Of course. Frank is predictable. It's always about others.'

'Yes, not like you and me.'

'True.' He caught their reflections in a large mirror. It startled him. 'We look like brother and sister now.' He walked in closer, observing the tiny lines at the corners of his eyes. *Those weren't always there. I'm only twenty-eight.* Half-formed thoughts needled him. *She said I'll get what I want . . . said she'll put me in ads . . . an anthem. Is it already too late? And look at her.*

'We do look good.' She stood beside him. 'We'll get you dosed as soon as we've settled the mess.' As if reading his mind, she added, 'Best not wait.'

'You wouldn't consider keeping Frank around. There's still bits we're not clear on. Like is this a one-time thing or not?'

'True. But as you said, he's predictable. What I predict, is not in our interest. Besides, his telomere formula is the logical extension of work I started thirty years ago.' She put a hand to her cheek. 'If I'd known then where it could lead . . . I might have stayed with Jackson. Though Frank's sugar coating . . . inspired, elegant. If there were any reason to keep him around it would be to see what else he might discover. He is truly brilliant, and that's rare.'

'Did you kill Lionel?' Dalton blurted.

'I never meant for you to see that,' she said, by way of an answer. 'Did you kill Jackson?'

'Yes.'

'Why? I didn't tell you to.'

And while she'd nearly convinced him that he'd get what he'd want, he knew by the tension in her jaw that he'd gone off script and it pissed her off. 'Necessity. Frank was frozen with indecision. It was painful to watch him, day after day. Do I go left? Do I go right? Do I have the ham sandwich or the BLT?'

'You could have asked me.'

'Yes.' He faced her. 'And I didn't. That a problem?'

She shrugged. 'Water under the bridge, and in hindsight a good move. But we're done with that . . . correct?'

'Of course,' he parroted her words. 'From now on we both get what we want.' He thought to tell her that he knew Jackson was his biological father, but held his tongue.

'Yes.'

'I should get going,' he said. A lyric formed, *Places to go and people to kill.* He grabbed his valise, and headed out. *A good title.* He imagined the music, suitable for a James Bond film, heavy on the strings and the brass. *I've got the voice for it.*

'Good luck,' she said. 'There's a new world for you and I on the other side.'

'Thanks.' *And off we go to fight Mother's battles. Stay on script. Don't diverge. What Leona wants Leona gets. Places to go and people to kill.* As he walked to his car he mulled over the moving pieces. Like chessmen on a board, Leona the red queen, Frank the white knight, himself the queen's bishop, the six children and their parents rows of pawns. He drove past the manor home that housed Merryvale's five-star restaurant and turned onto 202. He felt jazzed, but bothered. He replayed the everyone-gets-what-they-want conversation with Mother. It sounded good. Maybe for a second he believed her, but she would never change. Not for him, not for anyone. Maybe she'd give him a dose, but she could just as easily . . . *poison me. She killed Lionel . . . who was not my father.*

Rattled, he mulled the options as he took the right onto the dirt access road. Movement in the woods caught his attention. He slowed as the car bounced over deep ruts and tangled roots. *An animal,* he thought. *Probably a deer.*

He rolled down his window and breathed the woodsy smells.

'She can't be trusted,' he said aloud. *She'll be the only one left with Frank's formula. Unless* . . . He'd come intent on killing Grace and Frank. It would be a terrible accident. But thinking about Frank dead, hurt. It was unwanted and unexpected. *I like the guy.* But it went deeper. *What if he didn't have to die? What if?*

He pulled up outside the barn. He knew Grace would still be unconscious. And while killing never bothered him, he didn't like to make anyone suffer. *Best if she never wakes.* The sedative he'd given her, a UNICO special, so special that it had never been brought to market, broke down into common molecules. It would be undetectable at autopsy. If there was even much of a body left; fire is unpredictable. But beautiful.

He popped the hood and grabbed a sealed, and badly rusted, coffee can. It was filled with linseed oil. A bit of the sappy aromatic fluid clung to his fingers. The pine scent reminded him of junior high woodshop and turning wooden bowls on a lathe, which he gave to Grandma Karen, because Leona thought them childish and not good enough to put out.

He entered the barn and listened. A breeze through the trees, mice burrowing in bales of dry hay, and silence from below. *So much kindling*, he thought, excitement surged. The fire will be spectacular.

He squatted on an upturned feed bucket and stared back through the open bay door. It was a solid plan, people got trapped and died in fires all the time. It would look like she'd had an accident and fallen into the root cellar. He thought about going down and breaking her wrists as though she'd tried to brace her fall. He decided against it as the pain might wake her. The bruise from where he'd cold cocked her would give credence to the story. Death by misadventure. The fire would start from some rags, bad luck and amazing they hadn't ignited years earlier when they'd been forgotten in a corner of the barn by the previous owner.

But Frank? Can I control him? And what will Mother do if he is alive? Leona gets what she wants. And that's the problem. Like an unresolved melody, he searched for the notes to set it right. But there she was. *I will never get what I want. But what if* . . . *it's not her left standing? Could I do it? Could she?* He sat and pondered and realized he'd struck on a crucial truth about his mother. That not only was she capable of killing him, but the more he thought of it, the more certain he became. While it hadn't shown on her face, killing Jackson infuriated her. Based on a lifetime's observation, people who crossed Leona met with misfortune, not with pop star fame.

He got up, and as he had the night he killed Jackson, he rewrote mother's script. He glanced at his watch. Little Jen still had an hour left to her infusion, then it would take another fifteen minutes for Frank to get away and follow his directions to the barn. By then, it would be over. One less living repository of his marvelous formula. He pictured himself consoling Frank, while simultaneously giving him an ultimatum. He'd do it in a gentle way. They'd kiss. *Face it Dalton, you like the guy.* There was still the matter of the detective . . . but that could be a simple fix. Tell Frank to break it off, or else. Besides, Dalton knew he was a catch, better looking, younger, rich, and talented. Frank would want for nothing, and once Mother was no longer a factor . . . *We will be unstoppable. I will give you everything, Frank Garfield.*

He walked into a darkened stall. Using his cell's flashlight, he spotted a pile of rags. *Those will do.* He poked a hole in the can and dribbled the linseed oil and then arranged it on its side, as if it had rusted through in place. *DIY gone tragically wrong. People should read the warnings on the label.*

He pulled out a lighter. And touched the flame to a grimy bit of plaid. It flickered, nearly went out, and then blossomed with flashes of orange, blue, and gold. Oil trickled onto the straw-strewn floor, the flame danced across it. The air crackled and dense gray, almost black, smoke rose and spread.

'Nearly forgot . . .' He walked back to the trap door and pulled out the piece of wood he'd wedged through the ring. *That would have been stupid.*

He would have loved to stay and watch. But now was not the time for amateur-hour mistakes.

He walked away from the structure and searched for evidence he might have left. Just a barn, old hay, and an unfortunate woman who'd gone for a hike, had a bad fall, and . . .

The sky had darkened. A drop landed on his cheek, and then

another. *Not good. But OK.* Not even a full downpour would stop the conflagration. *Too much fuel. The thing is done. Sorry, Grace.*

He hurried to his car as the skies opened with a wind-whipped torrent. It pounded cozily on the roof as he bounced down the rutted path. The windshield clouded with condensation. He wiped it with his sleeve. He cranked up the defroster.

Something crashed into the hood. The windshield shook and nearly shattered. He slammed on the brakes. Through the misted glass a big animal flew back and landed with a thud. 'Shit!' The car fishtailed. It skidded on the loose surface, but not before hitting whatever it was a second time. The right front tire raised up and he heard the crunch of bones.

'Shit.'

He got out. Thinking it was a deer, and knowing that if it were badly injured or dead he'd need to get rid of it. What he found was quite different.

He stared in disbelief as rain soaked his hair and dribbled down his back. 'You have got to be kidding. Catalyst my ass.' There, sprawled flat, legs clearly broken, left arm half under his front tire, and blood trickling from her nose lay Candace Garfield in mud-caked hospital scrubs and a single rubber-ribbed hospital sock.

He nudged her in the ribs with the tip of his boot. She didn't move. He knelt and felt for a pulse.

Dead. Crap! One body charred beyond recognition could be an accident. Two, 'Not good.'

He lost no time.

Just get it done and get out of here. He backed up to free her arm, and drove around in front of her. He popped the trunk and with a grunt, hoisted her up. He hugged her into his chest, his nostrils filled with a rank mix of sweat, urine and feces. He bent her at the hips and shoved her head-first into the trunk.

He glanced back at the ruts his tires had made. *Not good.* Rain pounded down through the woodsy canopy, it formed jagged rivulets which pooled in the tire gashes. *I did not need this.* Something shiny at the path's edge pulled his gaze. *Great.* He retrieved a large kitchen knife. There was blood on the blade and smeared on the handle. He tossed it in back with Candace Garfield's body, slammed the trunk, and drove off.

THIRTY-NINE

I t was one p.m. when Frank pulled the IV needle from Jen's tiny hand.

'You look scared,' she said.

'It's nothing.'

'I wish you wouldn't lie to me.'

'This time it should work,' Frank said, aware his audience extended beyond Jen and her exhausted mother.

'The others are all doing so well,' Marnie Owens said. 'Why didn't it work with Jen?'

'I don't know,' he lied. Because to have voiced the truth, that pharma magnate Leona Lang stole it for herself, would have horrible consequences. 'Hold pressure,' he said as he applied a thin gauze pad and followed it with a Looney Tunes bandage. 'I have to go.' He smiled. *Everyone must think it's business as usual.* His gut churned. *Will they let me out of here?*

'You're going to look for Doctor Grace?' Jen asked.

He nodded and headed towards the door. He expected it to be locked. It wasn't. He thought there'd be guards outside. There weren't.

Like a white-coated rat led to cheese, he headed towards the elevators. Between the expansive glass, open atrium, and the cameras overhead he knew that everything he said or did was observed. *They can't see inside my head.* And that was the problem. Because however he turned things, he found no good solution. Dalton and Leona called the shots, they'd done so from the beginning. His attempts to keep control over the process now seemed naïve. *Past is past. I follow my breath as it goes in, and I follow my breath as it goes out.*

He smiled to the families, high-fived Ben and fist pumped Lakeesha. He managed a 'good afternoon' to the guards who seemed to have a new set of orders that included letting him walk out the front doors. *So much for worrying about me getting killed by my crazy mother.*

Outside, a driving rain sent roiling sheets of water down the U-shaped drive. There was an empty UNICO SUV parked and waiting. He looked around, thought of his mother who was out there somewhere, likely with a butcher knife with his name on it.

The wind and rain brought visibility down to near zero. *If I can't see her, maybe she can't see me. Right.*

He got in. There was a key fob on the passenger seat.

Even without Dalton's directions, he knew the place he'd been told to go. Grace, Sean, and he had hiked for several miles along the Shepaugh River. They'd speculated on what the various properties they'd passed would cost, including a strange one that was both modern, in an eighties kind of way, and derelict. There'd been a large barn out back. Lots of beer bottles and a few discarded condoms. A good spot for teens to hang out, get high, and mess around.

He headed out. The wipers on high couldn't keep pace with the downpour.

A siren wailed in the distance. And then another. Blinded by rain, he drove fast. A cop car came up behind him with lights and sirens. *You've got to be kidding.*

He pulled to the curb, and expected them to stop behind him. They flew past, followed by a fire engine, and an ambulance. With a sick certainty he headed after them. He rounded a curb. Through gusts of rain he glimpsed dense black smoke. The emergency vehicles disappeared down an easy-to-miss dirt road. He followed as more sirens screamed at his back.

The unpaved road was pitted and thick with mud and loose rock. Blue and red flashers filled the cab. He smelled smoke. He passed the weird house and an algae-filled pool. He caught glimpses of the swollen river below. Wind howled overhead, as if in competition with the sirens. Trees, thick with spring leaves, cracked, branches snapped and fell.

He hadn't remembered the barn being so far back. It seemed forever, but then he was there.

Orange flames engulfed the front of it and shot thirty feet high.

He slammed on the brakes, and ran out. 'Somebody's in there!' He shouted to the cops and fire fighters. 'Grace Lewis is in there.'

He didn't wait for a response as he ran around the back. His lungs filled with smoke. The rear of the barn had not yet been touched by the flames; he found a door, yanked it open and ran in.

It was a mistake. He was blinded by flame and smoke. 'Grace!' he yelled. 'Grace! Grace!' He covered his nose with his shirt. Waves of heat pulsed around him. 'Grace.' He pulled out his cell and dialed her number. He stood still and waited. His pulse raced. But through the sirens, the crackling flames, and driving rain, he heard the marimba setting of her phone. It came from deeper inside. 'She's in here,' he yelled.

A firefighter ran towards him. He shouted. 'Mister, get out of there.'

'No.' He pressed her number again and ran towards the source of the ring.

The firefighter was joined by a cop. 'Mister, if we have to pull you out of here . . .'

A section of the front collapsed. It kicked up clouds of dust and smoke. Hay strands sparked and ignited in midair as they whirled skyward.

'Grace!' He followed the marimba and spotted a pull-handle. The sound came from underground. *A cellar.* The metal ring was a few feet from the flames, but the heat was unbearable, like being cooked. He couldn't breathe. He dropped to his knees, and crawled towards the trapdoor.

He grasped the ring, and recoiled as it burned his palm. He ripped off his rain-soaked shirt and both heard and felt it sizzle as he covered the ring, and pulled. At first, there was no movement and then it yanked back and open.

Cool air rushed up.

'Grace.' He looked down. It was pitch black, but he could see a bit of light colored something. He flicked to the flashlight on his cell. 'Grace.'

She was curled on her side, not moving. 'She's down here,' he yelled and was overcome with coughing and raw fear. 'Down here,' he croaked, wondering if the cop and fire fighter had followed. There was a metal ladder beneath the trap-door hinge, and he climbed down.

The air was better, but he knew there was no time. He knelt

by her side. 'Grace. Grace.' He had a sick dread. He shook her shoulders and ran his knuckles hard against her sternum.

She moaned and pushed him away. 'Stop that. Where? Frank?'

'Can you get up?'

'What's burning?'

'We are if we don't get out of here.'

Something crashed above, as another portion of the façade fell. Flaming wisps of hay floated into the cellar. 'Where are we?'

He helped her sit. She coughed, and by the light of his cell he saw the dark red mark on her temple. 'He hit you.'

'I don't remember.'

Adrenalin, fear, and rage, surged. 'Grace. We need to climb that ladder. Don't stand, crawl.' *And then I'm coming for you, Dalton and Leona.* He wondered if it might not be better to ride things out in the cellar, but he felt heat through the floor above, and imagined the two of them discovered hours or days later, fully cooked, like a campfire Dutch oven cake.

'Let's go.'

Things fell all around. The trapdoor shook. Precious oxygen was sucked from the air by ravenous flames. 'Come on.' He dragged her up.

She was unsteady. He couldn't tell if it was from the blow to the head, the smoke, the heat, or something else. 'Grip tight,' he whispered.

'Ow.' She recoiled from the metal ladder. 'It's too hot. I can't. This won't work.'

'It's the only way. Here.' He gave her his shirt, wrapped it around her hands, and pushed her up the chain-link ladder. She paused as her head cleared the opening. 'Oh my God. Frank. No.'

'Can you see the back door?' He held his breath. And heard a different voice.

'Frank,' a man shouted.

Sean. Fear surged anew. 'Stay back.' He tried to shout, but doubled over with coughs. His throat and nose burned. His shirt landed at his feet. Grace was gone from sight. He tested the metal of the ladder with a finger. It burned.

He wrapped his hands and willed himself upwards. The metal

singed his bare chest and shoulders. He made it up but the smoke was too dense to see. He collapsed to his knees and with his head to the ground he squinted. His eyes burned. He couldn't find the door, or Grace. *I'm going to die.*

'Frank.'

He couldn't speak. *Move.* He ambled crablike towards Sean's voice. It seemed miles away, and he knew with certainty, *I'm not going to make it. I'm going to die.*

But then someone, *Sean*, and a firefighter grabbed him. They threw something over his head and half carried and half dragged him out. Not a word was said as they muscled him out of the inferno and through the blazing ring of fire around the door.

Frank tripped on the doorframe and tumbled forward. Sean grabbed him, lost balance, and the two of them landed on their butts. 'Where's Grace?' he wheezed, as rain landed cool on his fevered skin.

'She got out,' Sean said. 'We got to get away from this.' He grabbed Frank's hand, and with a fierce yank pulled him to his feet and away from the barn.

'Where is she?' Frank asked.

He blinked back and spotted her being ministered to by a pair of medics. There were fresh sirens in the distance. Sean's hand smoothed circles on the bare skin of his back. 'You're going to be OK.' His voice wavered.

Frank shook his head. 'No. None of this is OK.' He thought of the Langs. For the first time, things had not gone according to their plan. Grace had nearly died . . . as had he. They wouldn't stop. Dalton's threats hounded him. Even now, as the fire raged, he felt watched. And the danger extended beyond himself and Grace, to Sean, the children, their families. Anyone the Langs felt could control him. He also knew that he no longer served a purpose. They had what they came for. And now they wanted him dead. He turned into Sean.

'How did you find me?'

'I followed you from UNICO.'

'You've had me under surveillance?'

'Yeah. You didn't answer my calls.' Sean forced a smile. 'OK, I turned into a stalker.'

'You can't be near me, Sean. You shouldn't be here.'

Sean lowered his voice, and bumped his forehead to Frank's. 'I am exactly where I need to be.' Rivulets of chill water streamed down their faces, as his lips met Frank's.

Frank tried to think of all the reasons he needed to send Sean away. But couldn't.

Grace ambled towards them, an oxygen mask on her forehead, and a soaked white sheet wrapped around her shoulders. She clutched her throat. And silently mouthed 'Ow.' The medics trailed after with a gurney.

'Miss, we need to get you to the hospital.'

'I'm OK.' She coughed and couldn't stop. Her face, already red, turned vivid beet as she gasped for breath. A medic took the mask off her forehead and put it over her face as her partner attached it to the oxygen tank strapped to their stretcher.

Frank looked at his oldest friend. *This is because of me. My fault. She nearly died.* He pulled back from Sean. 'My mother. Did they find her?'

'No.' He tried to wrap Frank in his arms. 'No one is going to hurt you. You're safe.'

'You don't know that,' Frank said. He pushed away.

'I know this was no accident. And I know that someone is going to pay for it.'

'You don't know who you're up against.'

'I do. We've got to get you and Grace out of here, and far away from the Langs.'

Frank faced Sean. 'Please leave.'

Sean whispered. 'No. Not happening.'

Despite everything, Frank couldn't help but stare into Sean's eyes. What he saw was beautiful and too important to put in harm's way. 'They're vicious. They will use those kids to get to me . . . They already have.'

'What do you mean? And let's get out of the rain. There . . .' he pointed towards a small derelict lean-to. 'Come on.'

'They made me give them the compound . . . all of it,' Frank said. He shivered. 'They used the children.'

'We get them out of here,' Sean said.

Frank heard uncertainty in Sean's voice. 'They're two steps ahead. Now that they have what they want . . . none of us matter. If they thought they could get away with it, they'd get rid of all traces of this experiment. Oh my, God.'

'They're not invulnerable. They've made mistakes. Like this. They wanted Grace dead. She's not.'

Frank looked at the engulfed barn, the flames less high as the final walls caved. The firefighters hadn't attempted to save the structure, but focused on preventing the conflagration from touching off a forest fire in the fuel-rich woods.

Grace argued with the medics who tried to coax her into their ambulance.

'She's not safe. Once they know she's alive . . .' His teeth chattered.

'Understood.' Sean looked down at a molded plastic horse trough. It was filled with brackish water and tadpoles scurried in its depths. 'Sit, I'll be right back.'

Frank watched as Sean jogged over to the medics. He showed them his shield, and pointed back at Frank. One nodded and motioned him towards the back. Grace took the opportunity to ditch the oxygen and head towards Frank.

A pair of state troopers, the same ones who'd been dispatched to his car accident also approached. 'Dr Garfield, are you OK?'

It was a straight-forward question, but Frank knew he was far from OK. 'I'm not hurt bad.' And argued the point with a spasm of coughs.

Sean returned with clean sheets stamped with the logo of the volunteer ambulance company. He draped one over Frank and handed the other to Grace. 'You're burned. Let me see your hands.'

'They'll blister,' Frank said. 'Second degree at the worst.' He looked at Grace, there were soot marks beneath her nostrils and her eyebrows were gone. 'What about you?'

She nodded, and raised a finger as she tried to speak. She rasped, 'OK. Not great.' She closed her mouth and swallowed.

'I'll get you some water,' the male trooper said.

Grace nodded and mouthed, 'Thank you.'

'Can you give a statement?' the woman trooper asked. She looked at Grace, 'Maybe let him do the talking for now.'

'Sure,' Frank said.

She pulled out a notepad. 'How did you and Dr Lewis come to be here?'

And so, began the lies. He was glad that Grace was there, so she could tell the same story. 'She'd been hiking, and called me. She'd had an accident. I knew where she was, we'd been here before. I saw the barn on fire. I dialed her phone and heard the ring. So I went in.'

'Where were you when she called?'

'The UNICO labs at Hollow Hills.'

'You have people who can verify your presence there?'

'Yes, many.'

'Good,' she said. 'And when you got here, you figured she was inside.' Her tone was skeptical.

'Yes.'

'And you went in.'

'Yes.'

She looked back at her partner as he returned to the shelter with a six-pack of waters. 'Yesterday you nearly died in a car accident.'

'True.' Frank took a careful sip of water. The cool liquid burned his throat.

She looked to Grace. 'Is that what happened?'

Grace nodded, took a sip, winced and said, 'I fell into the cellar. I must have blacked out.'

The trooper noted it down and turned back to Frank. 'And your mother, who killed your father with an axe just escaped from her mental hospital.'

'It was a hammer, but yeah.'

She looked at Sean, who stood glued to Frank's side. 'Something of a danger magnet.'

'No kidding,' Sean said.

'You're a detective, right?'

'Brookline Mass.'

'Investigating a homicide of a professor,' the trooper stated.

'Jackson Atlas.'

'Don't you think,' she said, 'there's a lot of smoking guns around Dr Garfield?'

'Yeah, working on it,' Sean said.

'How did the fire start?' she asked Frank.

'I don't know. From the color of the smoke I'd say there was something combustible.'

'Like an accelerant?' her previously silent partner asked.

'Yeah. I can smell it.'

'That'll be for the marshal to determine. You think it was set?' he asked.

'I didn't see anything, but . . .' Frank cursed himself for not keeping it simple. *I was looking for my friend in trouble. Found her. Got her out. Why the fuck did I have to say accelerant?*

'But what?'

Frank stalled. *They're watching me.* He looked around. A barn on fire, woods, the sound of the swollen river, rain pounding and drip drip dripping into the trough from holes in the roof. 'Have they found my mother?'

'Not that we're aware,' the trooper said.

'I need to get out of here. We all do.'

'Good point,' her partner said. 'We'll escort you and Doctor Lewis.'

'Not necessary,' Frank said.

'We can keep you safe,' she said, believing the threat to be from his mother.

'Like witness protection?'

'It's not the worst idea,' Sean said.

'I can't. I've got six sick kids at Hollow Hills. I can't just leave them.'

'At least tell us where you're going,' the officer said.

It was a good question. For which Frank had no answer. He started to hack and couldn't stop. 'Back to my place.'

'Not the lab?' she asked.

'Not right now.'

'You're being deliberately vague,' she said.

'No. I need some space.'

'You should go to the hospital,' her partner said. 'You both should.'

Frank shrugged. 'I got some burns and some inhalation. I'm a doctor, I know what to do for that.' *And we'd be sitting ducks for my mother . . . the Langs.*

Sean grunted. 'A doctor who treats himself has an idiot for a patient.'

'Thanks,' Frank said.

'You going to stay with them?' the trooper asked Sean.

'Yeah.'

'No. Take Grace and get out of here,' Frank said without, conviction.

Grace said, 'No.' And would have said more but had to fight to hold back another wave of coughs.

'Not a debate.' Sean turned to the trooper. 'We'll get a hotel room, something his mother wouldn't expect.'

'I guess that can do for now. Though I don't feel good about it,' the trooper said.

They arranged a time for the following day for Frank and Grace to give statements. 'We can have the marshal there so you only have to do it the one time. That is, if everything checks out.'

'Thank you,' Frank said.

The trio stood and watched as the troopers headed back into the rain.

'Now what?' Grace rasped.

Frank looked from her to Sean.

'We nail the Langs,' Sean said.

'You don't know who you're dealing with,' Frank whispered.

'I've an idea,' he said. 'They're super rich and have done horrible things for a long time, gotten away with all of it, and think nothing of murder.'

'They're not stupid. Leona is brilliant, and Dalton . . .'

'Is a narcissistic prick,' Grace added, and proceeded to hack.

'Have you seen his YouTube stuff?' Sean asked.

'No. Why?'

'He thinks he's a singer. Kind of Edgar Alan Poe meets Justin Bieber. It's strange.'

'They've watched me for months,' Frank said.

Sean stared at the fire. The last of the barn walls fell, flames and coals sizzled and sparked in the rain. 'You're supposed to be dead,' he said to Grace. 'I'm not so sure about you, but what if you both were killed?'

'They'll know it's not true,' Frank said. 'I'm sure they're monitoring the emergency band.'

'Good point,' Sean said. 'But maybe not. You said they've been watching you for months.'

'Yeah.'

'There are easier ways to do that. You got your cell? And Grace, you?'

They pulled them out.

'Give them to me,' Sean said. He gripped them tight and hurled them into the fire.

'What the hell?' Frank said.

'How do you think I followed you? Your GPS and God knows what else they've planted on your phone. You and Grace end here. If they think you're dead, it could buy us time.' He looked back at the police cruiser. He clicked his tongue against the roof of his mouth.

'What?' Frank asked. And wondered, *is tracking your boyfriend normal behavior?*

'It wouldn't hurt to have something on the emergency bands about fatalities . . . but no.'

'We got to be careful,' Frank said. 'Those children, their families . . . Jackson was right and I should have listened.'

'Bullshit,' Sean said. 'You couldn't have known about the Langs.'

'He tried to warn me.'

'We'll deal with that later,' Sean said. 'We need to end this.'

'Dalton tried to kill me,' Grace wheezed. 'Isn't that enough?'

'You got witnesses? Evidence?' Sean asked. 'He said/she said won't even buy an arrest warrant. And where's the motive? By the time anyone listens, you'll be out-lawyered . . . and Frank's right, they'd use those kids as leverage. You willing to risk that?'

She shook her head no.

'There's got to be a way,' Sean said. He looked back at the fire. 'Frank, you got here after the fire had been set.'

'Yeah, Dalton told me where I'd find Grace. He neglected to mention the bits about the fire, or that she was underground.'

'He knew you'd try to save her.'

'Yes. And that we'd both die and it would look like an accident.'

Sean shook his head. 'That part doesn't jive. Too iffy. Grace was toast.'

She jabbed him in the ribs.

'Sorry, bad word choice. You are lucky to be alive. You both are. So even if Dalton knew you'd go in the barn, he'd have no way of knowing the outcome.'

'See that's the part you don't get, Sean. He's watching . . . everything.'

'Maybe,' Sean said. 'But if he had something on your phone, it's gone. There are no cameras out here. He'd be stupid to leave that kind of evidence, and he's not stupid. But he left your fate up to chance. Why?'

Frank hesitated. 'I think he likes me.'

'Excuse me,' Sean said. 'Something you haven't told me.'

'He tried to kiss me.'

'When?'

'Back in Boston. It's not important.'

'Just a kiss?'

'Yeah. I told him no and . . .' His words trailed off.

'Out with it,' Sean said. 'What aren't you saying?'

'He's said a couple things. But I thought that was just part of his sales pitch to get me to work for them. And we really need to get out of here.'

'Understood, we'll take my car.' Sean looked around. 'If they're good at surveillance you know they've got the UNICO vehicles wired.'

'Where to?' Frank asked.

'We take it to them,' Sean said. 'They can't see it coming. I'd say our boy Dalton is the weaker link. We need evidence, something airtight. And we have to get those kids and their families out of here.'

'Too many maybes.' Frank clutched the sheet around his shoulders; he stopped at the edge of the shelter, sheets of water beaded down. 'I made this mess. I have to clean it up.'

Grace came up behind him and rasped, 'Don't be stupid.'

'Sean, please get her out of here. The minute they know she's not dead . . .'

'Not leaving,' she croaked.

'Neither am I,' Sean said. 'We stick together, we don't rush into anything, we track down Dalton, and yes, lots of maybes. But it's what we've got.'

FORTY

D alton pulled into the lot behind the Inn at Merryvale. He had to do something soon with Candace Garfield's body before it reeked. But between the rain and the cool, he figured it could wait until tonight, maybe morning. He pulled up his GPS tracker for Grace, Frank, and a few others, including his mother and grandmother.

'Shit.' Not what he'd expected. Both Frank and Grace were at the barn, which meant they were dead. 'You're not gay.' *Frank is special . . . was special.* A dull ache throbbed in his chest. He grabbed a pad and pen from the passenger seat and scribbled.

> *Blood red chrysanthemum too soon we part.*
> *Blood red chrysanthemum, how could I know*
> *I had given you my heart?*

'Not bad. Needs pruning, but good hook and decent end.' He stared at his words, and then at the rain as it ran down his windshield. Frank's death ate at him. *It's what she wanted.* He glanced at the GPS. *Why is she here?* He spotted her white BMW in the lot.

Moisture welled in the corners of his eyes. He flicked back a tear and then another. 'What the fuck have I done?' Not prone to fits of conscience, an inventory of his recent deeds, from killing Jackson, his biological father, to Frank and Grace's fiery deaths, made him reflect. *Why do I let her do this? Why am I sitting in the rain, in Connecticut, with a dead body in my trunk? What the fuck is wrong with this picture?*

Maybe Frank's not dead. What if he's hurt? You can't go back, that's for amateurs.

He tapped another app and scrolled to the local emergency band. The frequency crackled and the reception was poor, whether because of the lack of towers or the rain, he couldn't figure. He strained to hear reports of the fire and if they'd found the bodies in the cellar. 'Useless.'

He stayed rooted as emotions swirled, disquiet, sadness, regret . . . but something else. 'Why is she still here?' Their last conversation fresh in his mind. Her promise to let him pursue his music, her absurd suggestion that he could become the face of UNICO. 'Anthem my ass. She's up to something.'

This felt familiar, the never-ending chess game with Leona. *They'll find the bodies and she'll do what?* Grandma Karen's voice rang in his head. *'Whatever Leona wants, Leona gets.'* And now that she's got Frank's formula, what next? *Who next?*

He pressed the ignition start and headed out of the lot. As he turned onto 202, she called.

He thought to ignore it, but pressed Accept, after first hitting a recorder app on his cell.

'Where are you?' she asked.

'I'm going to visit Grandma Karen.'

'What in God's name for? I need you here.'

'Yes, well we don't always get what we want.'

'We had an agreement, Dalton. No more fighting, no more games.'

'Why are you still in my rooms?'

'I'm waiting for you.'

'Why?'

'I'm your mother. I don't need a reason.'

'I did what you wanted. That should be enough.'

He heard her sigh. 'I'm glad. I had concerns. You had feelings for him.'

'What happens now?' he asked, hating how well she read him.

'Wait for the story and then control the spin.'

'We need to have our stories synced,' he said.

'Yes. Which is why you should be here . . . with me.'

'What about those test subjects and their families. Seems like a lot of loose ends, especially if you want to control Frank's elixir.' His throat choked.

'Done and done,' she said.

He held his breath, wondering just how far she'd already gone . . . would go. *Say it, Mother. What have you done?*

'Yes?' He pressed, hoping she'd say something incriminating that he'd catch and record.

'Standard stuff. Airtight confidentiality agreements.'

'He's altered their genes.'

'No, just tightened them up.'

'No one could examine their cells and reproduce the process?' He had nothing.

'No. End of the day he had a clever little trick. It's why no one else has done it, but we can.'

'And if one, or more, of them broke confidentiality and told of the experiment . . . which was never approved or even registered with the FDA—'

'Shit happens.' *She's angry.* 'Enough of the questions and get back here. There's work to be done.'

'We can do it over the phone. I'm tired of this place. I'm going to check on Grandma and then head back to the city.'

'I see . . . you know there's a witness.'

'To what?'

'You were seen with Grace Lewis before the fire. A stupid mistake.'

'By who?'

'Some kid who lives across from her. There's things you need to know and now is not the time for one of your adolescent tantrums.'

He gripped the wheel. Why did she always have to get the upper hand? 'I'll be there in twenty.'

'Good.'

He ended the call, slowed and pulled into an entrance to White Memorial State Park. *What is her game?* It felt familiar. This is what she does . . . before she gets rid of someone. Point the blame and shoot to kill.

It's her or me. It was funny. One dead mother in the trunk of his car. It was spacious. It could hold two. A queer lightness washed over him. It was unexpected. *Life without Mother. I could be who I want. Do what I want . . . and have all the money in the world to make it happen.*

If this is how you want to play it, Mother.

He made a surgical j-turn in the muddy parking lot and headed back to the inn at Merryvale.

FORTY-ONE

'Everything feels wrong.' Sean wiped the condensation from the windshield. He'd cut the engine and the lights and concealed his Jeep next to a wisteria-covered arbor behind Dalton's rented cottage. The rain crackled like pebbles on the roof.

'I know,' Frank admitted. The heat was cranked up and Sean had retrieved sweats and Brookline PD T-shirts from a gym bag in the back for Grace and Frank. 'You tell me there's any other way and we do it. We've got to confront them. Tell them to stop or we go public with everything.' His teeth chattered.

'I'm trying,' Sean said. 'I don't see it . . .' He peered through binoculars as a black BMW turned in. 'And enter Lang number two.'

They watched as Dalton parked beside his mother's car in the lot behind his two-story cottage at the renowned inn.

Through the lens of a high-power camera on video mode, Sean saw the trunk pop and Dalton emerge from the driver's side.

'What the fuck?' he said. 'There's something in the trunk.' The rain and now Dalton's back made it hard to see. He zoomed in and recorded images of what appeared to be a pair of feet one bare and the other in a grimy sock. 'Not something . . . someone. And whoever it is, they ain't moving.'

Before he could get a clearer shot, Dalton reached in, grabbed a black briefcase, and slammed the lid.

'Merry Christmas,' Sean whispered. 'We just got lucky. And he got sloppy.'

'What?' Frank asked.

Sean grinned. 'You can't get redder handed than a person, alive or dead, in your trunk.' Kidnap or murder, either will put an end to Dalton. Sean pulled out his cell and made fast calls. First to the FBI agents he'd lunched with. He gave them the address, GPS coordinates, make, model and license plate of Dalton's vehicle.

'Isn't this enough for probable cause?' Grace asked.

'Out of my jurisdiction and with these two, the closer we stick to the rules the better. Any evidence gathered not by the book will get tossed as inadmissible. We sit tight.'

'Did you see who it was?' Frank asked.

Sean hesitated. 'Just feet and a bit of ankle, like a woman's.'

'Wearing shoes?' Frank asked.

'A muddy sock.'

'The kind you get in hospitals?'

'Maybe. It could be her. You got the card for those state troopers?'

Frank fished it out of his soaked and wadded-up pants pocket.

Sean dialed and put the phone on speaker. 'Yeah hi, remember how you said Frank Garfield is a trouble magnet. Well, how do you feel about a body in a car trunk parked at one of the guest cottages at Merryvale?'

The by-now familiar trooper's voice was clear. 'Seriously? We're on our way. What's the number of the cottage?'

'Can't see from here,' Sean said. 'How well do you know this place?'

'Well enough,' she said.

Sean described the location. 'There's a big wisteria-covered arch thing behind it. Which is where we are.'

'You going to tell me whose car it is, or is that part of the surprise?'

Sean hesitated. He knew the Langs poured money into this part of the state. But how much, and how far that might influence a pair of state troopers was unknowable. To lie, would create downstream problems. He took the middle ground. 'I don't want to say.'

'Oh, fuck,' she said. 'What are we walking into?'

'Sorry.'

'We'll be there in ten.'

'I'd try faster, and just a thought, ditch the lights and sirens.'

A popping noise cracked from the direction of the cottage.

'Shit.' Sean unsnapped the holster of his gun, was out of the car and raced towards the cottage.

'What's happening?' the trooper asked over the car phone.

Frank opened his door. 'I think it was a gun shot?'

'Is that you Doctor Garfield?'

But he was gone. 'Get here fast,' Grace wheezed from the backseat.

'Five minutes tops,' the trooper said. 'Stay put, Doctor Lewis.'

But the trooper's directive fell on an empty car.

FORTY-TWO

Leona primped and studied her reflection as she waited for Dalton. *What if I gave myself another infusion? How far can I push?* She tilted her head from side to side; all the loose flesh was gone. Her chin returned to its pointed splendor. She thought about giving that young drug rep a call. *What was his name?* Mesmerized, she stared at herself. *You can do better.*

A door opened and closed downstairs.

And here's Dalton . . . Everything has its shelf life.

She waited as he bounded up the stairs.

'You got me here,' he said, from the doorway.

'Is it done?' she asked.

'Yes. I tried to get confirmation but either the rain or something else is making access to the local emergency bands impossible.'

'I see.' She wondered, if he weren't her son, how many years back he would have been fired. *Would never have hired him to begin with.*

'You don't. But, whatever. You wanted me here, what's so important that I couldn't visit Grandma Karen?'

'You mean bring her booze.'

'The store delivers. But yes, I always bring her something.'

'It's called enabling, Dalton.'

'She's old. What does it matter?'

'She's a bitch. I should never have bought her that place.'

She glanced from her reflection back to Dalton. 'You were right. We could be brother and sister.'

'Yes, hurray for you. You wanted me here. Say what you have to say.'

'Why so angry?' She stopped her self-examination and focused on him. Young, handsome, and petulant as a two-year-old. 'It's Frank. You had feelings for him. I'd thought that was an act.' She shuddered.

'Stop it,' he said. 'Who I like is none of your business.'

She snorted. 'You're wrong. Everything you do is my business. Is this something we need to talk about? Are you going to be gay now? I'm not certain how I feel about that.'

'Stop it. What's so important that you needed me here? I have things to take care of.'

'More important than me?'

Dalton stared at his mother. Years of practice schooled his expression. *Give her nothing.* The weight of his briefcase dangled in his right hand. 'What could be more important than you?' He headed towards the kitchen. 'Tea?' he asked.

'Sure.'

He rested his briefcase on a chair and filled the electric kettle. *Are you going to do this? Are you really going to do this?* He pictured the steps, the Glock in the middle compartment, loaded and good to go. *You killed your father . . .*

The kettle hissed.

He both felt and heard a loud pop. A sharp pain at the base of his scalp. A moment of clarity. *She shot me. Too late.* He pictured Frank. He pictured Grandma Karen, and then he died.

Leona, pistol in hand, stared as Dalton crumbled to the floor.

The kettle screamed, rain pounded on the roof, and she smelled ozone from the discharge. Her fingers tingled inside a soft kid glove. She held still and parsed her emotions. A tinge of regret, but something stronger . . . freedom. 'Sorry Dalton.'

She laid her pistol on the kitchen table, turned the kettle down, opened Dalton's briefcase and pulled out his Glock. As expected, it was loaded. She arranged her scene and alibi. 'He came at me. I had no choice.' She knelt and pried open her dead son's hand.

And the gunshot to the back of his head?

'The kettle distracted him. He turned. I grabbed my gun from my purse and fired.'

It will do. Not as simple and elegant as with Lionel. *He slipped and fell. He hit his head.* She arranged the Glock into Dalton's still supple fingers. She felt the calluses on the pads from playing guitar. *He was good. Such a waste. Is he still alive?* She stared at his chest. There was no movement.

Immersed in the moment she did not hear the front door, which Dalton had left unlocked, or the sound of three pairs of feet up the stairs.

Her concentration shattered at the sound of a man's harsh voice. 'Leona Lang, put your hands where I can see them.'

FORTY-THREE

Like the night his mother killed his dad, what happened in the next sixty seconds became seared in Frank's brain. Soaked, burned, and in borrowed sweats he padded silently behind Sean with Grace two steps back. The shot had come from upstairs.

As they cleared the landing Frank spotted Leona Lang with her back turned, kneeling on the ground by a wall of cabinets. At first, he couldn't see what she was doing. But then he saw a swath of flesh. *Dalton; she killed her own son.*

Sean, revolver drawn, moved fast towards the kitchen.

Frank followed, his gaze fixed on Leona who was oblivious to their presence. Her gloved hands wedged something into Dalton's.

A gun. Frank saw the dark elongated barrel fitted with a silencer.

Leona strained as she raised Dalton's hand in the two of hers. The gun pointed towards the door . . . and Sean.

'Leona Lang, put your hands where I can see them,' Sean barked.

'She has a gun,' Frank shouted, and moving fast he grabbed Sean and nearly tackled him.

'What are you doing here?' Leona spat out, her words punctuated by the pop of a bullet and the sound of a shattered mirror in the hall behind them. She wrested the firearm from Dalton's lifeless fingers, sprang to her feet and assessed her intruders. She glared at Frank and Grace. 'Shit, Dalton. Even this you couldn't do right.'

Frank stared at her, the gun . . . and Dalton. A cruel thought came to mind, *one down, one to go.*

Sean regained his stance and trained his revolver on Leona. 'Leona Lang, put down your weapon. You're under arrest for the murder of your son, and God only knows what else.'

Her eyes darted from him, to Frank, to Grace. 'No,' she said, as a siren sounded in the distance. 'This is not how this plays out. He came at me with a gun and tried to kill me. I acted in self-defense.'

'Not from where we stand,' Sean said. 'Put down the gun.'

'No.' She stared at Frank. 'Don't think for one second that any of you are safe. Or those children, those sweet innocent babes. One by one Frank, Logan, Tara . . . little Jen, and don't think I won't.' She turned to Sean and to Grace. 'I have resources you cannot imagine. You do as I say, or things will get very ugly.'

Frank caught her gaze and held it. He focused on her face, twisted with emotion, but so young. It fascinated him – *this is my doing. This is all my doing. This is why she stole Jen's dose. Jackson had been right all along and it killed him. I killed him.* He raked in the details of the space between them, two overstuffed chairs to the left and a sofa to the right, in between a glass-topped coffee table. Her gun pointed at Sean. He sensed the flurry of her thoughts, their three stories against hers, and one of them a cop. Her jaw twitched.

'Put down the gun, Leona,' Sean ordered.

She turned on Sean, her mouth twisted up in a half smile. 'I don't think so.'

Frank heard vehicles pull into the gravel lot behind the cottage. Their time was up. Her back was to the wall and he knew, *she's going to shoot him.* And without pause, *eye on the ball,* he charged her, *this ends now.* He didn't hear Grace scream or feel the bullet that tore through his left shoulder a centimeter from the arch of his aorta. He was pure momentum and forward force as his one-hundred-and-eighty-eight pounds barreled into her. The impact that connected his right shoulder to her larynx was deliberate and surgical. He heard the crack of her head against the maple-fronted cabinet, followed by a strange full-body spasm beneath him from the shock to her spinal cord as she sank to the floor with him on top.

Footsteps pounded up the stairs, as he tried to raise himself off but couldn't. He felt and saw the blood, not hers but his. He saw a look of confusion and wide-eyed surprise on her beautiful face, she seemed at a loss. Her lips quivered and pursed, like a fish with too little oxygen puffing at the surface.

'Active shooter!' a woman shouted from the stairwell.

Grace, furthest from the action, shouted, 'Frank. Oh my God, Frank! No.'

He stared into Leona's sapphire eyes. Jackson's words, 'the most beautiful girl I'd ever seen' – he felt light-headed and frozen. *She's not dead*, but then her lips stopped as did the tremors that rolled through her body.

He felt Sean behind him, a hand on his shoulder, there was pressure and pain. 'You've been shot. What the fuck? Why?' *Good questions*, but he couldn't find words, and he was suddenly so tired. And the last thing he heard or remembered was Sean's anguished voice, 'Shooter is down. We have a man shot. We need an ambulance now!'

FORTY-FOUR

Frank tried to focus on the silver haired UNICO executive across from him. Behind the man in the five-thousand-dollar suit stretched a panoramic city scape. It had been three weeks since Leona shot him, since they found his mother dead in Dalton's trunk, and two weeks since Sean last spoke to him . . . or at least with him as he was present in the hospital when he gave his statements to the FBI and then to detectives from

Connecticut's Major Crime Squad. He'd had two surgeries to his shoulder, slept little, eaten less, and felt separated from everything and everyone.

'Unprecedented, to say the least,' Matt Taylor, UNICO's CFO and acting CEO for the past week, said.

Frank sat silent; *unprecedented* was a comment not a question. It had taken everything he had to get dressed and into the UNICO limo that morning. He knew he'd had no choice, but everything to that point had been a series of mistakes. From not listening to Jackson, which he now knew cost him his life, to saying yes to the murderous Langs. He tried to pay attention to Matt, early fifties, perfect hair, bespoke suit and muted-red silk tie dotted with tiny paisleys.

'You'll want more time to recover. I can't imagine the shock of what you've been through.'

'Thank you,' Frank said. *He felt a trap. Why am I here?* His mouth filled with saliva. This morning he'd barely been able to suck down a cup of coffee and a dry piece of toast. He still felt the impact with Leona, the sound of her cervical spine as it fractured, the feel of her beneath him. Grace's screams. And then Sean's cold expression and hard words after he woke from the first surgery, 'you're going to be OK. But we're not. Was any of it real? Was it all lies?' Frank gasped.

'Are you OK?' Matt asked.

'No. Not really,' he admitted. 'Why am I here?'

'Good. Business. You're here because you signed a five-year exclusive non-compete contract with UNICO. And a generous one at that. There is a thirty-day buy-out option, but it's on our side only and at least while I sit here, we won't exercise it.'

Frank met Matt's gaze. This felt familiar. Had he survived Dalton and Leona only to encounter . . . 'What do you want?'

'Very little, Frank. At least for now. Leona was obsessed with your project at Hollow Hills. While I'm not a scientist anyone can see the results were astounding. Six children with terminal cancers, all . . . cured. How is such a thing possible?'

Frank held his tongue.

'Fortunately, they all signed nondisclosure agreements,' Matt said, 'and I've never met a group of more grateful individuals. You're quite the hero to them, and understandably so.'

Frank's internal alarms sounded. 'You met with them?'

'Of course. The Langs took the need for damage control to new heights. One thing that's clear, they all think you walk on water, Dr Garfield. But we have some problems to . . . fix.'

'Such as?'

'How many people are aware of the Hollow Hills study? As you now know, it was never vetted through a human study review board and was never submitted to the FDA for approval. From start to finish the whole thing is an illegal cluster fuck that needs to be buried. It never happened. So who knows about it?'

'Myself, Dr Lewis . . . various UNICO employees will know pieces. They're not blind to the changes in the kids.' He stared at Matt, 'Not to mention anyone who caught sight of Leona. Her transformation was – is – remarkable.'

'True,' Matt said. 'Although where she is, and will remain, should prevent further speculation.'

'Which is where?'

'A UNICO facility outside Mexico City.'

'And her condition?'

'Unchanged, a permanent vegetative state. She will never wake up, and I've got to clean up this shit.' Matt's gaze narrowed. 'Though I must say, her interest in you and your product makes sense. Cure cancer and look twenty years younger. And that's the assessment of an MBA. I wonder, what else can it do? Not that those two things wouldn't be game changers.' He sighed. 'But here's the deal, Dr Garfield, it's over. This project is shut down as of now.'

'You just said you wouldn't terminate the contract.'

'True. You've got five years to do what you'd like with a million-dollar salary, profit sharing, the whole package. It's all yours. None of that has changed.'

'What's in it for UNICO . . . for you?'

'Your silence. Even after the five years are up, whatever you created at Hollow Hills belongs to UNICO, though it appears you never committed it to paper.'

Frank tried to make sense of Matt's words. 'UNICO is a drug company, wouldn't you want something that actually cured cancer?' He wondered if the taped session of his frenzied night making Jen Lewis's dose had been for the Langs' eyes only. In which case . . . *a good thing. But what happened to it?* And Leona in a coma, was not Leona dead. He wanted to ask Sean about it, if the FBI would be able to break through her passcodes, and if they did, would anyone have the scientific background to understand his work? But none of his texts, or voicemails to Sean in the last two weeks had been answered.

Matt smiled, and with the tone of someone talking to a small, not-bright child, said, 'Dr Garfield, we are first and foremost a for-profit corporation that must turn a profit. Your product, while enticing, would torpedo a trillion-dollar industry.'

His bluntness stunned Frank. But he was being offered a way out that neither Leona or Dalton would have given. 'You shelve a product that could save millions of lives in the interest of the bottom line.'

Matt smiled. 'Yes. Do you have a problem with that?"

'Actually, no. And what am I supposed to do for UNICO during the remaining four years and nine months of my contract?'

'Up to you. But be aware while the contract is generous in many respects, should you pursue other research, all of the product belongs to us in perpetuity.'

'I could choose to do nothing?'

'Yes . . . or you could return to your medical practice, and to teaching, but we would be watching.'

'For?'

'Unusual success. Patients defying the odds, that kind of thing. Be a good doctor, just not too good.'

This felt familiar. Matt Taylor was another head of the pharma hydra, and he'd had enough. 'Here's the deal, Matt.' Frank stood and leaned over the desk. His shoulder twinged, but he bit back the pain. 'I may be under contract to you sick bastards, but I don't care about the money. Never have. Give it to charity. And yes, I think I will go back to practicing, and to teaching . . . if they'll have me. But the first hint I get that anyone from UNICO is following me, watching me, going into patient records, any of it, I will find a way to make it stop.'

Matt pressed back into his chair. He snorted. 'Idle threats, Dr Garfield.'

Frank shook his head. 'Tell that to Leona.' With that, he took

a last look at the long views over the park and walked out. In
the elevator, he thought of Dalton and the awkward kiss in the
park. The guy was a sociopath, but there was something quirky
and almost likeable beneath his Teflon good looks. In the weeks
since what he and Grace, in a stab at humor, now called *Macbeth
Act V*, he'd compulsively watched Dalton's YouTube videos one
after the other, repeatedly. They were good. The tune from
one of them had lodged in his head. As he headed down it played
in his mind, but with his own lyrics, *Pimps and whores, Pimps
and whores. I don't want to work for pimps and whores.*

He hit the street and looked up at UNICO's towering mother
ship. The mirrored glass obscured the activity inside. He looked
for cameras, knew they were there, but nothing the eye could
detect. *Are they watching me now? Probably.*

It was a cool day. Lots of people, and the sluggish dance of
stop-and-start traffic. He wandered aimlessly; his thoughts
jangled. Sean, not returning his calls . . . *I don't blame him. I
lied to him, kept stuff from him.*

Compulsively he pulled out his cell and checked for voice
mails and messages he knew weren't there. His words to him
in the hospital, 'Was any of it real, Frank?'

He blew out a breath and stared across the street at the weathered stone wall that girdled Central Park. He gauged the traffic,
caught a break and jogged across. In the distance he glimpsed
the turret of Belvedere castle through the trees. He rolled on the
soles of his sneakers and started to run with no direction in
mind. It helped to have pavement beneath his feet, a dull ache
in his shoulder and down his left arm, breeze against his face,
and the chance to shut down all the crap that tormented him.
From the news stories titillated by the discovery of his mother's
body. The headline in the *Post* had read, 'Junk in the Trunk.'
The coroner's final report had listed 'catastrophic blunt force
injuries'. She'd been struck by Dalton's car . . . more than once.
There had been extensive fractures and internal injuries, a savage
end to his mother's unhappy life. And while he tried to feel sad,
all that came was relief, and a sense of being cast adrift. No
family left, no biannual visits to the forensic hospital, no more
acid-tinged missives in her tiny manic script. But just like her,
he now had blood on his hands.

He hit a loping stride. The rhythm of his feet like the beat in one of Dalton's songs. *All my fault. Should have listened to Jackson . . . And what about Jen?* With the Langs gone, no one at Hollow Hills questioned Grace when she'd sent the families home the morning after Act V. They'd tracked him to the hospital in the northwest corner of CT and visited. He'd felt uncomfortable with their gratitude. Now, he worried about them. Leona would have made good on her threats. But what about this Matt guy? Different suit, same devil. He'd answered their questions as best he could.

'Will you stay here?' Marnie Owens had asked.

'I don't know. Don't think so.'

There had been a lot of tears, and he'd felt traces of what it must be like to be part of a family. True affection and love. They trusted him, but if they knew how close they'd skated to catastrophe . . . He pushed his legs faster, as their questions, some of them personal, tumbled through his head. He'd not hidden his budding relationship with Sean, and Daryl James-Morgan had asked, 'Thinking of marriage and kids? It's the best thing. You two should try it.'

But it was Jen, as only she could do, that brought him to the edge. 'I'm going to be seven,' she'd announced. 'I'm going to have a party and you better be there.'

He stopped. He turned around and took in the lush foliage, the beds of iris, top-heavy peonies, and lion-faced pansies. It was like a fog cleared from his head. 'I'm going to Jen's birthday party.' *After that, no fucking clue.*

A woman, tossing bread bits to pigeons from a bench, looked up at him. 'That's nice dear. I always like birthday parties. Celebrations of life, aren't they?'

'Yes, they are.' He pulled out his cell, pressed for Siri and said, 'Toy stores near me.'

Siri replied, 'Here's what I've found for "toy stores near me".'

He scrolled through the results, found one with over a thousand positive reviews, said, 'bye' to the lady and her pigeons and ran off.

FORTY-FIVE

Frank arrived at the Westwood home of the Owens at one. Cars crowded the semi-circular drive of the fifties-era split level and lined the edge of the busy two-lane road it faced, and onto an adjacent side street, which is where he parked his new-to-him used Element. Not one for crowds or social scenes, he gripped his rainbow-wrapped package tight. *Smile and get through this.* He spotted Grace's car and looked for Sean's Jeep. It wasn't there. He'd stopped calling. The message was clear. It was over and it hurt. Bad.

Ship sailed. As he approached, he heard the excited chatter of children and the background bass and treble of their parents. Balloons had been tied to the mailbox at one entrance to the drive and to a light pole on the other. While he treated kids, the normal joy of a little girl's birthday party outside a hospital wasn't something he got to see. It was all the other stuff. The sad stuff, like sitting in a family room outside a cancer ward to give bad news.

'Dr Frank,' a man's voice behind him, followed by a little girl's arms grabbing him around the waist.

'Dr Frank. You came.'

'Hey Tara, how's it going?' he asked the six-year old as he turned and shook hands with her two dads, Daryl and Douglas.

'Awesome. Everyone's here,' Tara said.

'Looks like.' He was struck at how well she looked, dressed in denim overalls and a vibrant tie-dyed T-shirt. Her dark hair covered her scalp, and she'd put on weight, no longer a bag of bones with a distended belly from liver failure.

'We tried to get her into a dress,' Daryl said.

Tara pouted and shook her head no.

'She wasn't having it. Insisted on farmer jeans.'

'They're new,' she said. 'I got two pairs. I'm having a birthday in two months,' she added with uncertainty, as though testing the temperature of a bath to see if it was safe.

'We're flooded with save-the-date cards,' Daryl said.

Douglas chuckled, 'But Tara's is going to be the best. Though we don't have your current address.'

'It's unclear,' Frank admitted.

'Not staying in Connecticut?'

'I don't think so. I'm trying to get my position back in Cambridge. But if not there, another medical school, another hospital.'

'Really?' Douglas asked.

'Yeah, but let's not talk about that stuff.'

'Sean coming?' Daryl asked.

'Also on the list of things not to discuss.'

'Sorry . . .' His voice trailed. 'You two seemed good.'

'We did. Things changed.'

A screen door banged open and Grace emerged in a figure-hugging floral-print dress. 'There you are.' She headed towards them. 'Jen has turned into a tyrant, "where's Dr Frank? Where's Dr Frank? Dr Grace go and see if he's here. Are you sure he knows the date? Did you give him the right address? Why isn't he here?" As for me, apparently not so important.'

'What's it like in there?' he asked.

'A zoo. Time to be a chimpanzee.' She linked an arm through his and headed towards the house.

Tara grabbed the wrapped gift out of Douglas's hands and ran ahead.

'Look at that,' Grace said.

Daryl said, 'I do . . . we do, every day.' His voice choked with emotion. 'A part of me doesn't want to believe it's real, like we're tempting fate. But she's OK, she's really OK.'

'Yeah,' Frank said. 'She is.'

'And it's because of you two,' Douglas said. He draped an arm around his husband's shoulders.

Frank kept quiet, as he watched the six-year-old, soon to be seven-year-old, Tara fly past the screen door and into the house wielding a purple and yellow box that likely held something cat related.

'It's OK,' Grace whispered.

'Why aren't you more . . .'

'Messed up?' she asked.

'Yeah.'

'You did what had to be done. It's that simple. She came at us with a gun . . . and a lot more. You did what had to be done. She would never have stopped. My one regret is that you didn't kill the bitch.'

'She has no cortical activity,' he said.

'Yeah, but brain dead is not dead dead.'

He grabbed the door and held it for her and Daryl and Douglas.

A young girl screamed from somewhere stories below. 'Dr Frank is here!'

There was a clamber of footsteps and children's voices and giggles. A little girl in a green dress with short blonde hair emerged. She raced towards him.

He almost didn't recognize her. 'Jen?'

'Dr Frank.' She threw her arms around his waist and squeezed like he was a giant stuffed toy.

The scientist and doctor parts of his brain gathered data. Like Tara, she was now free from the toxic chemo and radiation. Her skin glowed and her hair finally had a chance to rebound. Her follicles were thick and her blonde shimmered with highlights that only the young get for free. He squatted down to her level as other children and their parents, grandparents and whoever all else got invited, formed a dense circle around him in the cramped foyer. 'You look good,' he told her.

'I'm not sick. I'm not dying. This is my seventh birthday.' She sounded giddy. 'I'm supposed to get a special present. Do you know what it is?'

'I don't.'

'I'm hoping,' her voice quivered, she put her mouth next to his ear, 'for a kitten.'

Marnie Owens emerged from a crowded kitchen. 'Jen, let our guests inside. Daryl, Douglas, Tara . . . don't you look wonderful.'

Familiar faces surrounded him. Ken and Petra Jeffries, and little Carter, who if you didn't know his left leg was prosthetic, you'd never guess from how he raced around the other kids. Marvin and Shavon Thomas, and Lakeesha who sported an exuberant weave of yard-long braids dotted with turquoise beads, which a month ago her own hair could never have supported. Hands slipped into his and helped him up. They squeezed and clasped. Others patted him on the back and both children and adults demanded hugs.

Marnie Owens planted a kiss on his cheek, and her reserved husband James said, 'What the hell.' And did the same.

Marnie, to save Frank, shouted, 'It's time to open presents, everyone into the living room.'

A hand grabbed his. 'Sit with me,' Jen said. It was not a question.

'Of course.'

'You too.' She snagged Grace's hand.

'You bet.'

'Where's Sean?' Jen asked, she stopped and looked around. 'He's supposed to be here. Why didn't he come with you?'

Before Frank could formulate an age-appropriate response, she shouted, 'There he is.'

Frank turned back, because coming down the driveway, bright-green package in hand, was Sean. Dressed in jeans and a blue polo, the sun sparked gold off his hair, his expression unreadable behind blue-mirrored glasses.

'Now we can open presents,' Jen said, and then almost like reciting a prayer or incantation she murmured, 'please please please please please.'

With Frank on her right and Grace on her left Jen held court, as she ripped open packages. She was gracious, but Frank sensed, with each gift, her anxiety ratcheted higher. Every doll and stuffed cat was far from her heart's desire. Her little sister Kayla grabbed all the bows and ribbons. The ones with tape she stuck on her head and to her party dress.

Frank felt frozen. He glanced at Sean, who returned his gaze a single time and then looked away. There was no mistaking his anger. *I certainly fucked that up.*

Jen glanced at him, as she unwrapped a cat-themed jigsaw puzzle from the Jeffries. She bit her lip.

And while Frank had talked with all the parents about no longer needing to be super-cautious of infectious threats, such as a pet might carry, he understood why Marnie and James would hold back. Who could blame them? If it weren't for Caesar and Lavinia, Frank might not be so certain that the effects of his telomere compound would hold.

Jen stared wide-eyed at the mountain of torn paper and boxes.
Her smile was forced. Tears welled.

'You know,' Marnie Owens said, 'I forgot a box. James,
where did I leave that other box?'

On cue, he returned with an unwrapped box that had once
held a Samsung microwave.

Jen looked up. She bit her lower lip. And Frank again heard,
'Please please please please please.'

Marnie cleared a space on the coffee table in front of the
couch where Jen had opened her presents. James lowered
the microwave box.

Jen stood. She peeled back the flaps and gasped. She shot
her arms out to the sides, her fingers trembled. 'Mommy, Daddy,
thank you!' Tears streamed as she reached both hands into the
box and pulled out not one, but two, eight-week-old long-haired
tabbies.

Mesmerized, Frank watched Jen make eye contact with each
of the mewling fuzz balls. She looked at him; there was fear
in her voice. 'I can keep them?'

'Of course,' her mother said.

'Do they have names?' Jen asked.

'Not yet,' Marnie said. 'The one with a white patch is a little
boy, and the one that's all tortoise is a girl.'

'Then he's Frank and she's Grace,' Jen said, as she sat back
and cuddled the kittens in her lap. But the newly named Grace
was more intrigued by a piece of blue satin ribbon and little
Frank pawed at the air and wanted to get back into the box.

On the periphery Frank saw Sean turn towards the door. 'I'll
be back,' he said, and followed him.

He caught up with him half way up the drive. 'You're just
not going to talk to me?'

Sean stiffened and didn't turn.

Frank walked around. There was no mistaking Sean's anger.

'I'm sorry,' he said. 'I didn't see another way out. If there
had been any other—'

'What are you talking about?' Sean said.

Frank lowered his voice. 'Leona. I didn't see another way.'

'Jesus, Frank. For someone so fucking brilliant you are an
absolute moron.'

Frank started. 'Then what did I do?'

Sean looked around. He tapped his foot on the ground and shook his head. 'I don't want to do this here, or now. I shouldn't have come.'

'Jen would have hunted you down.'

'Yeah,' his expression softened, 'she would. You really don't get it, do you?'

'I don't,' Frank admitted, and like Jen praying for a kitten, all he wanted was for Sean to not go away.

'You lied to me . . . a lot,' Sean said. 'I get that you had your reasons . . . they could even be good reasons. But . . .' He winced and looked away. 'I need to get out of here. I can't be with someone I can't trust.'

'And that's it? We're done?'

'I don't know,' Sean spat back. He clenched and unclenched his fists.

'Tell me what I can do,' Frank said.

'Tell me the truth, but that ship sailed.'

'What do you want to know?'

'Did you sleep with Dalton?'

'No, but he would have.'

'Why didn't you tell me about your mother?'

'Seriously?'

'Fine. I can almost give you that one,' Sean admitted, cracking a smile that lasted less than a second. 'You nearly died, Frank. You and Grace both.'

'I know.'

'You still don't get it.'

'Tell me. I'm dying here now. You're about to walk away and then we're done.'

Sean moved in close to where less than a yard separated them. 'I can't be with someone who lies to me. It's too much like the day job. All this shit with Dalton and Leona was going on, and you never told me. Why? It plays over and over in my head. If you'd just trusted me, I could have done something. But you didn't. Why?'

Frank paused. 'I didn't want you to get involved, or hurt, or . . .'

Sean stared at him, he twisted the corner of his mouth, 'But that's the problem, how do I know what's true and what's not? It's like there are two of you running at the same time. The Frank you see and the one who edits out all this other shit. I've been with guys who've lied to me. I won't put myself through that again.'

His words hit like a punch. He'd never thought about the constant stream that ran through his thoughts. 'You're right.'

'I am. It sucks and it hurts. Goodbye, Frank.' He started to turn.

Frank felt Sean slip away and the weight of decades of needing to keep things back, to not let people glimpse his madness. The dragon to be faced was no longer outside, but within. 'You know about my mother, what you don't know is what came after.'

Sean turned back and met his gaze. 'Tell me.'

And out it poured. The voices inside his head, the psychiatric hospitalizations, the outbursts that left him tied down to a stretcher with blanks in his memory. And his darkest secret, one he'd never shared with Dr Stein or even Grace. The fundamental truth that he knew made him defective and unlovable. 'She's inside of me.'

Sean, who'd listened in silence, closed the space between them. 'No, she's not.' He ran a hand up the back of Frank's head. His words choked and tears welled. 'You are nothing like your mother. I really love you. You're brilliant and kind . . . and weird. But I need to trust you, Frank. Without that we're not going to work. You can't lie to me and that includes not telling me stuff.'

Frank shivered. He gripped Sean's waist. He felt winded and tried to make a joke. 'You want the telomere formula?'

'Don't be a wiseass. But either I'm in this with you all the way or none of the way. You have to decide.'

'All the way.'

'You're sure?'

'Yes.' His lips crushed against Sean's. Driven by hunger and passion they kissed and held one another close.

'Here's the thing,' Sean whispered, still holding him. 'I've thought about this a lot. I saw Leona, and those kids. I know what you and Grace can do. We now know that's why Jackson was murdered. But it's not going to stop, is it Frank?'

'No, but it's changed. UNICO wants me to bury it.'

'The formula? Why?'

'Economics. Killing people slowly with chemo and radiation makes a lot more money than healing someone.'

'Jesus. Someone actually said that?'

'Yes.'

'You're free of them now?'

'No. They intend to hold me to the contract and under no circumstances am I to pursue any research or clinical trials with the telomere formula. I think they have me under surveillance.' He smiled.

'Nothing in that was funny.'

'I pushed back. At least the current CEO, this Matt guy, is focused on dollars.'

Sean looked into Frank's eyes. He stroked the side of his cheek. 'You're not going to stop, are you?'

'I can't.'

Ben Bradley ran through the front door and shouted out to them. 'Doctor Frank, Sean, they're getting ready for the cake. You have to come inside.'

Frank felt Sean pull back. *And this is where he leaves me.*

Sean's hand sought out his. 'Right. How will *we* do it?' he asked, as his fingers entwined with Frank's and clasped tight.

'Don't know. But look at them.'

Holding hands and bumping shoulders, they headed back in as a three-tiered cake decorated with cats and lit with seven candles was wheeled from the kitchen to where Jen sat enthroned in front of discarded boxes and wrapping. She barely noticed the cake or the booming rendition of *Happy Birthday* as she dangled a piece of curly blue ribbon into her kittens' box.

When the cake stopped in front of her, she looked up. Her gaze went from her mother and father, to Grace, and then to Frank and Sean.

In a clear voice she shouted. 'I'm seven years old. I'm not dying. And when I grow up, I'm going to be a doctor who saves children like Doctor Frank and Doctor Grace.' And with that she sucked in a big breath in, the kind that would have been impossible a month ago and blew out the candles.